LUCKY

Praise for Kris Bryant

Temptation

"This book has a great first line. I was hooked from the start. There was so much to like about this story, though. The interactions. The tension. The jealousy. I liked how Cassie falls for Brooke's son before she ever falls for Brooke. I love a good forbidden love story."—*Bookvark*

"This book is an emotional roller coaster that you're going to get swept away in. Let it happen…just bring the tissues and the vino and enjoy the ride."—*Les Rêveur*

"People who have read Ms. Bryant's erotica novella *Shameless* under the pseudonym of Brit Ryder know that this author can write intimacy well. This is more a romance than erotica, but the sex scenes are as varied and hot."—*LezReviewBooks*

Tinsel

"This story was the perfect length for this cute romance. What made this especially endearing were the relationships Jess has with her best friend, Mo, and her mother. You cannot go wrong by purchasing this cute little nugget. A really sweet romance with a cat playing cupid."—*Bookvark*

Falling

"This is a story you don't want to pass on. A fabulous read that you will have a hard time putting down. Maybe don't read it as you board your plane though. This is an easy 5 stars!"—*Romantic Reader Blog*

"Bryant delivers a story that is equal parts touching, compassionate, and uplifting."—*Lesbian Review*

"This was a nice, romantic read. There is enough romantic tension to keep the plot moving, and I enjoyed the supporting characters' and their romance as much as the main plot."—*Kissing Backwards*

Listen

"Ms. Bryant describes this soundscape with some exquisite metaphors, it's true what they say that music is everywhere. The whole book is beautifully written and makes the reader's heart to go out with people suffering from anxiety or any sort of mental health issue."—*Lez Review Books*

"I was absolutely captivated by this book from start to finish. The two leads were adorable and I really connected with them and rooted for them…This is one of the best books I've read recently—I cannot praise it enough!"—*Melina Bickard, Librarian, Waterloo Library (UK)*

"The main character's anxiety issues were well written and the romance is sweet and leaves you with a warm feeling at the end. Highly recommended reading."—*Kat Adams, Bookseller (QBD Books, Australia)*

"This book floored me. I've read it three times since the book appeared on my Kindle…I just love it so much. I'm actually sitting here wondering how I'm going to convey my sheer awe factor but I will try my best. Kris Bryant won Les Rêveur book of the year 2018 and seriously this is a contender for 2019."—*Les Rêveur*

Against All Odds

"*Against All Odds* by Kris Bryant, Maggie Cummings, and M. Ullrich is an emotional and captivating story about being able to face a tragedy head-on and move on with your life, learning to appreciate the simple things we take for granted and finding love where you least expect it."—*Lesbian Review*

"I started reading the book trying to dissect the writing and ended up forgetting all about the fact that three people were involved in writing it because the story just grabbed me by the ears and dragged me along for the ride…[A] really great romantic suspense that manages both parts of the equation perfectly. This is a book you won't be able to put down."—*C-Spot Reviews*

Lammy Finalist *Jolt*

Jolt "is a magnificent love story. Two women hurt by their previous lovers and each in their own way trying to make sense out of life and times. When they meet at a gay- and lesbian-friendly summer camp, they both feel as if lightning has struck. This is so beautifully involving, I have already reread it twice. Amazing!"—*Rainbow Book Reviews*

Goldie Winner *Breakthrough*

"Looking for a fun and funny light read with hella cute animal antics and a smoking hot butch ranger? Look no further...In this well-written first-person narrative, Kris Bryant's characters are well developed, and their push/pull romance hits all the right beats, making it a delightful read just in time for beach reading."—*Writing While Distracted*

"It's hilariously funny, romantic, and oh so sexy...But it is the romance between Kennedy and Brynn that stole my heart. The passion and emotion in the love scenes surpassed anything Kris Bryant has written before. I loved it."—*Kitty Kat's Book Review Blog*

"Kris Bryant has written several enjoyable contemporary romances, and *Breakthrough* is no exception. It's interesting and clearly well-researched, giving us information about Alaska and issues like poaching and conservation in a way that's engaging and never comes across as an info dump. She also delivers her best character work to date, going deeper with Kennedy and Brynn than we've seen in previous stories. If you're a fan of Kris Bryant, you won't want to miss this book, and if you're a fan of romance in general, you'll want to pick it up, too."—*Lambda Literary*

Forget Me Not

"Told in the first person, from Grace's point of view, we are privy to Grace's inner musings and her vulnerabilities…Bryant crafts clever wording to infuse Grace with a sharp-witted personality, which clearly covers her insecurities…This story is filled with loving familial interactions, caring friends, romantic interludes, and tantalizing sex scenes. The dialogue, both among the characters and within Grace's head, is refreshing, original, and sometimes comical. *Forget Me Not* is a fresh perspective on a romantic theme, and an entertaining read."—*Lambda Literary Review*

Whirlwind Romance

"Ms. Bryant's descriptions were written with such passion and colorful detail that you could feel the tension and the excitement along with the characters."—*Inked Rainbow Reviews*

Taste

"*Taste* is a student/teacher romance set in a culinary school. If the premise makes you wonder whether this book will make you want to eat something tasty, the answer is: yes."—*The Lesbian Review*

Touch

"The sexual chemistry in this book is off the hook. Kris Bryant writes my favorite sex scenes in lesbian romantic fiction."—*Les Rêveur*

By the Author

Jolt

Whirlwind Romance

Just Say Yes: The Proposal

Taste

Forget Me Not

Touch

Breakthrough

Shameless
(writing as Brit Ryder)

Against All Odds
(with Maggie Cummings and M. Ullrich)

Listen

Falling

Tinsel

Temptation

Lucky

Visit us at www.boldstrokesbooks.com

LUCKY

by
Kris Bryant

2020

LUCKY
© 2020 By Kris Bryant. All Rights Reserved.

ISBN 13: 978-1-63555-510-3

This Trade Paperback Original Is Published By
Bold Strokes Books, Inc.
P.O. Box 249
Valley Falls, NY 12185

First Edition: June 2020

THIS IS A WORK OF FICTION. NAMES, CHARACTERS, PLACES, AND INCIDENTS ARE THE PRODUCT OF THE AUTHOR'S IMAGINATION OR ARE USED FICTITIOUSLY. ANY RESEMBLANCE TO ACTUAL PERSONS, LIVING OR DEAD, BUSINESS ESTABLISHMENTS, EVENTS, OR LOCALES IS ENTIRELY COINCIDENTAL.

THIS BOOK, OR PARTS THEREOF, MAY NOT BE REPRODUCED IN ANY FORM WITHOUT PERMISSION.

Credits
Editors: Ashley Tillman and Stacia Seaman
Production Design: Stacia Seaman
Cover Design by Deb B and Sheri (hindsightgraphics@gmail.com)

Acknowledgments

I have a lot to be thankful for in this life. I am a published writer, and I have a loving, supportive family and fantastic readers who make this dream a reality.

Always and forever, a giant thank you to Bold Strokes Books for continuing to publish my books and novellas. I love our family and how supportive we are of one another.

Thank you to Ashley for making everything I write sound better. I wish I could take all the credit, but she really has my back and is instrumental in my success. I also had the pleasure of working with Stacia this go-around as my copy editor. A big thank you to her for correcting all of my mistakes—trust me, there are always a lot because I can't seem to learn.

My friends are invaluable, especially during the writing process. Thank you, Melissa Brayden, for pushing me to write in third person. I'm still scared of it, but now I can say I did it! Paula is the BEST at pumping me up whenever I start doubting myself so a big kiss and hug to you. Fiona, Jenn, Georgia, Carsen, Elle, Nikki, A, and the rest of the gang. Thank you for supporting me and always having my back. Britt & Avery—we have the most interesting talks. Thank you for always being in my corner, too.

Deb always creates the best covers and catches my billion mistakes before the manuscript even gets to editing. You're wonderful and I appreciate your help every step of the way. Molly is my little furry heroine. Even with all the obstacles she has in her life, she is a fighter and never gives up. She finds joy in living. When I grow up, I want to have her courage and determination.

Thank you to everyone who picks up or downloads my books. Your support helps me continue to write and do what I love most.

To Mel
Thank you for being in my life.

Chapter One

"Just this hot dog, and can I get a lottery ticket?"

Serena Evans made a different choice that day. Digging through her purse, she managed to scrape up four dollars and eighteen cents. With a two-dollar hot dog in hand, she could've used her last two dollars on a large Diet Coke with extra ice, her go-to every time, but something made her ask Dougie, the Quik Stop cashier, for a lottery ticket instead. The jackpot was forty-two million, almost double the highest it had ever been in Colorado. People in town were talking about it and dreaming about the what-ifs if they won. Serena never played the lottery or gambled at all. Maybe it was the fear of missing out that made her buy one, or just the idea of having everything she ever wanted for the first time in her life.

"Good luck." Dougie handed her the ticket.

She mumbled "thank you" and slipped the smooth piece of lime green paper in her back pocket without even looking at the numbers. It was a decision she instantly regretted. That Diet Coke would have been a real treat considering the hot dog wasn't nutritious or even delicious. The only good thing about getting a Quik Stop hot dog was all the extras she could add. A thick line of ketchup paralleled a thicker line of mustard. She applied a generous amount of relish and nacho cheese under the scrutiny of Dougie, avoiding eye contact with him. She didn't want to have to defend herself, but she was hungry and it was there for the taking. This meal would have to carry her over until morning, when her deposit showed up in her account and she could afford a trip to the grocery store. Serena lived paycheck-to-paycheck and budgeted every penny she earned at the Hooked Bookworm. She scraped by using two-for-one coupons and took advantage of supermarket sales on chicken and beef every Tuesday. Even though a huge portion of her salary went to a tiny studio apartment above an antique store, Serena couldn't imagine living anywhere else.

Late spring in Vail, Colorado, was beautiful. Even though there was still snow on the ground, the sun was bright and warm and the crisp air was refreshing. Nothing beat the smell of fir trees and mountain air. Serena took a deep breath and two seconds to appreciate her surroundings, then quickened her step. The bookstore was four blocks away and she'd spent over half her lunch break walking to the gas station to pick up her cheap lunch. She cupped the flimsy cardboard boat that housed the messy hot dog with both hands and crossed in front of traffic, nodding apologetically at the drivers. She needed a few minutes to sit down and eat this before her lunch break was over.

"You have five minutes," Mrs. Brody, busy with a customer, said over her shoulder when Serena slipped into the store. Her smile had a bite that Serena didn't appreciate, but she tolerated it because she needed this job.

She rolled her eyes and closed the door to the ten-by-ten break room in the back of the store. It was windowless with faded yellow walls stained gray from old cigarette smoke and a wallpaper border that bowed out as if it, too, wanted to escape the dismal space. The long fluorescent bulbs hummed above her and flickered when she used the microwave. The room was a prison and she was sure it violated several safety codes. Mrs. Brody put so much love and care into the store, but was a complete slob behind closed doors. Serena had offered to paint the break room and hang pictures for her, but Mrs. Brody told her it would have to come out of her paycheck and be done after hours. As much as she loved what she did for a living, Serena wasn't that invested in her job. It afforded her the luxury of reading for free, but she had to be careful not to bend the spines or crinkle the pages or that, too, would come out of her paycheck.

She wolfed down her lunch, but refrained from licking the cheese that settled and hardened at the bottom of the disposable dish. Even though she was the only one in the break room, she was technically still in public. Serena wouldn't put it past Mrs. Brody to have hidden cameras in the vents or the smoke detector. She washed her hands and hit the floor with thirty-eight seconds to spare. She was good at budgeting not only every penny, but also her time.

"We have to move books around for today's shipment. The new

Stephen King book is out tomorrow and we want that front and center in the window," Mrs. Brody said.

Serena knew that meant her. The other employee was Hunter, Mrs. Brody's nephew, who sometimes closed the shop with her. He was cool, for a teenager, but also lazy. It was better if she got the work done before he came in. Then they could relax and have a good time instead of obsessing about who was supposed to do what before the next day.

"The books are late this time. Are they for sure getting here today?" Serena asked.

New books were shipped several days ahead of the release for stores, including the Hooked Bookworm, to set up massive promotional displays. Eight inches of fresh snow from the weekend had caused traffic delays that had a rippling effect on several town deliveries. It was a matter of waiting and stressing until the truck showed up.

"John said he was headed this way with the shipment. We can expect him by three," she said.

That meant overtime for Serena, and she was fine with that. She worked ten to six Monday through Friday, and opened on Saturdays. Hunter closed on Saturdays and Mrs. Brody worked whenever she wanted. Serena waited until Mrs. Brody left for her lunch break before pulling out her phone to text her best friend, Chloe.

I feel like I didn't get a weekend. How was the party?

I can't believe you didn't show. It was a good time. And no, Amber wasn't there.

Serena was forever running into Amber since they broke up over Christmas. Even though she lived across town, she was always in the area. Sometimes she would walk by the bookstore and wave to Serena, who almost always avoided eye contact with her. Serena knew she wasn't the most exciting person, but she had a good heart, and if Amber couldn't see it, then she wasn't worth Serena's time. At least that's what Chloe always told her.

I just wasn't feeling it. I'm sorry.

Truth was she didn't have enough money for gas and didn't want to show up empty-handed. She had the ingredients for sugar cookies, but who showed up to a party with cookies? Chloe and her wife would have expected wine or beer or even chips and dip. They never talked about money, but Chloe knew Serena struggled.

Nobody new for you but it was still fun. The usual suspects were there. Brian brought a new guy who was hot and very outgoing.

It sounds like fun. I'll be at the next one, I promise.

Chloe had parties every month. She said it was good for morale since there was snow on the ground six months out of the year and people tended to hole up if they weren't skiing.

We have too much food left over so I'm going to swing by tonight and drop some off. What time are you home?

We have inventory tonight. Probably not until seven thirty or eight.

Ooh. Well, if I miss you, check your refrigerator when you get home. Gotta go. Behave.

Never! Serena smiled and slipped her phone back into her pocket. They both knew that Serena was the most reliable person out of their small group.

The business phone rang. Answering it gave Serena anxiety. Mrs. Brody had an old push button phone from the eighties with a cord that twisted so badly, she had to bend down behind the counter to answer it. She hated not knowing who was on the other end. Phones today were such a luxury with caller identification. This relic didn't have it.

"Hooked Bookworm. How may I help you?"

"Hey, sweetie. It's Mom. I was wondering if you would like to come over for dinner tonight or later this week?"

To say her relationship with her mother was strained was putting it mildly. Serena resented her mother for so many things, and even though she knew a lot of bad family decisions were because of her mother's disease, it was still hard to forgive and forget. Serena managed to keep the heavy sigh to herself and eliminated all venom from her voice. "Tonight's bad because I have inventory and will be late. How about Wednesday?"

"Paul and I would love to see you again. I'll make spaghetti. Your favorite. Can you bring a salad?"

Panic fluttered in Serena's stomach as she wondered what the real reason for dinner was. Quality family time wasn't high on the list. Neither was just checking in. There was always a reason. Diane was a recovering alcoholic. Sober three years now, and Serena was still waiting for the slipup. How many times had her mother tried rehab and failed? Four or five? Serena lost count when she moved out at eighteen. It wasn't that she didn't love her mom. She just learned she had to love herself more to move on.

As much as she wanted to attend college and go on to Colorado State University's school of veterinary medicine, one of the best in the country, she stayed in town. Faith, her half sister, had needed her.

She was ten years younger and completely at the mercy of Diane and her abusive drunken outbursts. Serena hung around to ensure Faith ate every day and got to school. Someone had to make sure she had clean clothes to wear, even if they came from a thrift shop, and school supplies. College just wasn't in the cards for Serena. Taking care of her family and working full-time made taking classes at the community college impossible. Like every other spark in her life, the desire for continuing education was a flash of hope that fizzled out.

"I'll bring a salad and dessert," she said. Even though Serena liked a glass of wine with pasta, no way was she going to be okay with her mother and a bottle of wine in the same room. She thought of the scene in the book *New Moon* when Bella cut her finger and Edward fought off his family because Bella's blood was too tempting to them. She visualized her mother with the same crazed intensity as Jasper when he first smelled Bella's blood.

"You bring the salad. I'll ask Faith to bring dessert. We'll see you around seven."

Serena figured her mother called the bookstore because she had to answer the phone. It was her job. Most of the time, she let her mother go straight to voice mail on her cell phone and called her back when the mood struck. She placed the mauve handset back in the cradle and did her best to untangle the cord, a meaningless task to keep her mind from flooding with memories she'd rather tamp down. After a moment, she decided to text Faith.

I guess we're doing dinner on Wednesday night. Bring banana pudding fluff. Please. Serena quickly added the word "please" to her text so as not to still seem bossy. Even though she had a good relationship with her, the need to offer her guidance, whether she wanted it or not, was strong.

What's in it for me?

Spending quality time with your favorite sister.

You're my only sister. Appropriate eye roll inserted.

That we know of! Open mouth emoji, then a winking one.

Okay. Banana pudding. The good stuff. On it.

Thanks. It was dessert semester at Vail's Culinary Center, and Serena had offered to be Faith's guinea pig any time she needed a taster. The banana pudding fluff was Serena's weakness. Never mind the chocolate eclairs or vanilla bean soufflé, Serena was all about the simple, rich things.

Knowing Mrs. Brody would question what she did in her absence, she pulled the books from the window and switched out the pale backdrop to something darker and ominous for King's latest. While she enjoyed a good paranormal thriller like the next person, she couldn't help but wish the bookstore would give this kind of attention to romance writers whose books lasted far beyond a quick story. Their books gave her hope and made her believe in something she hadn't felt in a very long time. Love was always the goal, but finding the right woman seemed impossible. She was almost thirty and had never really been in love before. Giving her heart to just anyone seemed impractical, but damnit, she wanted it more than anything.

Chapter Two

"You've worked hard for this. You're hungry. It's yours. Take it."
Gabrielle Barnes leaned closer to the mirror, gripped the sides of the porcelain sink with both hands, and stared at herself. The charcoal gray suit and cream-colored blouse were conservative, but still very feminine. She tilted her head to the left, then to the right to ensure her makeup and french twist were perfect and professional. She hid behind glasses most days, but she'd opted for her contacts because today was going to be life-changing. Her amber eyes were her best feature, and she was going to show them off. She needed to look and feel successful.

Today the board was going to discuss partnership at Arnest & Max Architecture. Gabrielle had been with the firm for ten years and worked harder and longer than anyone else. She was the first one in the office and, more often than not, was the last to leave at night. A sixty-hour work week was normal for her. She was also the only female architect in a sea of conservative men whose jokes she was never privy to, nor their praise. Gabrielle didn't care. She was in it for a career, not a fraternity. Thirty-three years old with a promising career and no baggage; the latter only because she had no social life. Taking a final deep breath and squaring her shoulders, she lifted her chin, collected her water bottle and iPad, and walked out of the bathroom. The meeting was in five minutes, but Gabrielle wanted to get there before it started.

"Are you ready?"

Tom Gehrhart, an architect who was hired the same day she was, surprised her in the hallway. Their shoulders brushed as they headed to the conference room.

"Ready as you are."

Their relationship was light, almost friendly, but there was always a competitiveness brimming just below the surface. They were both very aware of each other's successes and failures. Gabrielle thought her list of successes outweighed his but wasn't going to be childish and actually pull out a list to share. She wouldn't be at the meeting if there was any doubt. Her only issue was that she was at the mercy of the firm's board of directors to decide if she was a better fit than Tom to make partner.

"Looks like they called in the big guns." Tom's voice was low enough for only Gabrielle to hear as they marched into the conference room and immediately split apart. Tom sat on the side closest to the owner, while Gabrielle preferred to have her back to the large, floor-to-ceiling windows. She carefully placed her iPad on the table in front of the open high back chair next to her immediate boss, Christopher. He gave her a brief smile when she sat down but immediately turned his attention to his iPad. Not a good sign, Gabrielle thought, but wasn't going to let his impersonal gesture derail her.

Lawrence Anderson, board director, stood and pulled at the hem of his single-breasted suit jacket, bringing all eyes to his stomach, which rounded out and strained against the oversized black button. "Let's get started. We've invited Gabrielle and Tom to the board meeting because with John's retirement at the end of the year, we will have an open seat in January." If Lawrence were to stoop down two inches, his girth would rest on the top of the conference table. Standing a mere five feet two inches tall, wearing shoe lifts, Lawrence seemed almost as wide as he was tall. At five foot seven and also in heels, Gabrielle towered over him. She hated when the men in the office teased Lawrence behind his back. She respected him too much to partake, but also didn't stop it. He was a powerful man at the firm and she appreciated his hard work of growing the company as much as he had over the last thirty years. Still, it was hard not to wince at his struggles with his ill-fitted clothing. "While a decision hasn't officially been made yet because both candidates are equally qualified, we're going to evaluate you both over the next six months on projects that come in. Tom, we've decided to give you the lead on the new Lexington Hotel and Conference Center in Aurora. Gabrielle, we want you to step in and finish Aaron's project. You'll also get the next large project that comes up."

Gabrielle kept her shoulders squared even though the wind had been knocked out of her sails. Blood pounded in her ears and flushed her neck and cheeks. Once again, she was swooping in to clean up a massive mess. She always told herself that her ability to salvage a hot mess was job security, but just once she wanted a large project from start to finish. They always gave her smaller gas stations and new pharmacies to design, but most of them were chains and the designs were pretty standard. Gabrielle wanted complete design control.

"Thank you," she said. She couldn't look directly at Tom. Her peripheral vision picked up his giant grin and the handshake he shared with one of the partners. She folded her hands in front of her and waited for the meeting to be called. Sexism and favoritism were still alive and kicking at Arnest & Max.

As much as Gabrielle wanted to scream and throw shit, she remained calm and collected. When the meeting adjourned twenty painfully sluggish minutes later, she slowly stood, trying not to draw additional attention to herself, and quietly left the room, nodding at those who dared to make eye contact with her. Everyone else stayed behind to talk about their weekends or lofty investments they were so smart to snatch up when they did. Gabrielle wasn't a part of their camaraderie, nor was she going to share her financial successes. Although her skin had toughened over the years, it still stung being left out of the jovial banter she heard all the way down the hall to her office.

"Gabrielle, Chad called twice while you were in your meeting. Sounds important." If her assistant wasn't so damn good at his job, Gabrielle would have fired him a long time ago. He was irritating in a way that wasn't legally terminable, but Miles consistently danced on her last nerve with his peculiar quirks. After the third gum pop in the ten seconds it took to hand Gabrielle her messages, Gabrielle snapped.

"Don't make me ban gum chewing. It's meant to be enjoyed, not heard by everyone in the office."

She turned on her heel and marched into her office, closing her door with more force than she intended. She winced at the noise but was far too irritated at this day to open it again and apologize to Miles. She plopped in her chair and sighed with defeat. An uphill battle. That was the best way to describe her career at Arnest & Max. The ridiculous challenge that was given to her after handing Tom the best project the firm had seen in years made her want to throw something.

She picked up a paperweight in her left hand and threw it at the couch. It bounced off the cushion and rolled to a stop on the rug in front of her desk. The barely audible whoosh did nothing to improve her mood. She needed to hear the satisfying crash of glass smashing into thousands of pieces or hear her tires peel against the asphalt as she stomped on the accelerator of her sports coupe. She couldn't stay in the office, but she couldn't leave either. People would speculate that she was pissed about the turn of events and how unfair the partners were to her. She had to remain calm and cool and stay put. If she thought they were watching her before, now she was definitely under their scrutiny. She was trapped. She did the only thing she could think of to escape. She called her best friend.

"I'm going to play the lottery and win the jackpot Wednesday," Gabrielle said as soon as Rosie picked up.

"As long as you take care of me, I'm all for it."

Gabrielle smiled at how quickly Rosie jumped into her fantasy.

"I'm having a shitty day. Tell me good things," Gabrielle said.

"Well, I love you and Muppet loves you and so does Kittypurrs. As a matter of fact, Kittypurrs wants to talk to you."

Gabrielle heard a thump and a loud rumble before Rosie yelped and then giggled.

"Sorry! I dropped the phone. Kittypurrs was a little too excited to talk and swiped the phone out of my grasp."

"As much as I dislike animals, yours are probably the only ones I will tolerate."

"Why is your day so s-h-i-t-t-y?"

Gabrielle laughed at Rosie's decision to spell. "Let me guess, Care Bear is right there." Rosie's precocious three-year old had a remarkable ability to understand and follow adult conversations.

"Ten-four, good buddy. Talk to me."

Gabrielle launched into the story and immediately felt better knowing she could always lean on Rosie for support. Friends since high school, they were inseparable until after college when Rosie met Anne. They were married within six months and started a family right away. Carolyn was their third and final child.

"Record everything in case we need to find a lawyer," Rosie said.

"It's not worth the effort." Gabrielle tried not to be upset about her downward spiraling fate, but it was hard when the continual climb got her nowhere.

"Maybe now is the time to start thinking about opening up your own company. Hell, I could even work for you part-time. Minimum wage, maybe even sweat shop wage. Just get me away from the children."

Gabrielle laughed. "You love your family. I'd never take you away from them. You need them as much as they need you." Rosie did plant a tiny seed in Gabrielle's mind. She was at the age and had enough experience and money where she could take the leap. She had clients who kept coming back because they respected her and enjoyed working with her. Tom didn't have that in his arsenal.

"I do love them, but I think getting away from them for a few hours a day might be exactly what keeps me sane. Maybe I'll join a book club or a gym," Rosie said.

"You hate reading and you have never worked out a day in your life."

"Book clubs are for drinking wine and gyms are for ogling hot bodies."

"I tell you what. If I don't make partner, I will quit and start my own business. Hey, Christopher. I quit." Gabrielle pumped her fist in the air in mock victory.

"You're doing that fist pump thing again that nerdifies you, aren't you?" Rosie asked.

Gabrielle slowly lowered her hand and looked at her phone as if somehow Rosie could see her. "No. I'm in my office sitting here professionally like a partner would."

"Sure, sure. Hey, why don't we get together for a drink tonight? Come over after the kids go to bed. Bring the wine," Rosie said.

"That'll give me time to work out. I certainly feel the need to hit something. Hard," she said.

"Instead of the air?" Rosie asked.

"I threw a paperweight, but I had to be quiet about it."

"Don't ever let them get the best of you. Stay cool. I'll see you tonight."

"Make cheesecake," Gabrielle said and hung up before Rosie could object.

❖

Gabrielle pushed herself harder than ever. She watched her name climb the board minute by minute. Her sleeves were drenched with sweat, and wiping her brow on them was futile. She refused to wear a headband, but now was seriously reconsidering fashion versus functionality.

"Great work, Gabby! Way to own it."

Blaine was leading the performance spin class, something Gabrielle didn't subject herself to unless she was feeling bloated or extremely angry at the world. Today she was both. Her adrenaline was off the chart, but it was fading fast and there were only thirty seconds left.

"Doing it." She choked out the words and then nodded coolly at Blaine as if they were buds, when in reality, she was surprised he even knew her name.

The class congratulated one another once the clock wound down. Twenty hard high fives made her arms match the numbness in her legs as she worked her way through the crowd on the way to the locker room. Gabrielle didn't know how she was going to have the energy to get cleaned up and make her way over to Rosie and Anne's. She leaned against the bench in front of her locker and drank her entire bottle of water.

"You were fierce out there."

A blonde stood in front of her and toasted her water bottle against Gabrielle's now empty one. She was tall and smooth and had a dimpled, lopsided smile that made Gabrielle sit up straighter.

"Thanks. Rough day at the office. I had some aggression to work out."

"I've been there. I'm Dani. And you're Gabby," she said.

"Gabrielle really. I'm not quite sure why Blaine shortened it." Gabrielle hadn't been called Gabby since elementary school. When her grandmother passed away when she was ten, Gabrielle made an announcement to the family that only her grandmother called her that and now that she was gone, so was that nickname. Some family members slipped during holidays, but by the time she hit high school, she was known by her full name only.

"My apologies, Gabrielle. Why was your day so horrible?" Dani stood opposite Gabrielle and leaned back against the top locker. The protruding metal slots couldn't have been comfortable in that tender spot between her shoulder blades, but she looked cool and sexy.

Gabrielle stretched her legs out in front of her and crossed her ankles to get more comfortable. Her foot grazed Dani's bright pink workout shoes. She took the time to appreciate Dani's smooth, toned legs and flat stomach. Her workout outfit was tasteful and expensive. Her compression pants clung to her ass, hips, and thighs as though they were a part of her skin. She was attractive and knew it. The space between them shrank as Gabrielle finally picked up on Dani's interest.

"Just a woman clawing and scratching her way to the top." Gabrielle shrugged as though all of her hard work wasn't important or the only driving force in her life.

"With what I saw back there, I'm sure you're very good at what you do." Dani smiled that adorable lopsided grin again and Gabrielle couldn't help but smile back.

"Thanks." She leaned on the bench to push herself up and get moving, unaware that Dani had reached her hand out to help her.

"Here. Your legs have to be jelly. I'm only standing because if I sit, I'll never get back up."

Dani's hand was warm and strong. Her fingers were long and her red nails filed and trimmed. She wasn't wearing any jewelry, but that didn't mean anything. Gabrielle removed her two rings and necklace during spin. It was hard to grip the handles of the stationary bike with the rings pressing uncomfortably into her fingers, or the slight wisp of a chain with a small four leaf clover charm hitting the underside of her chin.

"As much as I would love to stay and chat, and I do mean that, I'm in a hurry to meet up with some friends," Gabrielle said.

"Then we'll talk after the next spin class," Dani said.

Gabrielle nodded and smiled. The unspoken agreement that passed between them made her stomach flutter with promise. When was the last time she went out on a date? Hell, when was the last time she got laid? She gathered her caddy and headed to the private showers to quickly wash off. Even though it was a night in with Rosie and Anne, she wanted to be clean. Sweats, no makeup, a glass or two of wine, possibly cheesecake, and curled up on a couch talking to her best friends sounded like the best way to end her shitty day.

Chapter Three

"I hope everyone played the lottery. The drawing is tonight." Diane placed a basket of steaming garlicky breadsticks in the center of the table next to the spaghetti and sat next to Paul.

"I'm not old enough," Faith said.

Serena rolled her eyes. "The legal age to buy lottery tickets is eighteen. You're thinking of gambling." She backed away from mentioning the legal age of buying alcohol out of habit.

"The payout after federal and state taxes is roughly half. Twenty or so million dollars would go a long way," Diane said.

"I would definitely retire. As much as I love fighting fires and working with the guys, I could easily stay home and learn to whittle or build things," Paul said.

"You would miss your job too much. Besides, you don't even use the tools you have out in the garage now," Diane said.

"I wouldn't have a problem quitting my job," Serena said.

"I thought you loved working at the bookstore." Diane sounded surprised, like working in a bookstore was Serena's perfect job.

"It's retail, Mom. I'm almost thirty and my boss is a tyrant," she said.

"There's nothing embarrassing or wrong about working retail." Diane's voice was sharp, almost reprimanding Serena for having an opinion.

Serena held up her palms. "You're right. I just wanted more by now, but real life kind of got in the way."

The silence that followed was uncomfortable, but easy enough for Diane to maneuver around. She was a pro at it.

"Faith, I see you brought your famous banana pudding fluff. What else are you learning?"

"Crepes and all the possible things you can do with them."

"Have you heard back from any of the restaurants in town for a summer internship yet?"

Serena had to give it to her mom. When she was sober, she was charming as fuck. She knew she wasn't being fair, but Diane didn't call a family dinner unless something was up. It was a matter of waiting.

"I should hear something back this week. If not, I'll just work shifts at Buddy's like I have every other summer. They're pretty good at adjusting the schedule for me," Faith said. She reached for a breadstick and passed the basket to Serena.

"I'm sure you'll hear something soon. My little girl is going to be a hot commodity once she finishes school."

Faith's smile melted Serena. Any misgivings she had about her mother's intentions were put on hold as she smiled back at her sister. Pride pricked Serena's heart. She knew that as long as Faith stayed on track and finished school, she would succeed. And culinary school didn't require a four-year education. Faith was only four months away from graduating and spreading her wings.

"So, what's going on, Mom? Why are we having family dinner?" Serena couldn't handle the anticipation any longer. Her anxiety was already off the charts, and sitting at the table making small talk wasn't something they did as a family.

"Fair enough. I guess you do know your mother pretty well," Diane said. She held her glass of ice water as if she was giving a toast. "Okay. There's no other way to say this, but Paul and I are moving to California."

The news stunned even Serena. She reached for the salad and knocked her glass of water over in the process. "Oh, shit. I'm sorry."

Diane and Faith jumped up to rescue the breadsticks and wipe up the water before it dribbled onto the carpet. A few napkins thrown Serena's way and it was cleaned up in less than a minute. Paul returned with a fresh glass of ice water. She apologized again only for Diane to wave her off.

"Don't worry about it. It's fine. I know it's a lot to take in."

"Where in California?" Serena kept her voice from elevating. Why? When? How? Even through all of the emotional and exhausting abuse she endured her entire life, Diane was still her mother, and the thought of her not being around gave Serena a confusing mix of anxiety and happiness.

"I applied for a captain's position in Redding and got it." Paul held his hands up and shrugged like it was no big deal.

"That's so cool. When do you leave?" Faith asked.

"Well, that's why we're having dinner. We want to make sure you girls are okay with us moving and have everything you need before we leave," Diane said. She busied herself by filling plates with pasta and sauce and passing them around the table.

"I think Faith and I will be okay. I have her and she has me. As a matter of fact, we can help you pack if you need help," Serena said. The message was there, and delivered with a side of trademark Evans passive-aggressiveness.

Diane ignored Serena's barb. "Always so thoughtful. If nothing else, I raised my girls to be kind and generous."

Again, Serena bit the inside of her cheek. She could take a lot from people, but her fuse was always short with her mother. She needed to get over it. This was a clean slate for all of them. She would still be in town for her sister, and the dark, ominous cloud of her past would disappear with her mother.

"Congratulations, Paul. I think it's crazy you're leaving Vail, but at least you're going to California, which is second best to Colorado. I'll come and visit when we get breaks. And I'll drag Serena with me," Faith said.

"Mrs. Brody only gives me two weeks off. Northern California is at least a two-day trip by bus and we all know my car can't make the drive," Serena said.

"You should look at getting a new car soon. And demand a raise from that old biddy. You've been there long enough now."

"Easier said than done."

Faith softly touched Serena's hand. "You really should get another job. Your boss is a jerk and takes advantage of you."

Serena scoffed. "Mrs. Brody knows everybody in town. If she finds out I'm looking, she'll fire me on the spot. I have to be careful."

"What about where I work? The lodge will need a new front desk clerk since I'm going to give them my two-week notice on Friday. And you already know everyone there," Diane said.

She didn't want her mother's help, even if the idea had merit. Besides, she was the one who got her mom the job at the Waterfall Lodge. If it wasn't for Jackie being willing to give Diane a fresh start, God only knows where her mother would have ended up. A new job sounded great, but Serena didn't like being around a lot of people, and a ski lodge meant a lot of new people daily, even in the summer. That much interaction would force her further into her shell, and that was the last thing she needed.

"I'll be okay. I like my job. Yeah, my boss is a jerk, but I get to read anything and everything that I want."

"But only when Mrs. Brody isn't around. It's not even a real perk." Faith wasn't trying to hurt her, but it felt like an attack.

Serena took a deep breath. "Look, I appreciate everyone's concern, but I've done all right for myself thus far." She didn't tell them about how she ran out of money Monday and if it wasn't for Chloe dropping off a plate of cheese, summer sausage, and a box of crackers, she wouldn't have eaten last night at all. After inventory, she'd wearily walked home and found, much to her surprise and gratefulness, that Chloe kept her promise of leaving leftovers. She'd even added two longnecks and a piece of pie. It was the perfect dinner, at least in that moment.

"I'll still put in a good word if you want."

"Thanks, Mom. I'm sure I'll figure something out soon," Serena said.

"I want both of you to come over and take the things you want to keep. You know, report cards, art projects, old family photos. I think it will be a nice way to spend my last few weeks in Vail."

As much as Serena hated to admit it, her mother looked happy. Paul was a good influence on her. He was the first-long term relationship who stuck around. He was there during the last fallout and made sure she stayed on the wagon. Guilt washed over Serena. She had been burnt too many times before, but it was time to let it go. Her mother, the woman who made her grow up faster than she should have, was leaving. "Saturday afternoons work for me."

"Oh, we can stay the night on a Saturday. Make it a girls' night," Faith said.

Serena smiled and nodded. She could grit her teeth and do that for a day. Then she would only see her mother a few times a year, if that.

"I'll order pizza. It'll be so much fun. How about next Saturday?" Diane clasped her hands in front of her. She gave Serena a quick nod that went unnoticed by Faith.

"I get the guest room, you get the couch," Serena said to Faith.

Faith rolled her eyes. "Tell me something I didn't already know."

❖

"What do you think about all of this?"

Serena reached out and squeezed Faith's hand. Faith obviously had the better relationship with their mother. If Serena didn't have so many damn chips on her shoulders and scars on her heart, she would be in pieces at this news.

Faith squeezed Serena's fingers back. "It's a surprise and makes me a little sad, but I'll always have you. You've never disappointed me. Maybe pissed me off, for sure, but you've been more of a mother than Mom, I mean."

Serena's heart inflated at Faith's confession. "It's going to take a lot for me to leave you."

"Just don't forget to have a life in the process. Okay? Promise me you'll start to loosen up and have fun. As a matter of fact, me and the girls are going to have an almost summer cookout next weekend, if it doesn't snow. Why don't you come?"

Serena pulled up to Faith's apartment building and parked in the closest spot. "That sounds great. Just let me know what you want me to bring."

"Thanks, sis."

Serena looked confused. "For what?"

"For being the better person back there. Mom's finally in a place where she's a decent mother and she's leaving. You have every right to be angry with her, but you always take the high road. I know you love her. Deep down. I wish she was a better person, especially to you, but she's all we have." Faith leaned over and kissed Serena's cheek. "I'll see you soon."

Serena waited until she saw the light flip on in Faith's apartment to pull out of the parking lot. Faith acted young and immature at times, but every once in a while she would say something that plucked Serena's heartstrings.

"Did you survive family night?"

Serena smiled at Chloe's voice over the phone. "I did. It wasn't bad. Get this. Are you sitting down?"

"I'm on pins and needles waiting for whatever bomb you're going to drop."

"Mom and Paul are moving to California," she said.

"Shut up. Why?" Chloe asked.

"Paul got a captain's job at the Redding Fire Department. They leave at the end of the month. We're supposed to go over there some weekend before they leave to take things we want from our childhood."

Chloe snorted. "Like there's anything left. Is there?"

"I remember putting some things in boxes. It'll be new for her, too. I'm sure she doesn't remember much."

Chloe's voice softened. "How do you feel about this? Are you okay with her moving?"

"I was shocked at first. I thought I would be saddled with her for life, but now I have a new start. She'll be gone. Faith will eventually move once she graduates."

"Now you can focus on you," she said.

"Now I can definitely focus on me," Serena said. It still left her with a hollow feeling. She was forever taking care of her family and didn't know the first thing about taking care of herself.

Chapter Four

"I didn't win the lottery, so you are stuck at home with the kids." Gabrielle checked the numbers when she got to work. Falling asleep on the couch had done nothing to improve her mood. Now she was restless with the added bonus of a crick in her neck.

"Shit. Okay, I guess I'll get them up and feed them after all." Rosie gave a hard, audible sigh for effect.

"Don't make me call child services on you. Again." That joke always made them laugh. When Rosie quit work to become a full-time mother, Gabrielle wasn't surprised. Motherhood was her true calling, and Gabrielle had never seen Rosie happier. "Somebody did win it, though. The jackpot is back to the minimum."

"Maybe next time. Since you still have to work, what's on your agenda today?" Rosie asked.

"I have to fix the gas station mess Aaron left on his desk. Then I'm going to sit around and wait for them to deliver me the best design job ever."

"I love your enthusiasm and your belief in your job. I hope you get something incredible, and not another Target."

"I know. But doing these crap jobs just pads my résumé and makes me invaluable," Gabrielle said. She sat back in her chair and relaxed. Ever since the announcement, her entire body was tense with anticipation. Hotels were the cream of the crop for the firm. Most non-chain hotels allowed the architect to make suggestions, and Gabrielle thought her artistic eye was the best. But Tom got that job and she had to wait. Like always.

"I'm serious. You say the word and I'll be your office manager and do boring paperwork for you while you live out your dream job. Open up your own place."

"If things don't go as planned, I might take you up on your offer. And I should probably have a conversation with Christopher to find out what is really going on. This sexism thing isn't really working for me."

"Go. Go now, while you're still passionate about it."

"On it. I'll call you later."

Gabrielle hung up, grabbed her iPad, and walked to Christopher's office. She one knuckle knocked on the ajar door before peeking in. "Hey, boss. You got a minute for me?"

He leaned back in his chair and waved her in. "Sure. Come on in. Have a seat."

Gabrielle took her time getting situated and formulated her thoughts. "You knew I was going to come in here."

He smiled. "I would've been disappointed if you didn't."

"What do we have in the works? Big project wise? I want to know that the playing field will be even."

"Most of the things in the pipeline are pretty standard stuff. But the board came to the decision that you would get the next project, and I believe them. They're giving you a fair shake. I know it doesn't feel that way at the moment, but several of the members are anxious to see what you will do with complete control."

"Oh, please. It's an uphill battle and we both know it. I just want to make sure you've got my back in there and I have a fighting chance." Gabrielle commended herself for keeping her cool and not letting her anger over the unjust situation get the best of her.

"I promise you have more allies on the board than you realize. You've done a great job here and people know it."

"And I will continue as long as I know this isn't a way to keep me quiet and I really have a shot at partner. You know how long and hard I've worked to get to this point."

"Without a doubt. Let's just hope somebody closes a deal soon. I think we have a small soccer stadium and a closet company that wants to expand," he said.

Gabrielle perked up at the soccer stadium. That had the potential to be fun. "When do you think we'll know?"

"By the end of the month. Hang in there. We'll get something fantastic in."

He seemed so genuine that Gabrielle believed him. She left his office feeling inspired. When was the last time that happened? Grabbing all the files on Aaron's job, she headed to one of the conference rooms to spread out the drawings and put together the pieces. Since Aaron abruptly quit, there was a scramble to get a handle on this project. The customers were coming in next week for an update. Gabrielle had called them when the job became hers and introduced herself with as much confidence and excitement as she could muster. It was a shitty deal all around—for them, for her—but she was going to charm them. Aaron had fucked it up a dozen different ways. It had to have been on purpose. She sat down and sighed.

"That bad?"

Tom walked in, hands deep in his pockets, and looked at the piled chaos that was once Aaron's job. He skulked around the drawings, barely lifting up a corner of the top one as if he knew it wasn't his business. For some reason he was comfortable in her space, and that unnerved Gabrielle. After twenty seconds of review, he gave a low whistle and took a step back from the table. "I know you think I got the better deal, but if you can salvage this, they should make you partner."

Gabrielle honestly didn't know if he was complimenting her or buttering her up for something. She shrugged with indifference just to be safe. "I have a meeting with them next week to find out what they were going for and make it happen. This is tiny compared to a hotel. When do you meet up with the clients?"

"Next week, too. I'm still reviewing the contract and the final proposal. It actually sounds like a job for two architects and a handful of engineers," Tom said.

And there it was. He needed help. She couldn't help the smile that fought to remain hidden for professional reasons. This was too perfect. It had only been one day.

"Let's see. There's Jim, Michael, and any of the senior partners. Who has the lightest load?" she asked.

The old Gabrielle would have offered to help and they both knew it. The new and improved Gabrielle wasn't going to do a damn thing to help him. He would get all of the glory. Even if she was approved as co-architect project manager, that wouldn't help the board make a final decision. It would be both their stamps on the project and they would be in the same position. No, worse. Tom would probably get partnership because he would get the credit for managing the team.

"What about your boss? Do you know the projects he's working on?"

Gabrielle did, but she wasn't going to share. This whole exchange was making her uncomfortable. "I'm not too familiar with what

Christopher has going on, but I know he's in his office. You could probably catch him before lunch."

"Oh, okay. I might do that. Thanks for your help."

It wasn't until after he walked out of the conference room that it dawned on her. He was going direct to the source and get her on his project. She whipped out her phone and sent Christopher a message.

Don't even think about putting me on his project.

Bubbles popped up immediately. *What are you talking about?*

Tom's looking for another lead on his project. I'm out. I'll just patiently wait on the next one. It's only fair.

It was an excruciating long five-minute wait until bubbles appeared.

He's going to ask Michael. Christopher followed it up with a smiley face.

Gabrielle laughed and sent him back a smiley face. Christopher wasn't always the friendliest person, but he was fair, and that was all she could ask for.

❖

"Another late night?"

Gabrielle looked up to find Lawrence standing in her doorway. She sat up straighter, cleared her throat, and squelched the need to stand.

"I just want to ensure I'm prepared to meet with Turbo Gas next week. I'm reviewing the notes and taking some of my own." She nodded at him, insinuating she had things under control and he could trust her.

"Then I wish you the best of luck. You always do us proud."

He gave her the slow head nod and continued walking down the hall. Gabrielle glanced at the time. It was twenty after eight, and her favorite sandwich shop closed at nine. If she left now, she'd make it in time. If not, it was another fast food dinner night, and she and her waistline were getting tired of fried foods. She started to pack up her things. Her phone rang as she closed her office door.

"Hi, Mom. What's going on?"

"Are you just now getting off work? Honey, quit working so hard." Meredith's voice held a note of concern that made Gabrielle smile.

She hadn't told her mom about the latest events at Arnest & Max. The last thing she needed was her mother running into Rosie or Anne, which happened a lot, and finding out about the partnership competition that way instead of from her own daughter. She took a deep breath. "You're going to keep me company until I get to my car. That way if I get kidnapped or murdered I'll be sure to give you a complete description before I take my last breath or they destroy my phone."

"Don't even joke like that, Gabrielle." She smiled at her mother's panicked voice and pictured her wagging her forefinger sternly.

"Get away from me, strange man," Gabrielle said. She laughed to let her mom know she was kidding. "Listen, I wanted to let you know that I'm up for partner, but don't get excited just yet. It's a six-month evaluation and they are giving me and Tom the opportunity to show them our best work. Tom, of course, got the best project ever, but I get the next one that trickles in."

"Don't tell me it's another Walgreens or Costco," Meredith said.

"Well, that's just it. They promised me the next big project. Not a corner pharmacy. Anyway, I'm excited about it, and if it doesn't go my way, Rosie and I are going to open up my own firm." Gabrielle talked through Meredith's attempt to interrupt. "Don't get excited. Not yet. Ask me January first what my plans are."

"I'm not going to say anything right now for fear of jinxing it, but I'm holding you to it."

"I hope you do. Okay. I'm safely tucked in my car now. Dinner on Sunday?"

"Roast and potatoes."

"I'll see you then." Gabrielle disconnected the call, and even though loneliness crept into her thoughts, she refrained from calling Rosie. She was probably putting the kids to bed, and a phone call now would disrupt their routine. She dialed the neighborhood deli and tried to ignore how pathetic it was that it was number three on her speed dial list. She quickly placed her order, promising to be there within fifteen minutes. She turned up the music and lowered the windows. Nothing got her in a better mood than cranking boy band music and singing loudly and poorly. Her love for boy bands was a secret she was taking to the grave.

"I gave you an extra cookie since you're probably our last customer." Phillip, Tommy's Deli's sandwich engineer, greeted Gabrielle when she opened the door.

"Well, that sounds like a win in my book." She wasn't going to eat it, but she wasn't going to be ungrateful either.

"Another late night?" he asked as he rang her up.

"They all are. I'm so ready for the weekend. Maybe I'll enjoy it for a change."

"At least the weather is warming up. This winter felt like forever."

She grabbed extra napkins, added a twenty-dollar bill to the tip jar, and waved on her way out. "Have a good night, Phillip."

"See you Sunday, Aunt Gabrielle."

Chapter Five

"Somebody in Vail won the lottery!"

Chloe's voice was so loud that Serena had to turn down her phone. "Ow. Okay, good for them."

"Sadly, it wasn't me, but what if it's somebody we know? How cool would that be? Nobody's come forward, though."

"Why would they? Then everyone they knew, plus some fake relatives, would be crawling out of the woodwork for a handout. And it could have been somebody passing through town." Serena plopped on her couch and turned on the television. After thumbing through the basic channels, she shut it off again and gave Chloe all of her attention.

"I've seen the lottery shows, but how could money be a bad thing?" Chloe asked.

"Truer words have never been spoken. I would hate to have that problem. You know, the one where you can buy anything you want including groceries, a car that's reliable, a roof that doesn't leak, and clothes to keep you warm," Serena said.

"Quit whining. With your mom leaving, you can breathe a little sigh of relief and have fun again. Maybe even start dating."

Serena grabbed the pillow next to her and hugged it. "Let's not get ahead of ourselves. I still have Faith to worry about, and I think I'm done dating. Besides, I'd be happy to just have a dog."

"Stop it. Faith is a grown woman, and you know what Colorado is like in the summer. All the women come out wearing shorts and tanks. It's perfect. The Patio will be open and there isn't a better place to be than there, drinking a beer, surrounded by majestic mountains and staring at all the eye candy Colorado affords us."

"Now you sound like a commercial. Are you girls coming over tonight? Or should I start the movie without you?"

"Give us twenty minutes. We'll pick up a pizza."

"Bless you, my friend. If I don't answer, I'm doing laundry, so let yourself in."

"That basement is scary. Why don't you come over here and do your laundry? Warm safe place, lots of light, and all the snacks you could want."

Serena was tempted, but didn't want to lug everything over to her friends' house in a car that was as temperamental as the weather. Plus, she was always going over there, and for once she wanted to return the favor. "Thanks for the offer, but I'm good. They have a new light downstairs and there are only three tenants. I won't run into anybody. Besides, who does laundry on a Friday night?"

"Sad, lonely women do. We'll see you in twenty."

Serena looked around her apartment. It wasn't anything special, but she kept it clean and organized. The walls were painted beige and decorated with pieces she found downstairs at Fine Antiques or at the Goodwill in Colorado Springs. Her landlady and owner of Fine Antiques, Mary Rhoads, gave Serena first pick at anything she was rotating out of inventory. Serena didn't care much for antiques but appreciated the heavily discounted items. That's what she loved about her place. As oddly decorated as it was, everything was hers. The wrought iron statue of jazz musicians tucked in the corner was her favorite piece. It wasn't as if jazz was her favorite kind of music. Truth be told, she really didn't like music. She liked the quiet because it was the one thing she could control. The piece represented something she strived for. Unity, fun, togetherness. A display of old piano music from the nineteenth century hung to the left of the statue and an old gramophone with a broken horn sat on a planter stand to the right. It still worked, but the sound was so warbled that Serena never played it. It completed the look, though, and the few people who visited her apartment praised her for interior decorating skills.

She popped a cookie in her mouth to tide her over until the girls showed up with pizza and grabbed her laundry basket and detergent. She went through her pile of dirty clothes and picked out dark sweaters and jeans to start. They always took the longest to dry—two turns in the almost broken dryer downstairs—and Serena didn't want to monopolize the laundry room. Since no other tenant did laundry on Friday nights, it was the best time to get the heavy stuff out of the way. She turned her sweaters inside out and checked her jeans pockets for loose change or pieces of paper where she had written down quotes in books she enjoyed reading. When she pulled out the unfamiliar green piece of paper, she looked at it peculiarly until she realized it was the lottery ticket she'd bought instead of a Diet Coke. She'd completely forgotten she had it, even after her mother mentioned the lottery the other night. Before recycling it, she pulled up the state lottery on her phone, not because she thought she'd won, but to rule it out just in case.

She remembered waiting for the page to load, and the next thing she remembered she was on the floor, but she didn't remember how she got from the couch to the floor. Did she pass out? She looked at the lottery ticket still clutched in her hand. No. No way did she just win. She unlocked her phone and looked at the winning numbers again, then compared them to the piece of paper. Holy shit! She won! She was the mysterious winner in Vail. She forced herself to take deep breath after deep breath. Her heart drummed in her chest so hard, the noise was deafening. She felt nauseous and weak and her entire body shook.

"Oh, my God. Are you okay?" Chloe asked.

She rushed across the room and gathered Serena into her arms. Jackie stood behind her looking nervous. Serena wasn't sure when they'd arrived or how long she'd been on the floor. She couldn't find her voice. She was crying so hard she could barely make out her friends' faces through the stream of tears.

"What's going on, honey? Are you hurt?" Chloe asked. Her voice was filled with concern as she gently rocked Serena against her body.

Serena managed to shake her head. She thrust the ticket at Chloe.

"Shut the fuck up! Really? You won the fucking lottery? You're the one the town is looking for? We were just talking about this twenty minutes ago. Jackie, look at this." Chloe showed the ticket to Jackie, who promptly squealed and pulled Serena up. She jumped up and down until Serena joined her. Thirty seconds later they were all dancing, laughing, and crying together.

"So now what?" Jackie asked.

"I have no idea. There are instructions on the back with who to contact. But listen, I don't want people to know it's me," Serena said.

"I don't think that's a choice. I think you have to come forward," Chloe said. She googled and found the six states where a winner could remain anonymous. Colorado was not one of them.

"Shit," Serena said.

The room sobered quickly.

"Look, maybe your mom will still leave town. Maybe you don't have to come forward just yet. What's the lead time? Look it up, babe," Jackie said to Chloe.

Serena sat on the couch and anxiously waited for the news.

"Okay, it says depending on the state, the winner has anywhere from sixty days to one hundred and eighty days to claim. Wait. Some are even three years. Who would wait three years? Anyway, there's tons of advice what to do. Photograph the front and back of the ticket and take a video of you with it," Chloe said.

"Like I need that leaked on YouTube or to the news station, but okay. We can do that. What else?" Serena asked.

"First thing tomorrow, we're going to your bank and getting you a safety deposit box. Some articles say sign the back of the ticket, but some say don't. And don't tell people, whatever you do. Get a post office box and change your phone number. Maybe. That might be for people who still have landlines," Chloe said.

"This is so overwhelming."

Chloe knelt down in front of Serena and put her hands on her knees. "Listen to me. It's going to be okay. We won't say anything about this to anyone. We're going to help you figure this out. We know a lawyer in Denver who can help. Her specialty is corporate law and finance. We can start there and see what she advises."

"My lips are sealed. I won't breathe a word of this either," Jackie said.

"I trust you both. You're my best friends," Serena said. She leaned back against the couch as the adrenaline finally left her body. "But can we eat something, because I feel like I'm going to pass out."

Fast as lightning, Chloe threw pizza on paper plates and handed everyone a beer. "We definitely should toast."

"Definitely," Serena and Jackie said at the same time.

"Here's to never wanting again. I mean, once I actually get the money," Serena said. "I wonder if it's quick or not? Shit. I'm going to have to keep my job for a few weeks, I bet."

"Probably so. They advise not to change your routine right away. We'll find out everything Monday. Can you get the day off?"

Serena shrugged. "I'll just have to tell Mrs. Brody it can't be helped and she'll have to open the store and run it until I can get in."

"You just won the fucking lottery. Take the whole day off!" Chloe tossed a pillow at her.

"You just told me to be normal and do normal things." Serena caught the pillow and threw it back.

"Well, one day off is not out of the ordinary. Say it's a family emergency," Chloe said.

"She's heard all of that before, and I'm a horrible liar." Serena shrugged. She wasn't sure what she was going to tell Mrs. Brody.

"Okay, let's talk about fun things. You'll probably get a lump sum, right? What are you going to do with twenty or whatever million dollars?" Chloe asked.

"First thing is to get a newer car. One that runs. Maybe a Jeep," Serena said.

"Or a brand new one," Jackie said.

"Too much attention."

"People are going to find out. Stay with us once the news breaks. They won't look for you at our place. And it's a gated community, so the paparazzi can wait outside."

"Do you really think people are going to stalk me? This is just so unreal," Serena said. She rubbed her face and tucked her long, honey-colored hair back behind her ears. "I mean, I don't have any family except for Faith and Diane. Technically, Paul, but I'm not really counting him."

Chloe shook her head at Serena. "Money changes people. Think of all of the scams people commit just for money. And that's only a little bit. Maybe you should move. Start over fresh."

"You could go to California with Diane and Paul," Jackie said.

She was immediately barraged with pillows, napkins, anything and everything Serena and Chloe could throw at her.

"I'm kidding, I'm kidding." Jackie held up her hands in surrender.

"Even if Serena moves, the world will still know she won the money. Stay here where you're comfortable. Buy a big house, drive a fancy car, open up a coffee shop or something you've always wanted to do. What do you want to do?"

Serena chewed on a piece of pizza before answering. She covered her mouth and swallowed. "You know what I really always wanted? An animal rescue place or a place where people can drop off their pets while they vacation here. Vail has a lot of rich people who have a lot of pets. I can't tell you how many people came into the bookstore and told me how much they missed their fur babies."

Chloe waved her hands at both of them for attention. "Yes. That's perfect. People will pay top dollar for somebody to give their cats or dogs top-notch care while they ski and party. And still cuddle with them at night. Great idea, Serena."

Serena smiled as her brain snapped a picture of her future. A Grand Cherokee with the windows down and a scruffy-looking medium-sized dog hanging her head out of window, gulping the fresh air. "And I'm going to get my own dog. First a car so my new-to-me dog can go with me everywhere." Serena thought about King, her sweet golden retriever mix they had to give away because their new apartment didn't allow pets. Another victim of Diane's selfish life choices. Getting kicked out of seven places during her childhood made having a pet nothing more than a dream.

"I want to go with you. Make sure you don't rescue them all," Chloe said.

"Hey, now I can afford it." She repeated it and pressed her fingers against her mouth as if the words weren't true and she had to hold them there until one of them confirmed.

"Yes, you can. Anything you want. For the rest of your life. It's karma. You winning the lottery after your mom tells you she's moving is like the universe's way of high-fiving you." Chloe hugged Serena again until they both started crying.

"I just can't believe this. I bought the ticket on a whim. Everybody's been talking about it and I forgot I even bought it. My mouth just told Dougie to give me a ticket instead of a Diet Coke." Serena relived that scene over and over, still cringing at scraping her change for that day and how Dougie kept his eye on her like she was going to steal something.

"Dougie at the Quik Stop? Oh, shit. I think the store gets cash for you purchasing the ticket there. It's like one hundred grand or something," Jackie said.

"I'm sure he'll get some money for being the one on duty. Let's watch how fast he burns through his and learn what not to do with money," Chloe said.

"I'm sure I'm going to make a ton of bad decisions."

"Are you kidding me? I've never seen anyone know the value of a dollar more than you. And I mean that in a nice way. You've done an amazing job and got back up every time you got knocked down. I couldn't be prouder of you," Chloe said.

When Serena met Chloe ten years ago, she was juggling several jobs trying to pay rent and survive on her own in Vail. The cost of living was outrageous, but Serena was determined to stay for Faith's sake. Chloe was a customer who frequented the little diner Serena worked swing shift at. She always tipped well even though they kept their relationship professional for the first year. They were both polite with one another and spoke of the weather and daily specials. When Chloe brought Jackie into the diner, the three of them hit it off immediately and their friendship grew into something Serena had never experienced before. A trusting relationship. She was hesitant to open up, but after ten years, Chloe and Jackie had proven themselves as true friends.

"You know I'm going to buy you anything you want, right?" Serena said.

"You save your money. We don't need a thing," Chloe said.

Jackie rolled her eyes. "I really want a vacation to Jamaica or somewhere super warm. This winter lasted forever." Chloe nudged her. "What? That's a shit ton of money. You seriously think she won't do something for us? Come on."

"I'm with Jackie. You can either come up with something massive and frivolous, or I will surprise you. I don't think you want that," Serena said.

"Let's just wait until you have the money in your hand. Then we can plan our getaway or whatever you two decide," Chloe said. She squeezed Serena until she grunted. "I can't fucking tell you how awesome this is. Seriously, the best thing ever. Call it karma, hard work, luck. You deserve this break."

Serena brushed the tears off her cheeks. "I can't believe this. I really can't. Who knew that one spontaneous decision, and one I instantly regretted, could change everything about my life?"

"Pack a bag. You're coming with us. Take a good look around. This life? The one you were drowning in? Yeah, that one's over. As a matter of fact, leave all the keys on the counter. On to the bigger and way better things." Chloe pulled Serena up from the couch and pointed to the bedroom. "You have two minutes to pack. Go."

Chapter Six

"What's up, boss?" Gabrielle looked up to find Christopher leaning on the doorframe of her office with a huge grin. She instantly touched her face to check if she had lunch crumbs stuck to her cheek or a smudge of ink on her chin from when she'd replaced the toner in her printer just a few short minutes ago. She leaned back in her chair and tucked her hair behind her ear.

"We have the perfect job for you."

Gabrielle sat up straight in her chair and almost stood out of sheer excitement. "Tell me all about it."

Christopher sat across from her and leaned forward. "We got something. Something that you're going to like. And it's all yours."

"Don't keep me in suspense. Tell me about it."

"Tomorrow Brad has a meeting in Vail, and I want you to go with him. He's meeting with someone who wants a daycare or some type of center built. Lots of potential, and it's all yours," he said.

Gabrielle nodded and chewed the end of her pen. "Is that all you know about it?"

"Brad had initial contact with the client. I'm going to tell him that you'll be point architect on this project and you're going with him. I wanted to clear it with you first."

Gabrielle looked at her calendar and nodded. "I can free up some time. I'll talk with him and get more information."

"He said money was no object, so this is perfect for you to show the client and us what you can do."

"Thank God because I was getting really worried the last month when nothing major came in. Tom already has a head start on his project," Gabrielle said.

Neither of them said anything about Tom's project and how behind he already was. The customer made a few changes, but it was a massive job and even with help, it was proving to be a bigger bite than he could chew. Gabrielle almost felt sorry for him. Almost. She knew the firm would grant him more help because they couldn't afford to lose the client.

"I told you the next big thing was yours." Christopher stood, suggesting this little office visit was over. "On Friday, tell me how it went. I'm out tomorrow and Thursday." He rapped his knuckles twice on her desk. "Good luck. Let's hope this is your lucky break."

"I won't let you or the company down." Gabrielle nodded at him as he left her office. She called Brad's cell phone, but it went straight to voice mail. "Brad, I'm going to head to Vail tonight. I have a friend there, but call me later and give me the details of the meeting. I'm excited to meet with the client and get started." She hung up and called Rosie's younger sister who lived in Vail to see if she was free for dinner.

"What a nice surprise." Elizabeth never said hello when she answered the phone. She'd told Gabrielle a long time ago that it was wasted effort. Gabrielle didn't disagree.

"Hey, baby sis. I am going to be in your neck of the woods tonight and wanted to see if you had time for dinner." Even though they weren't really related, Elizabeth always seemed like the little sister Gabrielle never had. She followed them around during high school and tagged along at college parties. Gabrielle was the person she turned to for guidance even though she had Rosie.

"That sounds great. Dinner, then zip-lining. I'm in," Elizabeth said.

"Hold up. I didn't agree to doing anything athletic."

Elizabeth snorted. "Oh, please. They strap you in and you glide through the air and you just have to sit there and let gravity happen."

"And you want me to do this after dinner? On a full stomach? Sounds disastrous." It's not that she was against the idea. Zip lining was fun. The two times she'd gone before were exhilarating. It just wasn't a good idea after dinner and alcohol.

"Weird. I thought you were only three years older, not twenty years older," Elizabeth teased.

"Okay, okay. Where should we meet and at what time? I'll hit the road in a bit and we can meet for happy hour. How about Franklin's?"

"Five thirty. I'll see you there."

Gabrielle hung up and immediately texted Rosie.

Two things. I finally got my big project AND I'm having dinner with Elizabeth tonight.

Have a drink for me and call me on the way there. I want to hear all about it.

Gabrielle put her phone down and finished everything on her desk. She uploaded her billable hours, signed off on design changes, and marked herself out of office until Friday. An afternoon off sounded like a great idea. She would pack a bag and stay at least tonight in Vail. Maybe more to get a feel for the town if she was going to be designing something to fit in. Vail was quaint, and she was sure the town had design requirements. She hoped the clients would be open to any suggestions. She knew she would have to learn about safe playground equipment and the right number of bathrooms per children. She wasn't going to dwell on it now. She would have the meeting and then start designing. But really, how hard could it be to design a daycare?

❖

"Excuse me, but does anyone work here?"

Gabrielle tapped her fingers on the counter, her irritation at the lack of staff at the lodge apparent by the continuous clicking of her nails in rapid rhythm. When nobody responded immediately, she rang the tiny bell incessantly until feminine hands gently pulled the bell away from her.

"Hi. Can I help you?"

"Well, I've been standing here for a good five minutes waiting for somebody to help me." Gabrielle snapped at the clerk and then took a deep breath. "I need a room. Is there anything available?"

"I'm sorry nobody was here when you arrived. We are unfortunately short-staffed today."

"That's not my problem. You should always have somebody at the front desk because you never know who's going to walk through those doors. That's just good customer service." Gabrielle knew she was being a jerk, but she was on her last nerve and had never had to wait this long for service before.

"Duly noted. Hello, I'm Serena, and yes, we do have rooms available. How many nights would you like to stay?"

Gabrielle studied the woman in front of her. She was surprisingly calm for somebody who was the recipient of her rudeness. She was attractive with long light brown hair and blue-green eyes. Gabrielle guessed her to be in her mid-twenties. She had that quiet controlled personality that wasn't exactly confidence, but just an acceptance of life. If Gabrielle wasn't so irritated at her long drive and the ridiculous traffic, she would have tried a little harder to be her normal charming self. "Just one night. And can I schedule a zip-line excursion for tonight?"

Serena quirked her eyebrow at Gabrielle. "Are you sure you're in the right frame of mind for outdoor fun?"

Gabrielle should've been offended by Serena's judgement, but instead of getting upset, she laughed. "Okay, you're right. I'm meeting a friend for dinner and it's entirely her idea to go zip-lining. She's obviously more adventurous than I am. Personally, I could go for a long hot bath, a glass of wine, and my laptop for the rest of the night." It didn't feel weird to share this information. There was something calming about Serena that made Gabrielle take another deep breath and relax.

"Your idea of a good night is my idea of a good night. Not to sell the lodge's excellent zip-lining experience short. It really is fun and exciting."

"I think I might need both. There was a bad wreck on the highway that backed up traffic for miles. I was supposed to arrive two hours ago and now I'm pressed for time."

"Oh, I'm so sorry. Here, let's get you a room," Serena said. She quickly toggled over to the reservations screen on the computer and asked for Gabrielle's information. "Looks like we have a nice suite far away from the elevator."

"I just want a regular room," Gabrielle said. She patted her hair and tucked her shirt tighter to reduce the disheveled look. She handed Serena her credit card but delivered it with a smile this time.

"One key or two?" Serena asked. She swiped one and handed it to Gabrielle, who shook her head to a second key. "Just head for the elevators. Your room is on the third floor."

"Ah, the penthouse." Gabrielle smiled so Serena would know she was joking.

"Nothing but the best. Enjoy your stay. And if you want to sign up for activities the lodge offers, please check with Katie over in customer service over there in the corner and she'll hook you up."

Gabrielle picked up the key card, looked at the map of where her room was, and thanked the woman who not only helped her get a room quickly, but who had lightened her mood. An overturned truck had spilled corn all over the highway and she'd grumbled and huffed while it took the crews over an hour to clear a path for cars to get through. Her nerves were at a critical point when she pushed through the lodge's doors. It was an impressive lodge with hundreds of windows and fireplaces in all the rooms. When Gabrielle opened the door to room 318, she gasped. Serena still gave her a suite, even though she specifically said she only wanted a basic room. Before unpacking, she picked up the phone to call the front desk.

"This is Serena. May I help you?"

"Hi, Serena. This is Gabrielle. I just checked in. It appears you put me up in a suite and I requested a regular room." She worked to keep the irritation out of her voice.

"It was a rough day for you. I gave you an upgrade. That way you can still have your bubble bath after zip-lining and we can even send up a bottle of wine."

Gabrielle was taken aback by Serena's kindness. After being rude even by her own standards, why would anybody be nice to her? "Thank you very much. It was unnecessary, but appreciated. I'll be sure to tell your manager how helpful you've been. Unless you're going to get into trouble for the upgrade?"

Serena laughed. "Oh, no. The boss won't care at all. Thank you, though. Please enjoy your stay."

Gabrielle hung up and checked the time. Elizabeth was meeting her downstairs at Franklin's in ten minutes. Hell, she was probably already there. She quickly slipped into jeans and a fresh shirt, and brushed her hair. She grabbed her warm fleece jacket because it got cold at night. If they were zip-lining after dinner, she was going to be out in the elements, and she hated being cold.

"Sorry I'm late. I got caught up in that snafu on the highway. How are you?" Gabrielle leaned down for a hug and a kiss from Elizabeth.

"You're not too late." Elizabeth handed her a cocktail as she sat down. "And I didn't want you to miss happy hour, so I took the liberty and ordered you a mojito."

Gabrielle nodded her approval and took a sip. "Good choice. What's good here to eat? I skipped lunch, so I'm famished. And before I stuff myself, are we really going zip-lining? I can't feel sick or break any bones because I'm meeting a new client tomorrow, and this one is a make or break deal."

"Oh, fun. You'll have to tell me all about it."

"I really don't know much about the project other than it's a daycare for rich babies."

"Well, that sounds boring."

"That's because you're young and you hate kids. I see it as a challenge. Hopefully they'll be open to my suggestions. I'm anxious to find out the class size and what the clients are thinking design-wise." Gabrielle thought about all the fun and educational things she could recommend during the meeting tomorrow. With her experience with Rosie and Anne's three children and their obsession with the best educational toys, Gabrielle truly believed she was going to knock this one out of the park.

❖

"Where's the meeting?" Gabrielle asked Brad as she slipped into the company car. He waited until she got situated before driving off.

"It's on location. The customer purchased two acres just on the edge of town. GPS says it's only a six-minute drive from here. Cheaper and free of all the zoning restrictions," he said.

Gabrielle thought it was strange that a daycare wasn't right in the heart of town where parents could visit children on their lunch hours if they wanted, but six minutes wasn't a long drive at all.

"So, what do we know about the client?"

"Not a whole lot. She came recommended to us from a previous client, one of Lawrence's from way back when. He designed the Waterfall Lodge in 1996. Did you know that? He was a badass a long time ago."

"He's not doing too shabby now either."

"Now he just collects his money. He does very little legwork. He attends the big meetings, but for the most part, he just collects fat checks," Brad said. He leaned over toward Gabrielle and pointed. "What does that sign say?"

She squinted until the letters came into view. "Bear Camp Road. Who would name a road Bear Camp?"

Brad turned and took an immediate right onto a partially hidden gravel road.

"You're not taking me out here to kill me, are you?" Gabrielle asked.

"Nah. Not this close to the road." He wagged his eyebrows at her. "Oh, look. There's our client."

Another squint. Gabrielle saw a woman standing outside a dark Grand Cherokee. "Hold up. Is that a dog? Does she have a dog with her?"

She and Brad watched as the woman called the dog over and secured it to a leash.

"Looks that way." He put the car in park and hopped out. "You coming or are you going to work from there?" He pointed at the passenger seat.

"I'm coming. Let me grab my stuff." A chill shook Gabrielle's shoulders while sweat gathered at her lower back and on her palms. She wiped her hands on her skirt and took a deep breath. She had to do this. This was everything right now. She opened the door and followed Brad to where the woman and her dog, now on a leash, were standing. No. It couldn't be. She knew two people in Vail, and one of them was standing in front of her.

"Serena. Hi. You're our client?" Gabrielle couldn't keep the surprise or confusion out of her voice. "I just saw you at the lodge last night."

"I was only helping a friend out. Three people called in sick yesterday, and I didn't have anything else to do so I stood in."

Gabrielle was in shock. She instantly cringed recalling the way she had initially treated Serena. She wasn't a total jerk, but she wasn't on her best behavior last night either, something she regretted at this moment. "Okay. So, you want to put a daycare here?" Gabrielle stood to the left of Brad and stepped back when Serena's dog moved her way to say hello.

"Oh, I'm sorry about L.B. Here, let me put him in the Jeep." Serena opened the door and L.B. jumped in without being told.

"He's very well behaved." Gabrielle felt she had to say something.

"I just rescued him three weeks ago. He just looked up at me and I knew we were destined to be together. That's why I want to open up a doggie daycare. The Pet Posh Inn. For anybody who wants to bring their dog on vacation with them, but still be able to ski and have fun around the area."

"Oh, I was under the impression it was a child daycare. So, you want us to design a doggie daycare?" Gabrielle shot Brad a look to tell him they would talk about this later.

"Is that a problem? Have you done anything like this before?" Serena asked.

"We helped design Denver's ASPCA shelter. The one off 470. It blends well with other businesses around the area. Since you don't really have any close neighbors where you'll have to keep a similar décor, your vision can be whatever you want it to be. We're here to look at the land and talk about what you see happening here," Brad said.

Gabrielle stopped herself from rolling her eyes at his syrupy sweet ass-kissing sales technique. Instead she studied Serena's reaction to what he was saying and watched her nod as she absorbed all of his clichés. She couldn't blame her. Brad was smooth and nice looking. She wondered how many times he slept with clients to seal the deal. Another cliché.

"What do you think, Gabrielle?" Serena asked.

Gabrielle cleared her throat and looked directly at Serena. Her blue-green eyes were stunningly pretty, but they were guarded. Her posture was straight, but the confidence she had was fragile. This was a woman who'd just made a major decision and was trying to get comfortable with it. The Jeep had temporary tags on it and she'd just revealed that L.B. was a recent adoption. Everything about her said new money. Maybe she had just received an inheritance. How else could she afford to do this at her age? She was definitely younger than Gabrielle.

"We can do whatever you're envisioning. I can get the surveyors out to mark the property. Then we can put our heads together and design exactly what you want," Gabrielle said.

Serena smiled warmly and Gabrielle knew she'd said the right thing. They started a walk around the property. Gabrielle followed and took notes as Serena explained her vision. She wanted people and their pets to feel comfortable here. This needed to be a safe and trustworthy place for people who either came to town and wanted their pets with them or for people leaving town who couldn't take their pets, but wanted to place them with people they trusted. It wasn't a new idea, but Gabrielle felt Serena's passion for her vision and knew it was going to be a success. Especially since she was going to plug a lot of money into it. Curb appeal spoke volumes.

"I'd like to have a sit-down somewhere and discuss this further. Do you have time to grab lunch with us?" Gabrielle asked.

"If we head back to the lodge, we can set up in one of the meeting rooms and have Franklin's cater us lunch," Serena said. She looked at Gabrielle's three-inch heels. "And you probably want to slip into something more comfortable. Those shoes and this property aren't a great match."

Brad snickered and Gabrielle shot him another look. He had to have known all of this. She didn't figure him for a saboteur, but nothing shocked her anymore. "That sounds great. We'll meet you back there."

The second they slipped into the car, Gabrielle turned on Brad. "Seriously? You told Christopher it was daycare. Did you not know it was for pets?"

"Absolutely not, but you have to admit, her idea is brilliant." Even though Brad was laughing, he shook his head. "At least you won't be bored. And this isn't a hotel. Well, at least not for humans." He was still laughing when they pulled up into the lodge's parking lot.

Chapter Seven

"Don't mind Lucky Baxter. He's really a sweet dog." Serena reached down and stroked his wiry fur. He looked up at her so trustingly from his bed inside the small conference room the lodge reserved for their meeting. Serena felt her heart melt at his utmost trust in her.

"What kind of dog is he?" Gabrielle asked.

"He's a mutt. I think terrier and maybe labradoodle? I suppose I could do one of those DNA kits you can get for your dogs now." Of all the people Serena could have a meeting with, Gabrielle was not at all who she expected. It was a blessing and a curse. She made Serena nervous because of her confidence and good looks, yet both of those traits excited her, too. Was her skin as soft as it looked? And even after being outside for half an hour, Serena could smell her lotion or shampoo. She smelled like freshly baked cookies. It made her smile. Why, yes, I'll take a crumb, thank you, she thought.

"He's very well behaved."

Serena noticed the way Gabrielle's voice wavered and how her eyes darted from Lucky Baxter to the door and back. "If you'd like, I can put him in the office. He probably needs to spend some quality time with his Aunt Jackie. He's pretty much the mascot here. I'll be right back." When Serena stood, L.B. did, too, and followed her as if he was born at her side. She left him in the office with explicit instructions at the front desk to keep him in there until she was back.

Serena returned the same time lunch was delivered. The next fifteen minutes were punctuated with small talk and praise over the delicious food. It was hard for Serena to keep her eyes off Gabrielle. She was very attractive, but not overtly. She could have accentuated her features with different makeup and let her hair down, but Serena guessed this was her work persona. Her eyes were captivating. She wore glasses, the fashionable kind with thick black rims that made it hard for Serena not to make eye contact. Gabrielle fascinated Serena. Brad was attractive in a jock turned model kind of way, but Serena wasn't interested in him. All of her attention was on Gabrielle.

"If you're interested in working with us, I have the paperwork for you to sign and then I can let the two of you work out the details." Brad slid the paperwork to Serena. "Gabrielle is one of our best. She won't disappoint you."

Serena reviewed the paperwork, wishing Chloe was here to give her the go-ahead. It was Chloe who had recommended Arnest & Max so, with a burst of confidence, she signed her name on the proverbial dotted line. It wasn't the full contract, just a retainer so they could get started. The most she'd be out was a few thousand dollars of design time.

Serena shook Brad's hand and watched as he gathered up his things and nodded to them on his way out. "Let me know if you need anything else. It's a pleasure doing business with you."

There were a few moments of awkward silence as they settled in to discuss Serena's vision.

"First of all, I'd like to know why this? What made you want to buy land and open up the Pet Posh Inn?"

Serena liked the way Gabrielle kept eye contact with her and made her feel like her answer was the most important thing. And her eyes. Had she ever seen that color before? They were light brown with a copper ring along the outside of the iris.

"When I was thirteen we had a dog that we had to get rid of because of our living circumstances. I never knew what happened to him." Serena's mind wandered for a bit as she thought about King and the last day she'd hugged him and kissed his perfect black nose. She shook her head to snap herself back into the conversation. "Now I'm in a position where I can have as many pets as I want. That's not logical, so I decided to find a different way to surround myself with animals."

"I get it. Let's talk about capacity and the overall look. What are you envisioning? Rustic? Clean?" Gabrielle had her iPad ready for note taking and her Apple pencil in her bag in case she needed to do some sketching.

"I think it should be a log cabin style, but clean. I want it to look new, not like a place Abraham Lincoln grew up in," Serena said. Gabrielle's soft laughter set adrift a sea of butterflies in Serena's stomach. The feeling was so foreign that she put her hand across her midsection to hold herself down. She wasn't getting anything other than professionalism from Gabrielle, so she was conflicted by the sudden desire that filled her. It was probably because this was the first time she'd been alone with a woman who wasn't her friend in a long time. When was her last date? Six months ago? How long had she and Amber been apart now?

"How many rooms are you thinking? And what kind of rooms? Big? Small? Both?"

The questions swirled around in Serena's head. She had barely considered specifics. "I want a dog area, but I also want a cat area. And while we're at it, a room for small pets like rabbits, turtles, guinea pigs, and even birds.

"So, at least a dozen large rooms for big dogs, and double that for the medium and small dogs. Definitely posh. Heated floors, but easy to hose off and clean." Serena rattled off her vision while Gabrielle continued to type. Activity rooms, outdoor corrals for the different-sized dogs, a play space for cats, large windows for the bird room, and a quiet space for the little pets who were sensitive to noise and light. "Oh, and we'll need a few offices. At least one for me, one for the office manager, and one or two for the vets on staff."

Serena watched as Gabrielle scribbled the last of her notes.

"I'll have our surveyors mark off the land so I know where it is and we don't build on something that isn't yours. I'll come up with a few ideas based on today's conversation. Give me a week and I'll be in touch," Gabrielle said.

"What do you need from me?"

"I'm going to need the title or the plot called out on your paperwork. If you don't have it, that's fine. I can get a copy down at the courthouse. It's so our civil engineers know how to plumb for water and sewage. I need the property dimensions so we are maximizing the area."

"Do you know how much this is going to cost me?"

"Once we come up with a design that you like, then I'll have to figure out hours it will take to engineer—both structural and civil—and you'll need to find a builder you like."

Serena sat up straight. "Wait. I have to come up with the builder?"

Gabrielle touched her hand lightly. Serena held her breath at the softness of Gabrielle's fingertips. "Not at all. We are happy to give you a list of the companies we've worked with and trust."

"If you don't mind recommending a company, that would help me out immensely." Serena realized she was putting all of her eggs into one basket trusting Gabrielle so quickly. It was completely out of character for her, but Arnest & Max came highly recommended.

"Serena, I'll go back to Denver and work up some ideas. Let's plan to meet next week. Are you up for coming to my office? I have better equipment there to show you my vision."

Serena liked the way Gabrielle said her name. Her voice was honey—smooth and thick, and made Serena stumble a bit before committing. "Yes. I can come over whenever. Just give me the address and when and I'll be there. L.B. will stay home."

Gabrielle opened up a small silver case from her purse and pulled out a business card. She flipped it and wrote down her cell number. "If you can think of anything at all or need to just talk, please don't hesitate to call me. I'm available any time."

"So, you're a workaholic," Serena said.

Gabrielle shrugged. "I love my job and I love it when I get to do creative things. I'm looking forward to this. You have so much potential, and I'm excited to get started."

If Serena wasn't convinced before, she sure as hell was now. It was nice to talk to somebody about her vision and not have people judge her for her decision. She'd broken down and told Faith about winning the lottery two days after Diane left for California. Faith was angry at first that Serena had waited to tell her, but after her initial shock, she understood and cried with Serena at her good fortune.

There was a bit of a struggle on whether Diane should be notified. Faith wanted to tell her right away, but Serena stood her ground. It was her story to tell, and Faith was going to have to give her time until she found the courage. She knew Diane would want money. Not just a little bit like Faith, but millions. It wasn't a conversation Serena was ready to have with her mother. She wanted most of it invested so when her mother asked for a handout, she would only be able to hand over a small amount. She loved her mom, but she also saw what excess money did to her. More drugs, more booze, more weekends away.

Everyone Serena had told was supportive, but there was always a layer of fear, whether for her or themselves or someone else. Gabrielle didn't have that. She seemed like she simply wanted to make Serena's vision come to life.

"I'll be sure to call you if I think of anything else. This is all new to me. You've probably done this a million times." Serena fidgeted with the business card until Gabrielle looked at her hands to see what she was doing with it. She quickly slid the card into her pocket.

"Well, not really a million, but I've been an architect for ten years. Most of my projects have been pretty standard, but I'm excited to have a bit more of a creative license with your dream." Gabrielle's smile made Serena's body swell in all the right places. She took a step back, suddenly nervous at her nearness.

"I look forward to seeing what you come up with. I'd better go find L.B. and get home," Serena said. She grabbed her messenger bag and opened the door for Gabrielle, sneaking a peak at her long legs and noticing the dirt on one of her heels. "I'm sorry you didn't know we were going to the site."

Gabrielle looked down at her shoes. "It's my fault. I assumed we were just meeting in town. I should have asked questions."

"Or Brad should have told you," Serena said.

Gabrielle playfully shrugged, but Serena saw a little spark of fire in those beautiful, unique eyes. There was tension there, but she didn't want to pry. It was too soon.

"Or that. In all fairness, I slipped out early to meet my best friend's little sister, so he might have told me and I wasn't paying attention."

"Did you go zip-lining?" Serena asked.

"Sadly, no. We spent most of the night at Franklin's appreciating a new wine they were promoting. Which, by the way, was excellent and we gave them thumbs up."

"There's always next time. I have a feeling you'll be spending a lot of time in Vail," Serena said.

"I have a feeling you are probably right. Call me if you need me," Gabrielle said.

Serena slipped behind the front desk to pick up L.B. but watched Gabrielle until she disappeared behind the elevator doors.

She opened the office to find him on the small office couch curled up on Jackie's lap. They were both eating pizza. Serena put her hands on her hips. "Really? People food?"

Jackie held her hands up in surrender. "Hey, when a millionaire pup wants pepperoni and sausage pizza, I oblige. I mean, you did put me in charge of him until your meeting was over. How did that go?"

Serena plopped down in the chair opposite the two snugglers and sighed. "The architect, Gabrielle, is smart, has legs that go on forever, smells good, is charming, and has these beautifully light brown eyes with copper circles that are mesmerizing."

"So, let me get this straight. She's gorgeous and smart and you'll spend a lot of time together during this project, yet here you sit all mopey. What's the problem?" Jackie asked between bites of the pizza.

Even though she wasn't hungry, Serena grabbed a piece of pizza to have something to do. "It's the worst news, really."

Jackie sat up, prompting L.B. to jump down and onto Serena's lap. "Oh, my God. She's married. Son of a bitch."

"Worse. She hates dogs."

"What? You're kidding. Did she actually say that? Because that's not professional at all."

Serena waved her hand at Jackie. "No, no. She didn't say anything, but she wanted nothing to do with L.B. That's why I had to put him in here."

Jackie shook her head. "That doesn't mean anything. Maybe she loves dogs but she's allergic. Or maybe she's scared of them. Maybe you can be her heroine and either give her Allegra or show her how sweet and loving this handsome boy is." She waved her crust at L.B., who looked at Serena for approval. Serena nodded once and L.B. jumped down and was on Jackie's lap within two seconds. "When do I get to meet her?"

"Oh, she's staying here. She's the one I gave the suite to."

"That means she's going to check out. So, I can check her out." Jackie wagged her eyebrows at Serena.

"I'm going to tell Chloe that you're hitting on my architect."

"I'm going to take a photo and show Chloe. Then we can all talk about her."

Serena gasped and whispered, "No, you won't."

"You're right. I'm entirely too lazy to get up at the moment, but just know that we will meet her. And I'm sure she will be fabulous. When do you see her next?"

"She said next week sometime. I don't know how that's even possible, but she said she'll have a starting point for me. And she's excited to get to be creative on my project. From what I gathered, she does a lot of franchises and buildings that already have a set structure," Serena said.

"Just don't let her talk you into something you don't want. This is your dream, your vision. You make sure she hears what you say, and you stick to your guns. I don't care if she has a great ass or not."

Serena smiled at Jackie's passionate nature and how protective she was. If she only knew just how tight Gabrielle's ass was, she wouldn't be so fierce with her words.

Chapter Eight

"I can't even begin to tell you how conflicted I am about this project," Gabrielle said as soon as Rosie picked up the phone.

"Hold on, let me get away from the kids. Anne, honey, can you keep an eye on them? I have a nine-one-one from Gabrielle right now."

Gabrielle pictured Rosie pointing at the phone and either rolling her eyes or tapping her four fingers repeatedly against her thumb, insinuating she was talking up a storm. She didn't care. Whatever had to happen in order for her to get away for a few minutes to help Gabrielle keep her sanity was worth it.

"Talk to me," Rosie said.

"Okay, so my daycare project?"

"The one you were given complete freedom on and the one that was going to make you partner? Yes, I know of it. What happened?" Rosie asked.

"It's a pet daycare. With dogs and cats and all sorts of animals. Rosie, there are dogs, and the client showed up with her faithful companion at her side. I almost passed out," Gabrielle said.

"Hey, I'm sure if you explain to your client that you have an issue with dogs, then she won't bring the dog around."

"Okay, now listen to what you just said. Really listen." Gabrielle could hear the panic in her own voice. "I can't tell the one client who is going to be the reason I become partner that she can't bring her dog to her own project. Then I look like the worst person to do the job. What if she fires me?"

"Stop. She's not going to fire you. You need to take a deep breath. It's going to be fine. Why don't you spend some time over here with Muppet and see how it goes. We can take it slow."

"I don't know. I'm hoping this is just a one-time deal. I mean, she's coming to Denver next week and she said she wasn't bringing the dog with her. I'm only going to be on the project for a few months, at the longest. Then it'll go to the engineers and the builder. Maybe I can get away with only a few visits," Gabrielle said.

"Tell me about the client. What's she like?"

"Oh, my God. Get this, don't say anything to anybody and I'm not one hundred percent sure, although I'm almost positive…"

"Good God. Spit it out already. You're driving me crazy."

"Sorry. Yeah, I know I'm all over the place right now. I'm processing everything that happened in the last four hours. I think my new client is Colorado's latest lottery winner."

"Get out. Seriously?"

"I don't know that for sure, but I'm going to google it when I get home. She's young, attractive, building her dream business even though she clearly has no idea how to approach it, has a new Jeep, a new dog. There's just something about her. She's quiet, shy, and doesn't seem to have a lot of confidence," Gabrielle said.

"What's her name? I'll google it right now. I'm in my office."

"Serena. Serena Evans." Gabrielle heard Rosie's fingers click against the keyboard.

"Here! Latest Vail resident Colorado state winner of forty-two million dollars. Twenty-nine-year old Serena Evans. Most of the winners have photos of them holding up a big check, but she doesn't. Can't say I blame her. That's a lot of money, and probably a lot of people want some of it," Chloe said.

"She's really nice. I think it's great that she won, but I can't imagine the headaches and all the people hitting her up for a handout." Gabrielle pulled into her driveway and waited for their conversation to wrap up.

"What's going on tonight? Are you going to start on the project?"

Gabrielle leaned her head on the steering wheel. "No. I think I'm going to the gym to blow off some energy. It's been a hell of a day. I don't know how to unwind."

"Find a girlfriend. You're welcome," Rosie said.

"Ha, ha, ha. You're hilarious." The blonde, what was her name? Dana? Dena? Flashed through Gabrielle's mind. There was interest, that was a given, but was she in the mood for fast and disconnected? There was only one way to find out.

❖

"Gabby, what's happening? Are you really letting Dani beat you?"

Blaine's voice boomed out across the room. His callout was embarrassing, but effective. Gabrielle pedaled harder, faster, but so did Dani. After a five-minute battle for first place, Dani pushed herself harder and won.

Gabrielle walked over to Dani and smiled even though she really wanted to win. "I demand a respin." It wasn't the competition per se, it was just the one part of her day she had control over and failed at that, too. Today was not a notch in the win column.

"You almost had me a couple of times," Dani said.

Gabrielle watched as Dani wiped the sweat off her face with a towel she had hanging over one shoulder. "You won fair and square. Let me buy you a smoothie to celebrate your big win."

"I have a better idea. Let's get cleaned up and go out for a drink. We both just burned a ton of calories. I could use a good appletini."

Gabrielle lifted her eyebrow and nodded. The plan to start Serena's project was going to have to wait until morning. "That sounds like a great idea." She was a little bit unnerved to be in the dressing room with Dani, but blew out a sigh of relief when Dani turned down a different row. She quickly grabbed her bag of clean clothes and slipped into one of the private shower rooms. She wasn't sure how long Dani would wait for her, so she showered fast and got dressed in under fifteen minutes. By the time she applied a thin layer of makeup and blew her hair mostly dry, thirty minutes had passed. Dani was waiting for her in the lobby and smiled when she saw Gabrielle.

"I thought you already left," she said.

How did she look this good in such a short amount of time? Her hair was slightly wavy and loose around her shoulders. She was wearing skinny jeans, heels, and a sleeveless blouse. Gabrielle looked at her own outfit of ankle pants, sandals, and a simple black top and decided she looked good enough. "I'm sorry it took me longer. I was probably moping at my loss."

"Aw, come on. You can't always be on top." Dani tilted her head as if challenging her.

Gabrielle quirked her eyebrow. She never really considered herself a top. She was more of a whatever happens in the bedroom happens kind of woman. Sometimes she took control, but every so often she'd give it up. Her sexual encounters were quick, short lived, and to the point, so it wasn't much of an issue. Now it seemed like a chore to date. "I'll give you the honors. Tonight." She followed it with a quick wink and hoped she didn't cross a line.

"Then we'd better get started." Dani stood and held the door for Gabrielle. "Follow me. I know the perfect place."

Gabrielle slipped into her car and followed Dani's black Mercedes out of the parking lot. They playfully weaved in and out of traffic until Dani turned into the well-lit parking lot of a loft building. Gabrielle pulled up next to her and rolled down her window. "This doesn't look like a bar."

Dani walked over to Gabrielle's window, her hips swaying gently. She smiled when their eyes met. "You haven't seen my well-stocked bar. Besides, I make the best cocktails. Come on up. I promise to be gentle."

Gabrielle locked up and followed Dani to the elevator. Dani slipped a key into a slot and hit the button for the fifth floor.

"Oh, the penthouse."

"Well, not really, but one of the nicer places in the building."

Gabrielle was surprised when the doors opened. The simplistic brick building with large windows didn't do the inside justice. Dark hardwood floors were the perfect contrast to the creamy pearl color walls. The artwork was original. Based on what she could see of the space, there were only two condominiums on the top floor. "This is a gorgeous place, Dani. What exactly do you do?"

Dani flipped on the lights and dropped her gym bag beside a table that housed a plant, recent mail, and her discarded keys. "I'm a boring lawyer."

Gabrielle set her purse and phone on the same table, knowing she wouldn't need either for the next few hours. "I know firsthand you aren't boring. And being a lawyer is a reputable profession." She smiled when Dani looked at her and put her hands on her hips.

"You must know my mother. She tells me the same thing." Dani waved Gabrielle to the kitchen island and pointed to a high back chair. "Have a seat. I'm about to blow your taste buds with the best appletini you've ever had. Interested?"

Gabrielle nodded and slipped into the seat. She looked around the white and glass kitchen with the stainless steel appliances and found it extremely sterile. Nothing distinguished it from a kitchen one would find in an extended stay hotel. The black canisters tucked in a corner broke up the vast whiteness of the counters. Even the dishes, visible through the glass cabinet doors, were white. Great, she's a serial killer, Gabrielle thought. Nobody was this clean.

"I know what you're thinking," Dani said. She pulled out two martini glasses from below the island and dipped into the refrigerator for simple syrup, vodka, lemons, and a single apple.

"What am I thinking?" Gabrielle asked. She prayed that her assessment of Dani's place wasn't written all over her face.

"That I need more color in my house."

Gabrielle looked around and noticed that the open kitchen wasn't the only thing that was clinical. The black leather couch and white rug were tasteful, but lacked personality. "You could use a splash here and there." She turned back around and watched Dani's graceful movement as she mixed up two apple martinis. She even cut a sliver of apple peel and decorated the rims.

"Voilà. My signature drink."

Gabrielle took a sip. "It's very good."

"The advantage of having drinks here is that it's quiet. I mean, how would we be able to have a conversation if we were in a bar?" Dani asked. She softly ran her finger over Gabrielle's hand. Gabrielle stifled a shiver. When was the last time she was touched?

"What should we talk about?" Gabrielle took another sip, careful to maintain eye contact with Dani to let her know she was definitely interested. She watched as Dani walked around to her side of the island and leaned against the smooth, cool slate countertop.

"Let's see. You know what I do, you know where I live and the kind of car I drive. I have no pets and very little free time. Tell me about you," she said.

Gabrielle swiveled so Dani's body was almost between her legs. "I'm a boring architect. A hard worker, though. I'm up for partner and you know what kind of car I drive. I also have no pets and very little free time. I think that catches us up."

Dani slid closer to Gabrielle and ran her thumb along Gabrielle's lip. "You had a little something there."

"And your thumb was the best you could come up with?" Gabrielle's voice held a note of challenge. Somebody had to make the first move. The newness and excitement between them was the kind of tension Gabrielle appreciated. She knew when she walked through the door what would happen. They both knew. The cat and mouse game that was so common in her life was fun, too, but there was something so decadent about knowing exactly what was happening at the moment.

Dani answered by leaning down and pressing her full lips against Gabrielle's. It was a great first kiss. "Is this better?"

Gabrielle's body tingled with anticipation. She slipped her hand behind Dani's neck to keep Dani's warm mouth close to hers. "Definitely." She stood and pressed herself against Dani. Within a matter of seconds, the consensual understanding of what was about to happen incited a frenzy in both of them. Gabrielle wasn't sure who started undressing first, but by the time they had made it down the hall to the bedroom, Gabrielle was down to her bra and pants. Dani had even fewer clothes on.

"I'm glad you decided to come over for a drink," Dani said right before kissing Gabrielle so hard, she momentarily lost her balance and fell back against the wall. She felt Dani's hands slide down her abdomen and fumble at the button of her pants.

"You make a delicious appletini and your service is second to none," Gabrielle said. She slid the zipper down to make access easier. Dani didn't hesitate. She slipped her hand inside Gabrielle's panties, and they both moaned with pleasure. Gabrielle tugged the pants down past her hips, anxious to feel Dani inside her. Dani ran her fingertips along Gabrielle's folds and entered her with enough force to almost make her come on the spot. "How far away is the bed?" Her voice was deep and shook with need.

Dani pulled away from Gabrielle. "Ten steps." She pointed to the doorway that was a mere two feet away.

Gabrielle's body felt like lead, but she pushed off the wall with her shoulder. She pulled up her pants high enough to make the ten steps Dani said it would take. On step nine she kicked off her pants so that by step ten she was back in Dani's arms and ready to pick up where they left off in the hallway.

Chapter Nine

"It's nice, it's just not as exciting as I'd hoped." Serena liked the design Gabrielle came up with, but thought it was a little flat. "I mean, don't get me wrong, it's everything I asked for, it's just too much like a shelter instead of something warm and cozy."

"Okay, well, this is just a starting point. We can take each area and talk about improvement," Gabrielle said.

Even though Gabrielle had a smile on her face, Serena could see the tension in her shoulders and the tightness in the corners of her mouth. She regretted being so candid with her. Maybe being sequestered from society for over a few months had broken her filters. She needed to dial it back. "I think this is really good. I like the overall design and the large logs on the outside. I like the different options for the open play area outside. I think chain link would be easy for a bear to climb, so I like the vertical wrought iron fence you've drawn in here."

"I made them eight feet tall for that reason. It'll keep predators out and jumpers from escaping. If a dog can jump that, they should be free," Gabrielle said. She flipped to the next screen that showed the interior play area. "What about changes here? Your reaction wasn't a positive one when I showed you the two areas."

Serena bit her lip and studied the design. "I don't think I want anything the dogs can climb on and possibly fall off. We're going to have a vet on staff, but I don't want animals to get hurt during their stay." She pointed to the workout area that Gabrielle had designed. It looked like an obstacle course that she found online or from a dog show. She didn't think Gabrielle had an inkling of how dogs played.

"Let's focus on the structure. What do you think of the size of the place? Is it big enough? Too big?"

"I want more inside because of the weather. I do like the pools.

They're a nice touch." Serena didn't want to make Gabrielle feel bad, but she didn't think she really understood the vision she had for the Pet Posh Inn. "Maybe we can have a field trip to a doggie daycare and pick up some ideas." Again, Serena saw Gabrielle visibly stiffen. She automatically put her hand on Gabrielle's forearm. "This is a good start. I mean that."

Gabrielle nodded. "Let me google a few places and we can hit them today if you have time."

"Of course. I'll even buy us lunch," Serena said. She instantly regretted the offer when Gabrielle's shoulders stiffened again. "Or not. We can just go to the places and take notes."

"I refuse to let a client pay for lunch. It'll be my treat," Gabrielle said.

Serena wondered if Gabrielle knew she won the lottery. Even though she was required to reveal her name, she didn't do any interviews and only had one picture taken. It was the hideous one of her holding the giant check for forty-two million dollars that her lawyer somehow managed to keep off their website. Chloe and Jackie were right. The press camped out at her apartment once her name was released. She had to quit the Hooked Bookworm on the spot once they found out where she worked. Not that it broke her heart. She actually enjoyed seeing Mrs. Brody's reaction at the rushed news. It was a mixture of pure shock and jealousy.

"Deal." Because of the escalating uneasiness of their conversation, Serena decided to keep the words to a minimum for fear she'd continue to upset Gabrielle. It wasn't as if she wasn't trying.

"There are two doggie daycares close by. The shelter isn't too far away. I think we can hit one before lunch and the rest after. Does that sound good?" The look that Gabrielle shot Serena was one that made her heart beat quicker. Not because it was sexual, but because it was intense. Those amber eyes were, for lack of a better word, dreamy. She wanted to see them without the thick black-rimmed glasses perched perfectly on her delicate nose. And maybe see Gabrielle with her hair down. Serena didn't know if her hair was shoulder length or longer. It was always pulled back in a twist or braid. In such a male-dominated profession, Serena didn't blame her for toning down her femininity. She just wanted a peek at it.

"I can follow you," Serena said.

"Absolutely not. We can take my car. That way we can discuss it on the way there and on the way back."

"Okay." Serena grabbed her bag and followed Gabrielle out of the conference room. She felt bad that they were going to places with animals and Gabrielle was dressed in a suit again. With heels. No wonder she was perturbed.

"My car's the gray one."

Serena followed the direction of Gabrielle's nod and smiled when she saw the Jaguar. It was definitely a car she was interested in, but the Jeep was reliable. It was going to take her a bit of time to adjust to having cash for things like frivolous cars. "Is this your only car or do you also have a winter car?"

"No, she's all I have. I'm close enough to work that I can walk, and I can also work from home on snow days."

For a brief moment, Gabrielle stopped behind the car. It was as if she was going to the passenger side first, but stopped and turned to the driver's side instead. Maybe she was going there to open Serena's door, but thought better of it. Serena swore heat crept up Gabrielle's cheeks straight from under her white pressed shirt. The top button was undone, revealing creamy, smooth skin at the base of her neck, and a thin necklace with a charm that disappeared under the second button. It was hard for Serena to maintain eye contact.

"Can we put the top up? I'm sorry, it's just that I'm so pale I burn easily."

"Of course we can," Gabrielle said. She made a few adjustments, hit a button on the dash, and the top was securely in place. "And now you're safe." Her smile was the first genuine one Serena had seen. It was breathtaking. Maybe it was because Gabrielle was away from the office and the people she worked with, but Serena already noticed a difference.

"Tell me about the company you work for. How long have you been with them?" Serena adjusted her seat belt and waited as Gabrielle plugged the closest doggie daycare into her GPS.

"Ten years," she said.

"So, you started there when you were fifteen." The genuine laugh from Gabrielle forced Serena to look the other way. Her stomach did a flip-flop at the huskiness of the sound.

"I'm thirty-three years old, but thank you for the compliment. Arnest & Max pursued me at the beginning of my junior year of college. I was interning at a different firm during the summers, but they made me an offer I couldn't refuse." Gabrielle gripped the steering wheel tighter, either from determination or anger. Serena wasn't completely sure. The motion made thick white scars on Gabrielle's right hand stand out. They looked old, but serious. Serena was afraid to ask because it was rude, but her interest was piqued.

"Are you the only woman in the company?"

"The only woman architect. We have a few women engineers, the office manager is a woman, and most of the assistants are women," Gabrielle said.

"It's a male-dominated industry. I'm glad you're making a dent. I worked as a clerk in a bookstore. The owner is a woman, but she kind of gives women owners a bad name."

"That sucks. You don't work there anymore?"

"No. I quit about two months ago." Serena waited for the barrage of questions, but they never came. Gabrielle didn't press. How could an ex-bookstore clerk afford a multi-million-dollar project? "You know who I am, don't you?"

Gabrielle sighed. "I kind of guessed." She left out the part about Rosie googling her name and finding the info online.

"How did you know?"

"Actually the new car and new dog gave it away. I think it's great. For once somebody who's young enough to do something good with that much money actually won," Gabrielle said.

"Yeah, it was a massive change to my life." Serena looked out the window and watched the trees and small shops go by.

"Hopefully all for the better."

"It has its ups and downs, that's for sure," Serena said. She didn't know why, but she wanted to share with Gabrielle. Making friends now was virtually impossible. Not that she was great at it before, but forty-two million dollars richer and suddenly a lot of people wanted to be her friend for all of the wrong reasons. Chloe said Amber called her weekly wanting to reconnect.

"Here's the first place. I'm sure they'll give us a tour." Gabrielle pulled into a close spot and parked. "How do you want to handle this? Do you want them to know what we are doing or are we just looking for a place to board our dog?"

Again, that genuine smile made Serena's knees weak. Up close, Gabrielle seemed flawless. Perfect eyebrows, full lips with a touch of color on them, and not a single hair out of place. She was too put together. No freckles, no moles, not even a wrinkle. Serena leaned back because Gabrielle's presence was overwhelming in the small coupe.

"We can just say we are looking around at daycares. We don't have to tell them why."

Gabrielle nodded. "Okay. Let's do this."

Serena watched Gabrielle unfold her long legs and step out of the car. She grabbed her messenger bag and quickened her step when she noticed Gabrielle was holding the door to Pet Paradise open for her. "Thanks." She mumbled and smiled awkwardly at her.

Gabrielle walked up to the counter and asked for a tour of the place. Kelly, the new intern at Pet Paradise, was more than happy to accommodate them. She walked them through the play area which, much to Serena's embarrassment, had several ramps and obstacles for the dogs. The outside area had awnings, which Gabrielle didn't have on her design, but Serena thought was a good addition.

"I like the idea of artificial turf on the inside instead of just plain concrete," Gabrielle said to Serena.

"It's very easy to hose off and keep clean," Kelly said.

"Do you have heated floors?" Gabrielle asked.

"No, because our facility is heated. Follow me and I'll show you the newly renovated individual rooms."

As assertive as Gabrielle was in the play areas, she was extremely standoffish when they reached the individual guest rooms. She stood back while Serena walked with Kelly and discussed some of the perks they offered for the dogs. Although they were asked not to touch the guests, Serena couldn't help but talk to them.

"Look at you, you big boy." A St. Bernard was in the largest room they had available. It was a good-size room with a bed that was up on tiny legs so the room could be cleaned easier. Kelly explained that the dogs were taken out five times a day, not including play time. The dog, Samson, was a regular at the daycare. Serena fell in love with him instantly. "I just recently became a fur mama."

"Lucky you. Do you just have one pet?"

"For now, yes. Once I get settled in my house, I'm sure I'll pick up a few dozen more." Serena noticed that Gabrielle didn't laugh along with them. She stood behind them and didn't show an interest in Samson. "What about areas for other animals?"

"Oh, we also have a cat area. It's on the other side for obvious reasons."

Serena noticed Gabrielle's shoulders sagged in what appeared to be relief when they left the dogs. She was more involved when they entered the cat room. "We have cat towers, and scratching walls for them."

"Do they all get to be out at once or in stages?"

"Oh, the easygoing ones are out most of the time. They only go in their spaces at night. The cats who aren't happy to be here usually either stay in their spaces or go into the special rooms we have for cats that need a safe, quiet zone."

The rest of the tour lasted only a few minutes, but it was so helpful that Serena couldn't help but thank Kelly over and over again. She left with so many ideas that she couldn't wait to talk to Gabrielle.

"That was incredible."

"Very valuable field trip. I certainly learned a lot." Gabrielle checked the time and asked Serena what sounded good for lunch.

"I like just about anything." Serena came from a life of scraping. As long as it filled her up, she didn't care what she ate. "I bet I'm not as picky as you are."

Gabrielle's shoulders stiffened again. "I don't know about that."

Serena realized her faux pas and quickly backpedaled. "I mean, if you know my life, you would know that I will eat anything you put in front of me."

"High metabolism?"

"Raised poor."

Gabrielle nodded. "I understand. If you don't mind deli, I know a great place. It's smallish, but we can get a table at this time of the afternoon."

"Sounds delish. I'm in."

To be honest, Serena was getting tired of really nice food every night. She just wanted simple stuff like meatloaf and mashed potatoes, but living with Chloe and Jackie while waiting on the papers to close on the house she finally picked was all filet mignons and steamed asparagus and smoked, shaved Brussels sprouts. There wasn't anything normal. The last thing they ate together that was remotely fun was pizza the night Serena found her lottery ticket.

"This place is famous for its sandwiches, but their pasta salad and coleslaw are pretty great, too."

Again, Gabrielle held the door for Serena. She slipped into the cool restaurant but stopped short as she looked around to figure out where she needed to be. The "order here" line was opposite of where she thought it would be. She also wasn't expecting Gabrielle to bump into her. The feel of Gabrielle's curves against her back almost made her moan out loud.

"I'm so sorry."

"Completely my fault. I'm sorry to just stop."

"No worries. The line starts over here." Gabrielle pointed to a small line to their right.

Serena's body was still tingling from their innocent bump, but she followed Gabrielle and listened to her suggestions as she read off the best items on the menu.

"What is your favorite? I'll just go with whatever you suggest," Serena said.

"Sounds perfect. I'll order for us."

Serena was always attracted to women in charge. She loved the power they had over all situations. She wasn't meek. She just liked it when other people made the decisions. If life taught her anything, it was to go with the flow. If she didn't expect things, she was never disappointed.

Gabrielle had no problem telling the worker behind the counter what she wanted, what she didn't want, and how much she wanted. Serena wondered what she was like in bed. Was she as demanding? Or did she like to give up control? Amber had most of the control in their relationship. Serena never fought or argued with her. She was happy to be in a relationship that worked most of the time. The one thing she couldn't handle was infidelity. One time was forgivable. The second and the third time couldn't be overlooked. With Chloe and Jackie supporting her, she was able to cut that toxin out of her life. It was hard, and she almost caved a time or two, but with Amber gone, Serena felt stronger and more in control of her decisions.

Gabrielle turned to Serena. "Is there anything you don't like? Tomatoes? Onions?"

Serena took a small step back and wished Gabrielle's nearness wasn't such an issue. "Um, I could probably do without the onions, but if you think it tastes better with them on, then we can keep them."

"Good point. No onions." Gabrielle turned back around to the sandwich engineer and gave him very specific instructions on how much of everything she wanted.

"I think I've got this," the young man said. He slid both sandwiches into the toaster for thirty seconds and filled their side orders of coleslaw and pasta salad and potato salad.

"Then do it right, or I'm going to complain," Gabrielle said.

Serena was surprised at Gabrielle's rudeness with the young man. He didn't back down, though. He remained positive and friendly.

"Don't make me sneak jalapeños on your sandwich. Or over-pepper it," he said.

"I'm standing right here watching you," she said.

In an amazing turn of events, they both busted out laughing. Gabrielle explained that the sweet young man was her nephew. Serena breathed a sigh of relief and laughed nervously.

"What are you bringing to the barbecue on Sunday?" Phillip handed Gabrielle their tray after taking her payment.

"Sandwiches from here. You?" Gabrielle winked at him.

"I'm manning the grill. And I'm probably going to bring some cookies."

"I'm going to make peanut butter brownies and probably bake a pie," Gabrielle said.

"Oh, can I make a request?"

"Let me guess. You want a whole pecan pie to yourself."

His wide grin was a dead giveaway that she was right.

"Okay. I'll bring peach for everyone else and sneak you a pecan pie."

"You're my favorite," he said.

Gabrielle slipped a twenty in the tip jar. "See you on Sunday." She grabbed the tray and found an empty table near the back of the deli.

"He's very sweet. I'm glad you know him because I was getting a little nervous," Serena said. She waited for Gabrielle to divide up what was on the tray, not really knowing what was for her.

"You thought I was being rude like I was at the lodge, didn't you? I promise you that was a one-time deal. I'm not normally rude. That day was very stressful. Getting stuck on the highway was such a helpless feeling, and I knew Elizabeth was waiting." She handed Serena a plate with her sandwich, half the salads, and silverware.

"This is a lot of food," Serena said. She wasn't quite sure where to start. Gabrielle didn't waste time and took a hearty bite of the warm turkey and provolone sandwich.

"The secret sauce makes this so yummy," Gabrielle said between bites.

"What's in the secret sauce?"

"Phillip refuses to tell me. He said he has a nondisclosure with

Tommy's, which is completely untrue. He won't tell me just because I want to know. He's such a brat."

"He's adorable. Is he your brother's son or sister's? And by the way, this is delicious. Normal food. I love it."

"My brother and his wife adopted him when he was about three. He's been a perfect kid the entire time. Seriously, if I was going to have a kid, I would want to clone him. Honor Society, works all the time, helps around the house, and is super smart."

"That's amazing. My sister is twenty, and she has been a handful since the time she was three. I mean, she's smart and adorable now, but she rebelled when she was a kid."

Gabrielle wiped her mouth. "Not an easy life, huh?"

Serena sat back in her chair to take a break from eating. "It wasn't the worst, but I had to grow up fast, so I have a strained relationship with my mom."

"What about your father?"

Serena gave a half laugh, laced with sarcasm and bitterness. "What about him? I honestly don't even know his name. Truth be told, I barely remember Faith's dad. He wasn't around for long, thankfully."

"I'm sorry it was hard for you. I hope that now you can live the life you've always wanted to." Gabrielle sounded sincere and not at all jealous of Serena's fortune.

"Speaking of which, I thought the field trip was great. It gave me a lot to think about."

"Are we going to have a lot of changes?" Gabrielle lifted her eyebrow at Serena.

She shrugged. "Let's wait until we see a few more. Maybe the next one will give us even more inspiration."

Chapter Ten

"Christopher, I have to redesign the whole thing. This will be the third time."

Gabrielle sat down so hard her chair rolled back and she had to grab her desk to keep from falling over. Her boss was kind enough to not laugh at her.

"You've only been working on it a few weeks. You know you have to give it time."

"Here's the shitty part. She's added back things we scrapped from the original design. We went from plan A to plan B, then a combo of both. Now she wants so much on a relatively small amount of land." Gabrielle was frustrated. After their field trip and lunch meeting, Gabrielle was full of ideas and was excited to revise the drawings. Friday afternoon and they were almost back to square one. The designs she'd shared with Serena weren't met with the same enthusiasm. "She added the obstacles in the play area back in, but wants safety rails so the doggies don't fall off." Gabrielle stood because sitting was too much. She paced the little area in front of her desk as she shared her frustration.

"What do you need me to do? Do you need my help?"

She sat down. His tone was genuine and instantly deflated her bad mood. "No. I'm just being a whiny baby. It's all relatively easy. I'm just used to knocking it out of the park the first go around. This rejection is killing my artistic groove."

"You're one of our best. Don't worry. I know you will shine on this project. The client has written you a blank check. Do what you need to and make her happy. Keep me posted." He stood and looked at his watch. "Don't stay too late. You need a night off."

Gabrielle nodded as he left, thinking she did need a break. It wasn't that it was taking her forever, she just couldn't see Serena's vision. It was her fault. Her fear of dogs really blocked her creative ability to move forward on this project. She wasn't giving Serena the best she could. If the prestigiousness of partner wasn't on the line, Gabrielle would have handed it off to a junior architect. But everything was riding on this project. She couldn't fuck it up. The last conversation with Serena that afternoon made her want to throw something. Instead, she took a deep breath and did the one thing that always helped her mood: called her mom.

"Hey, Mom. What's going on?"

"Finally planning the barbecue and sending the lists to everyone, reminding them what they're supposed to bring." Meredith's voice instantly soothed Gabrielle's ruffled feathers from the day's rejection.

"Are you texting everyone? I already know I'm bringing pies. And making an extra one for Phillip," Gabrielle said.

"When did you see him?" Meredith asked.

"I took my client to Tommy's. She's the one who wants me to build the pet hotel. We keep running into walls. Mom, I've tried everything. She's very stubborn and has all of these ideas, but they aren't practical. She almost doubled the size of the big dog room, which takes away from their indoor play area. It's not that it's impossible, but she only has two acres. It's amazing how fast that real estate fills up with normal things like parking lots."

"Honey, remember that the client is always right. And she's obligated to pay you for your time. If she wants to drag it on and on, you just have to roll with it. What's she like?"

"The client?" Gabrielle wasn't prepared to answer questions about Serena. "Well, she's very quiet and stubborn, but not rude about it. She has a dog that travels with her everywhere, which you know I don't like."

Gabrielle heard her mom sigh on the phone. "You're not used to nice people who are stubborn. You're used to fighting to be heard and diving right into a project. Do you want my advice?"

"That's why I called. I always need your advice."

"Get to know her better. If this is the most important job of your life, try harder. As a matter of fact, why don't you invite her to the barbecue this Sunday."

"I'm not going to mix business with pleasure. You know I don't do that." Gabrielle was irritated because it was a solid solution, but she didn't want to cross the line with Serena.

"How many women clients have you had?"

There was a pause in the conversation as Gabrielle counted them in her head. "Maybe three or four." She had to dig back to the very beginning of her career, when she shared projects with other junior associates. Nothing really stood out. There were a few female clients who were secondary contacts if the main contact was unavailable for consultation. She always kept it professional. Serena was the first client who didn't fit the mold, and it threw Gabrielle off.

"Invite her. And have her bring her dog. Trust me on this."

Gabrielle clenched the receiver tighter. "That's a horrible idea."

"It's a great idea. You're going to do better if you really get to know her. Kiddo, this is your make or break moment. Do you want to be partner? Then include her. Make her feel welcome. Make her the best client you ever had."

Gabrielle took another deep breath. "Okay, I'll invite her." She didn't tell her mother Serena lived in Vail. The ninety-minute drive was probably going to be a deterrent.

"Tell her she doesn't have to bring anything. She's our guest."

For a brief moment, Gabrielle wondered if her queerness was going to be an issue for Serena. She tried to remain as asexual as she could at work. If Serena showed up to the barbecue, she would meet Rosie, Anne, and their three children. Not to mention all the other lesbian couples who were friends with her family. Gabrielle loved that her family was so accepting of her sexuality. Gabrielle's parents were the ones who showed up to Pride events wearing *Free Hugs* and *We love you* T-shirts long after Gabrielle stopped attending parades and events. She was proud of them for being accepting, but slightly embarrassed by how open they were. They were forever trying to fix her up with the nicest lesbians and bisexual ladies they'd ever met, according to her mother.

"Okay, but I can't guarantee she'll come. She's very private."

"All I ask is that you invite her. Do it now. I'll see you Sunday."

Gabrielle didn't feel any better after calling her mom. She'd gone from one set of problems to another. She placed another call.

"So, here's something. My mom wants me to invite my client to the barbecue."

Rosie's voice was instantly animated. "Oh, I think that's a great idea. Then we can finally meet the most difficult client you've ever had." She dragged out the last part of the sentence to goad Gabrielle.

"Yeah, yeah, I know. She's not that bad. Just really indecisive. And I'm not doing her any favors by not being really into her vision."

"Then get to know her on a personal level. Your mom is right. This can only help things. All those stuffed shirts at your office always invite clients to go on their yachts and private jets. I don't think a family barbecue is going to make or break the deal. Plus, I want to meet her."

"I confessed that I know she's the winner, so don't be all weird around her, okay?"

"What? Me? Never."

Gabrielle smiled at Rosie's exaggerated voice. "Yes, you."

"I'm going to ask her for a cool million, okay?"

"No. You'll ask her things like 'How are you? Where do you live? Isn't Gabrielle fabulous?' You know, important questions."

"I know we're always late to these things, but I promise we're going to be there on time. Maybe even early. I want to meet the woman who's got you in a tizzy."

Gabrielle rolled her eyes and playfully huffed. "You're going to like her. She reminds me of you. Kind of rolls with the punches and doesn't seemed fazed by a lot."

"Move over, woman. I just found a new best friend."

❖

Gabrielle hit the gym knowing full well she was really looking for Dani. She was wound tight and needed release. If Dani wasn't there, she was going to spin her way to the top of the class and work it out that way. Sex sounded way more fun, though. She scanned the room but didn't see the blonde anywhere. There were several other beautiful women, but she liked the no-nonsense vibe she shared with Dani. Their encounter had been fast and furious and was the first time Gabrielle didn't feel guilty after.

"Get on the bike, Gabby. You have two minutes to warm up." Blaine had his headset on with the microphone turned up loud so the entire class could hear him. His voice boomed without it, so the microphone was a bit much.

She climbed on a bike near the back to get away from the noise. She stretched out her legs, pedaled slowly, flexing her calves and pointing her toes to loosen up. Today had been the longest day, and she couldn't believe she was here instead of at home soaking in her oversize tub.

The changes she'd made to the Pet Posh Inn were for naught. Most of her day had gone into redesigning the space that Serena still had issues with. It wasn't like she felt she nailed it, but it was a vast improvement over the initial design. Serena was struggling with what she wanted.

"Ten seconds." Blaine's shout at the front of the class killed the low murmur of conversations people were having around her.

After such an emotional day, she didn't even know why she was there. She just knew she needed a win today. Any kind of win. When Blaine blew the whistle, she pumped her legs as fast as she could for as long as she could. Her stamina fizzled near the end and she finished in third. She was going the wrong way.

"What happened out there, Gabby?" Blaine threw her a towel, which she happily caught.

She wiped the sweat from her face and neck. "It was a bitch of a day and I let it get to my head," she said.

"Did you work it out?"

She shrugged. "If nothing else, I'll fall right to sleep tonight, so that's something."

"You'll get it next time."

Then he was off to motivate the next loser hanging around for bits of motivation and high fives. Gabrielle didn't know what made her feel worse: coming in third, or being dismissed by him. If only Dani was here, then she wouldn't feel so inadequate, but they'd never exchanged numbers or even last names. She sighed, grabbed her bag, and decided to shower at home. She was tired of people. She slipped into her car and checked her phone for messages. Rosie mentioned a T-ball game at ten for her older daughter, Rue. The text from her mother packed the most punch.

Don't forget to invite your client to the barbecue on Sunday.

Gabrielle groaned and checked the time. It was nine on a Friday night. Serena didn't strike her as the partying kind, so she took a chance and sent her a text.

My parents are hosting their annual barbecue on Sunday. We would love it if you could join us. It's very casual. Don't bring anything. Oh, and L.B. is invited, too.

She tried to make it sound as chill as possible, thinking she'd balk at the invite.

Sounds great. What time do I need to be there? And what's the address?

Whether out of panic or excitement, Gabrielle's heart fluttered for a moment. Exposing her personal life to a client was a big step. Never mind that Serena was an attractive woman. Gabrielle kept her distance for professional reasons. She took a deep breath and shot a text back with the address. *Great. We'll see you at two. It will be very laid back and fun.*

Gabrielle slipped into traffic and thought about Serena. She'd confessed her upbringing was rough and she didn't even know her dad. Gabrielle grew up with a support group who rallied behind her every step of the way. Her parents, still together after forty years of marriage, were always there for her with advice, discipline, and structure. She'd had the perfect childhood. Gabrielle hoped that Serena would fit in, knowing full well that if she didn't, her mother and Rosie would make her feel welcome.

Chapter Eleven

Serena stood in the doorway of her new house and waited to cross the threshold. This was a big moment. Her first house. She ran her hand along the smooth wooden door with the wrought iron door knocker and smiled. This was all hers. L.B. trotted off to investigate the house while she remained in the foyer. It wasn't a big house. Real estate was expensive in Vail. Too many people wanted to live there, and most of them were insanely rich. Serena's house was just over two thousand square feet with vaulted ceilings, but the location and view were both spectacular. And she had a garage for the first time ever. The furniture wouldn't arrive until Monday, but she was so excited at getting the house keys and having her own home that she bought a blow-up twin mattress to sleep on. She'd slept on worse things.

"L.B.? Where are you, boy?" Her voice echoed against the emptiness in the room. She smiled when she heard the clicking of his nails in the kitchen as he continued his investigation of new smells in a new place. He was like this at Chloe and Jackie's house. Only then she followed him around, afraid he might mark the new territory, but he never did. She trusted him. There was a doggie door that led to a decent-size backyard. She was going to have to show him what it was and how to work it. When he returned to her side after inspecting all the rooms, she squatted down and kissed his nose. "This is all ours now. Can you believe it?" She stood and looked around again. She felt like the most fortunate person on the planet. There was a good-size kitchen, four bedrooms, three baths, and a dream garden full of perennials. She didn't want to plug all of her money into a giant house. This was plenty big enough for her, all of the fur babies she was going to rescue, and maybe even for anyone who wanted to rescue her.

Her phone rang and Faith's face popped up. "Hey, don't even tell me you're canceling."

"Hell, no. I can't find your driveway. Can you come out to the street and wave me down?" Faith's voice held a note of irritation.

"Did you look for the red mailbox before the curve?"

"Um, no. I completely ignored your directions. Of course I did."

"Your new car has a GPS built in. Hang on, I'll be right out." Serena gave explicit instructions for L.B. to be a good boy and she'd be right back with Aunt Faith. She walked down the driveway, phone in hand, and waited for Faith's new Chevrolet SUV to approach. After waiting two minutes, she saw the car and waved for her to pull into the driveway.

"That's not a red mailbox. That's almost black," Faith said. She pointed at the stone structure perched near the road with a rust color door.

"That's red," Serena said.

"Maroon at best." Faith rolled her eyes and parked on the concrete slab beside the garage. "Is this good?"

Serena gave her a thumbs-up and opened up the back of the SUV. "Sleeping bag and camping mat. Perfect choice."

"I can't believe my millionaire sister is making me camp."

"We've done it for years. Consider it a night of nostalgia." Serena hugged Faith and grabbed her overnight bag. "I'm so excited for you to see the house in person." Faith had given her approval after looking at dozens of houses with Serena online. They both loved this one.

"It looks fantastic. I love all the windows." Faith waved at L.B., who was waiting for them at the door, his tail wagging so fast and hard that his whole body shook.

"Wait until you see the inside." Serena opened the door to a very anxious L.B., who jumped up on Faith and lavished her with kisses. She made the mistake of stooping down only to be knocked over.

"Stop, you furry beast." Faith tried to be stern, but her laughter gave her away. That only encouraged him. Serena had to pull him away while Faith scrambled to stand. "Wow. Well, he's happy here. And why wouldn't he be? Look at this!" She stood and looked at the ceilings and around the open space.

"Come on. I'll give you the tour."

"When does the furniture get here?"

"Monday, but I couldn't wait. I wanted to get in here as soon as I could."

Faith squeezed Serena's arm. "I don't blame you for a second. I would want to be here, too, furniture or not."

"You know you can stay here if you want. It's not super close to the center, but my door is always open."

"I know, sis. My lease isn't up for a few months, and hopefully by then I'll have a job lined up in Denver."

They walked through the house pointing out what they loved the most about it. Serena loved it the way it was. Faith wanted more color.

"I promise I'll add color to the walls."

"Stay away from antiques." Faith gave her a look.

"What's wrong with them?" Serena had brought the broken phonograph with her. Besides some of her clothes, it was the only thing she'd packed when Chloe and Jackie kidnapped her the night she learned she won the lottery.

"They're old. You aren't. Leave the antiques to the people who were alive when those things were popular," Faith said. She unrolled her sleeping bag near the fireplace even though it was hot outside. That stemmed from being cold for a lot of her youth. Serena thought they would adjust to the harsh Colorado winters, but they never did.

"What are we ordering for dinner?"

"Anything you want. You're picking because you're the chef and I don't want you making fun of my choices."

"You mean McDonald's, which is one hundred percent salt and unidentifiable meat? Yeah, no. Let's get food from that new Mexican restaurant. I've heard nothing but good things." Faith gave Serena her order and cuddled on the floor with L.B.

Serena ordered enough food for at least two meals. The electricity was on and in her name as of that morning. She threw a case of water and a case of Diet Coke in the otherwise empty refrigerator. L.B. had a bag of food that would last him until next week, so she was only worried about breakfast. Since joining the culinary center, Faith rarely ate fast food. What was once a staple in their lives was now snubbed. And this was all before the lottery. "Let's go to the diner tomorrow morning, but I can't eat a lot. I'm going to a barbecue."

Faith looked up at her in surprise. "Anyone I know?"

"It's the architect who's designing the Pet Posh Inn. She's pretty cool." Serena tried hard to act nonchalant, but Faith knew her better than that. The prodding had begun.

"Is she cute? Single? A lesbian?"

Serena held up her hands. "Whoa, whoa. Hold up. Yes, she's

pretty, but very professional. I don't see any rings on her fingers, but in today's world that doesn't mean anything. And as far as her being a lesbian, I have no clue."

"How pretty is pretty?"

The way Faith looked at her made Serena want to share the truth. She sat down in front of her and opened up how they used to when they were younger. "She has brown hair, darker than mine, but it's always pulled back so I don't know the length. Her skin is the softest I've ever seen. The best part about her is that she has these fantastic eyes that are golden brown with a darker brown circle on the outside of the lighter brown. They're amazing."

"What about her personality?"

"Well, I don't know. She's usually all business and very serious about this project."

"That's her job. You can't fault her for that," Faith said.

"I know, but still. It would be nice if she was as excited as I am." Serena leaned her head on Faith's shoulder and sighed. "Maybe tomorrow she'll open up more."

"Are you nervous? Do you want me to go with you?" Faith rested her head on top of Serena's.

"I'll be fine. I'm sure it'll be fun. I met her nephew. He's sweet. Worst case scenario, I hang with him all afternoon."

"Is he cute?"

Serena sat up as an idea popped up in her head. "You know what? Maybe you should come with me. That way you'll already know people in Denver if you get a job there. It can't hurt to have an arsenal of friends." She didn't look at Faith, knowing that if Faith saw the look in her eye, she'd know immediately that she had an ulterior motive. If Phillip was as perfect as Gabrielle said, he was perfect for her little sister.

❖

"This place is gorgeous. You never told me your architect was filthy rich." Faith opened the car door before Serena had the Jeep in park.

"Wait for us." Serena had neglected to text Gabrielle about bringing Faith, but she couldn't imagine it would be a problem if it was as casual as Gabrielle said it was going to be. She tethered L.B. to his leash and walked down the winding driveway to the backyard, where the smells of grilled food assaulted her nose and laughter and singing could be heard over music. This was definitely a good time. "Hey, this isn't Gabrielle's house. It's her parents' place, but yes, apparently they're rich." Serena didn't think she would ever get used to the posh life. Being a part of it now was surreal. It would take her a long time to stop scraping and looking for coupons. They both stopped when they reached the backyard, not knowing where to go. Even L.B. stopped next to them, overwhelmed.

"Hi. You must be Serena." An attractive woman with brown hair and eyes like Gabrielle walked forward and shook Serena's hand. "I'm Meredith, Gabrielle's mom. Welcome to our crazy start-of-summer barbecue."

"Hi, nice to meet you. This is my sister Faith, and the furry little guy here is L.B. Thank you for the invitation." For the first time in forever, Serena was completely at ease. Meredith introduced them to several people. She promised to find Gabrielle and send her over.

"It's nice to meet you. I'm Piper and this is my wife, Shaylie. Our daughter, Maribelle, is over there on the swings. She's going to love this guy." Piper leaned over and kissed L.B.'s head and rubbed his floppy ears in the process. "What's your name?"

"That's L.B," Serena said.

"L.B. That's an interesting name."

"He also answers to Lucky," Serena said.

"He's adorable. We're in the process of looking for a dog. Maribelle has been pushing us hard for a pet and we just don't know if she's old enough," Shaylie said.

The memory of three-year-old Faith crying and clutching King's fur in her tiny fists as she begged Diane to let them keep him popped into her head. "I don't think she's too young. And there are so many sweet dogs that need a good home."

"Where did you find him?" Shaylie squatted down and loved on him along with Piper.

"We're from Vail. There's a shelter on the west end of town where we picked him up." Serena watched as L.B. flopped over and offered up his belly for more rubs.

"If he comes up missing at the end of the night, we know nothing about it," Shaylie said.

"You made it."

Serena turned and did a double take. Gabrielle, completely casual in jeans, sandals, and a V-neck, stood a few feet away holding a toddler who was happily eating an ice cream cone. Gabrielle didn't seem to mind the sticky mess.

"Hi. Yes. I brought my sister. I hope you don't mind." Serena couldn't believe Gabrielle's transformation. Her hair was loose and rested just below her collarbone. It was gorgeous. Prettier than she had imagined. And her eyes weren't hidden behind the black rimmed glasses. They were bright and full of happiness. It was as if a different person was standing in front of her.

"The more the merrier. I see you met two of my favorite people." Gabrielle nodded at Piper and Shaylie.

"Yes. They have threatened to steal L.B. by the end of the night," Serena said. She noticed Gabrielle took a step back when she realized L.B. was on the ground, belly up, between Shaylie and Piper. "This is Faith."

Gabrielle shook Faith's hand. "I've heard a lot about you. All good things."

"Thanks for letting me crash your awesome party."

"Help yourself to anything you want. Everyone here is pretty friendly."

"I'll take L.B. with me. I'm sure to get more attention this way." Faith took the leash from Serena and walked away.

"Serena, how do you know Gabrielle?" Piper asked.

"Um, I'm her client. She's working on the Pet Posh Inn for me." She was surprised that Gabrielle didn't reveal who she was to her friends.

"Oh, is that a daycare for dogs?" Shaylie seemed completely invested in the conversation.

"I'm having it designed for all pets. Dogs, cats, birds, turtles, hedgehogs, anything really. Within reason, I mean. We're still in the design phase of it," Serena said.

"I love that. People treat their pets like family, because they really are a part of the family," Shaylie said.

"Hey, what's going on here? Everyone's having a good time and we weren't invited?"

A woman who looked Serena over several times reached for the toddler cuddled in Gabrielle's arms. She smiled at Serena and introduced herself as Gabrielle's best friend, Rosie. The little girl was Carolyn, but everyone called her Care Bear.

"My wife is over on the swings with Maribelle and our two older children, Rue and Dominique. You must be Serena."

Serena didn't miss the quick elbow jab by Gabrielle and the soft grunt that escaped Rosie. She nodded and pretended to miss their blatant interaction. "Nice to meet you."

"Have you eaten anything yet? I don't see a plate or a drink in your hand. Here, let's grab some food and get to know one another better." Rosie linked her arm with Serena's and all but dragged her away from the group. Serena liked her immediately. She liked all of Gabrielle's friends. And they were all lesbians. Was Gabrielle, too? And if so, was her girlfriend here or was she single? "You need to try the chicken. It's amazing. Meredith makes the best marinade. And Gabrielle's brownies are second to none. You're Gabrielle's client, aren't you?"

Serena didn't think she'd be able to get a word in edgewise, so she nodded.

"Gabrielle mentioned that she invited her client, but she failed to mention how adorable you are."

Serena looked over her shoulder at Gabrielle, who met her gaze but quickly looked away. It was unusual to see Gabrielle unnerved, and Serena didn't know if she should be concerned.

"She looks nervous, doesn't she?" Rosie whispered in Serena's ear. "Don't worry about me. I'm completely harmless, but I know her better than anyone, so if you want any dirt on her or have any questions, ask away."

The first thing out of Serena's mouth, completely unfiltered and ridiculously revealing about herself, even stopped Rosie in her tracks. "Is she seeing anyone?"

The grin on Rosie's face grew exponentially as the horror for asking the question in the first place grew on Serena's. Rosie reached out and squeezed her forearm. "No, she isn't. She works too hard, and even though we all tell her it's not healthy, she won't listen to us."

That still didn't answer Serena's underlying question. The chances were good that Gabrielle was a lesbian based on all of her friends, but Rosie never said the word. Serena needed a different approach for confirmation. "It's hard to date when work takes precedence. I have a hard time, too."

"So, you aren't seeing anyone either?" Rosie handed her an iced tea with a splash of raspberry juice. She guided Serena to the deck where a few chairs freed up as a rousing tournament of cornhole began.

"No, I had a girlfriend, but we broke up last winter. She was entirely too controlling." She took a bite of the chicken but didn't miss the giant smile on Rosie's face. Her being single was good news. Was Gabrielle interested in her? Had she said something to Rosie?

"Gabrielle hasn't had a girlfriend in years. She dates, on occasion, but nothing serious. Work is always in the way. She has to work twice as hard to prove herself worthy in that company." Rosie clamped her mouth shut even though Serena thought she had a lot more to say about Arnest & Max.

Serena clenched the arms of the chair and forced herself to remain seated. What did all of this mean? "My job wasn't glamorous, but it was something I was good at."

"What did you do? If that's not too personal."

Serena waved her off. "No, it's fine. I worked at a bookstore. But now I'm building the place of my dreams. And Gabrielle is helping me."

"She really is good at her job. They just take advantage of her, I think."

"I feel like we'll make this work." At Rosie's shocked expression, Serena quickly elaborated. "The project. We'll make the project work."

"Ladies, may I sit down?" Meredith waited until they extended the invitation. Both Serena and Rosie gestured to the empty chair.

Serena scanned the crowd until she found Gabrielle. This time Gabrielle didn't turn away. She playfully smacked the palm of her hand against her forehead. Serena smiled and winked. She winked! Mortified, she quickly looked at her plate and listened to Meredith and Rosie talk about the cornhole tournament that everyone took too seriously. Serena had never played and was entirely too nervous to try in front of a giant crowd. She looked for Faith and found her sitting on a lawn chair, talking to Phillip. Her plan, although under no execution on her part, was working. It was all fate. She smiled at how comfortable Faith was in a crowd. How different they were. Faith was carefree and didn't stress as much as Serena did.

"Serena, what do you do when you aren't working with Gabrielle?" Meredith asked.

"I've been taking it easy. Last night was the first night in my new house. Faith spent the night. That's why she's here with me."

"The more the merrier. What does she do? Is she in school?"

"She goes to Vail's Culinary Center. She's graduating this fall."

"How exciting. Does she have anything lined up?"

"She wants to try to get a job here in Denver. Vail has limited options for a recent culinary school graduate, but she wants to stay close to home." Serena didn't want to get into detail, but nobody pushed. It was a very pleasant conversation about families and fun, and Serena felt herself relax for the first time in forever.

"So, nobody's talked you into cornhole?" Gabrielle sat in a chair next to her mother.

Serena thought it was sweet how Meredith touched Gabrielle's knee and Gabrielle squeezed her mother's hand for a moment. It was a loving exchange, something Serena had longed for her entire life but never experienced. It was so casual, as if they did it all the time. That was one thing she wasn't going to ever take for granted. A touch from a loved one. She wondered if Gabrielle knew how lucky she was.

"No. I've never played it and I'm not about to embarrass myself in front of your friends and family," Serena said.

"Did you ever play sports in high school?"

Serena had to break eye contact with Gabrielle. "Not really. I was more of a bookworm. Playing sports wasn't my thing." Besides not being able to afford to play sports, she was never popular in high school. Being invisible was a survival skill that she applied in every aspect of her life growing up. Not much had changed in the last ten years.

She pretended to look around for Faith and L.B. even though she knew exactly where she was. She needed an excuse to look away from Gabrielle. Without her glasses and with her hair loose and flowing around her shoulders, Serena found her stunning. Dressed conservatively for work she was attractive, but here in the comfort of her friends and family, she was a knockout. And completely relaxed. This didn't seem like the same woman she'd battled with for the last few weeks. It was unnerving and exhilarating at the same time. How was she going to be able to work with her now that she knew Gabrielle on a more personal level? Especially since they couldn't seem to see eye-to-eye on a simple project.

Chapter Twelve

"You told her about the attack?" Gabrielle turned and stared at her mother. Meredith held her hands up as if surrendering before the onslaught even began.

"We were just sitting there, talking about animals and her pet project, and it just came up."

"Mom, it doesn't just come up. It's very private and personal. And now she has a reason to fire me if she wants to." Gabrielle threw a towel on the counter in frustration and crossed her arms.

Meredith walked over to her daughter and put both hands on her shoulders. "You listen to me, Gabrielle. She was very understanding and felt bad about having L.B. around you. She mentioned that you seemed skittish around dogs and I explained what happened. It's a fact."

"Yes, but one I didn't want her to know." Gabrielle moved out of her mother's grasp. "There are a ton of other things you could have told her about me like playing softball at State, or getting arrested at a protest, or even the fact that I graduated top of my class in college."

Meredith walked slowly back to Gabrielle. "None of that came up. Just the pet project. I know I shouldn't have said anything, but I'm glad I did. Something in her just clicked."

"Yeah, like let me get a new architect." Sarcasm dripped from Gabrielle's voice as she sat at the kitchen table.

"She's not going to fire you for being attacked by a dog as a child. You have a legitimate reason to fear them."

"But now she knows how unfamiliar I am with dogs."

"Is there a pity party going on that I wasn't invited to? Because I'm usually the host." Rosie walked into the kitchen and dramatically fell into the chair next to Gabrielle. "I brought the wine."

"You're still here?" Gabrielle slid an empty glass over to her.

"Anne took the kids home, so I'm either staying the night or you're taking me home. I heard the magical word 'Serena' and had to join in."

"Mom just told me that she told Serena about my dog attack."

"Yeah, so?"

Gabrielle threw her hands up. "What the hell? Am I the only one who sees this as a problem?"

"Yes," Meredith and Rosie said in unison.

"Okay, so tell me everything she said. Every word, how it sounded, her hand gestures," Gabrielle said. If they were going to talk about this, she was at least going to control the conversation.

"Can I just point out one very important thing that I need to share before we start this?" Rosie grabbed the bag of chips and shoved a few in her mouth. She held her finger up and chewed while both Barnes women waited not so patiently for her to finish. A quick sip of wine and she continued, "I found out that Serena is single."

"Big deal." Gabrielle acted unimpressed, but her heart sped up and she forced herself to refrain from wiping her instantly sweaty palms on her jeans.

"Normally, I would agree with you, because who cares, right? But the interesting part, the part that made me sit up a little straighter, is that your client, also known as Colorado's latest lottery winner, is also a lesbian." Rosie stood and bowed as both of them bombarded her with questions at the same time.

"She's the big winner? She won the lottery?" Meredith asked.

"She's gay? Are you serious?" Gabrielle asked.

Rosie held up her hands as both women questioned her. "Whoa. Hang on. One question at a time. Meredith, yes. That's how she is able to hire Gabrielle's firm and create her dream come true." She turned to Gabrielle next. "Yes, she's a confirmed lesbian. Ex-girlfriend and all. Once I mentioned that you're a single lesbian as well, things got interesting."

"Holy shit, Rosie. You outed me to my client?"

Rosie shrugged. "After she outed herself. It's Colorado. You had nothing but gay friends at the party. She met my wife. She met Piper and Shaylie. This isn't an issue."

"Let's hope not. I can't afford to lose her under any circumstances." Gabrielle put her head in her hands and groaned between her fingers. "This didn't go as expected."

Meredith leaned forward and rubbed Gabrielle's back. "You're blowing this way out of proportion. Serena seems like a very nice young lady, and I doubt she's going to fire you because you're a lesbian. But since you both are, that's probably an even stronger bond."

"Moms know everything. It's going to be okay. I guess now is a good a time as any to tell you the rest of the conversation." Rosie sat back, crossed her arms, and smiled wickedly.

"You're enjoying the shit out of this, aren't you?"

Rosie nodded. "Who wouldn't, Miss Perfect?" She high-fived Meredith, who didn't say a word and wisely avoided eye contact with Gabrielle.

"I'm waiting."

"I might have mentioned to Serena that you were single, too."

Gabrielle played like she didn't care. "That doesn't mean anything. We don't know what she looks for in a girlfriend."

"Or do we?" Rosie asked. Gabrielle raised her eyebrow. "No. I didn't ask. Even I know when to quit. But the good news is that we have a new friend. She gave me her number. We're going to get together for a play date. My girls and L.B., the greatest dog in the world," Rosie said.

"So, my client and my best friend are going to start texting. Should I be jealous?"

"This is only going to help you, you know that, right? I'm going to say all good things about you, and who knows? Maybe this rich, hot single woman might be into you." Rosie wagged her eyebrows playfully at Gabrielle.

"Can we talk about something else?" Gabrielle acted perturbed, but secretly she liked the idea of Rosie having a relationship with Serena. Serena needed strong people in her life, and Rosie was the best at making everyone feel loved and a part of something good. She knew Rosie was her personal champion and would never say a bad thing about her. "Mom, what did you think of the party?"

"It was a success. It's always nice to see our friends and make new ones." She winked at Gabrielle, who shook her head and smiled at her.

❖

"There's a Serena Evans here to see you."

Gabrielle knocked over one of her containers of pens and almost dropped the coffee she was holding when she heard Miles's announcement through her intercom. She took a deep breath, grabbed the pens, and straightened everything on her desk.

"Send her in." Gabrielle stood and waited for Serena to enter. This wasn't planned. Fear and dread stirred in the pit of her stomach. Was Serena here to fire her?

"Hi, I hope you don't mind that I'm just dropping by." Serena shyly walked into Gabrielle's office.

"Come on in. Hi. It's good to see you." Gabrielle gave herself an imaginary eye roll and tried hard to not blush at the way she stammered. There was a different charge in the air. She was more vulnerable now. She smiled again and sat down. Serena sat opposite her and handed her a casserole dish filled with something. "What's this?"

"Your mom insisted I take home some barbecue, so I wanted to get her dish back to her, and the best way was through you. Plus, it gives me a chance to see how things are going and see if there is anything we need to talk about."

Gabrielle could tell Serena was nervous. She took the dish and peeked under the lid. "There's something in here."

"Chocolate chip brownies. It's impolite to return an empty dish."

"You're sweet. My mom is going to love this."

"You're laughing."

"I'm laughing because my mom will be mortified. She didn't know she was sending leftovers home with Colorado's latest lottery winner," Gabrielle said.

"Your mom didn't know about me? You mean she's always this nice?"

"She's pretty amazing. We finally told her about you after the barbecue."

"We?"

"Rosie did. She felt the need to share a lot with us while we were cleaning up." Gabrielle broke eye contact first.

"Oh? A lot?"

Gabrielle slipped off her glasses and pinched the bridge of her nose. It was now or never. "Yes. She mentioned she outed me to you. I hope that's not going to be a problem."

"A problem how?" Serena seemed genuinely confused.

"I keep my private life private so that it doesn't become an issue for our clients."

Serena laughed. "It's not a problem, trust me."

"That's good to hear." Gabrielle made a big production of wiping her brow.

"I'm also here for another reason. The dish was a great reason, but I want to apologize for not understanding the problems you have with my project."

"I don't have a single problem with the Pet Posh Inn. I'm going to try to give you exactly what you're paying me for."

"Your mom told me about what happened when you were little," Serena said.

Gabrielle subconsciously rubbed her scars again. When Serena looked at her hands, Gabrielle thought about hiding them but ended up stretching her hand forward so that Serena could see.

"It's not that bad anymore, but I had several surgeries to save my fingers."

Serena reached out as if she was going to touch them, but pulled her hand back. "You almost lost them?"

"My ring and pinkie fingers were partially torn off."

"I didn't realize it was so bad. Do you have feeling in your fingers?"

Gabrielle nodded. "Sometimes they hurt because of the weather, but most of the time I don't even notice."

"I'm sorry L.B. scares you. I shouldn't assume that everyone loves dogs."

"I used to love them. Ever since then, I avoid them. Rosie has a really sweet dog, but I'm not going to lie. It's hard. I'm sure it sounds ridiculous." Saying the words out loud made her cringe. She'd never cared about her phobia until right now.

"Well, when we are working, I'll make sure you aren't in the same room with him ever. Even if we aren't working," Serena said.

What did that mean? Did that mean they would be together while not working? Gabrielle stared at Serena, trying to figure out what she meant until it was apparent Serena was uncomfortable under her scrutiny. She slipped her glasses back on and looked at her computer. "Thank you. Since you're here, do you want to see what I've been working on?"

"Definitely." Serena scooted the chair closer to the desk. "I mean, if you have time. I just showed up unannounced, which isn't ideal."

"Nonsense." Gabrielle turned her monitor so they both could see the redesign of the rooms. She zoomed in on the deluxe room with the individual air conditioner and heating unit. "If you do it this way, it's super posh and you don't have to worry about the heat strips on the floors getting damaged. There's a loft for the sleeping area. The steps will have traction so the dogs won't slip and fall. It's easy to clean up when they're done with their stay."

"I really want carpet. I think it adds to the warmth of the place," Serena said.

Gabrielle bit her lip to keep from groaning out her disbelief. "I don't disagree, but I think this is more practical for dogs. You won't be able to replace the carpet every time they go to the bathroom if they aren't taken out as often as they would like." She was careful not to accuse Serena's not-even-hired-yet staff of not letting the dogs out enough. Accidents were going to happen. It was a fact. "Okay, how about throw rugs? We can add some industrial-sized washers and dryers. We can add them to the pantry over here and just extend the east wall eight feet."

"That takes away from the outside area."

Gabrielle made a few adjustments and showed Serena the new backyard. "The area is still large and we can move this fort thing over so it's up against the wall, but fully functioning." After seeing Pet Paradise and the fun obstacles for the dogs, Serena had a change of heart and decided to add back some of the pet playground equipment she had Gabrielle take out.

"It just seems so small."

"It's larger than a backyard. There are only enough rooms for two dozen large dogs. There's plenty of room. More so than what we saw at any of the places we visited." Gabrielle was getting tired of trying to justify every change. She wasn't an expert on dogs and other animals, but she was an expert on space.

"You're right. It's just hard to see it from a two-dimensional perspective. I should trust you more," Serena said.

Neither one of them believed her.

"Are you okay with throw rugs, then? I'm sure there are carpet stores that would be more than happy to donate scraps of carpet they have left over from big house or apartment jobs."

"I can afford it."

Gabrielle looked directly into Serena's eyes and was surprised how quickly her blue-green eyes escalated from happy-go-lucky to do-not-insult-me. She had fire after all, and that knowledge gave her a ripple of excitement. "I never said you couldn't. It's my job to get the most bang for your buck, and I just know that carpet isn't easy to dispose of and donating it to the Pet Posh Inn might be beneficial to you and to them. Only a suggestion."

Serena leaned back in her chair and sighed. "I'm sorry. I didn't come here to argue. You're right. You're the professional."

"I want to give you what you want." Gabrielle cleared her throat at the implication of that. "You're paying me to design your dream business. We can have twenty rounds of changes. I'm charging by the hour."

Serena threw her head back and laughed. "You're totally right. I'm sorry. Yes, let's add the washer and dryer. That's a good idea even for towels and stuff. That way we don't need to use a service to wash linens. I was going to cart things back and forth to the house, but Faith pointed out I should keep work at work."

"So, you won't bring work home with you. I like it." Gabrielle winked at Serena, their testy moment already defused. "It's lunchtime. How about we get out of here and not talk about animals."

"I'm meeting with my lawyer, so I can't today. I'm sorry. Maybe next time?"

For some reason, that stung a bit. "That's fine. I'll probably just go harass my nephew into giving me free food."

"Phillip's a really a nice kid. Faith has been texting him since the barbecue," Serena said.

"Did you fix my nephew up with your baby sister?" Gabrielle could tell Serena was trying to hide her smile.

"Guilty. He's a nice young man, and Faith could use a break in the dating department."

"They did hang out at the party pretty much the whole time." Gabrielle couldn't recall a time when Faith and Phillip weren't together last Sunday.

"I coaxed her into going because I want her to know people here in town. Thanks to you, she knows Phillip, Piper, Shaylie, Rosie, Anne, and a few of Phillip's friends. I think she's starting to get excited about moving here."

"And the travel time isn't bad. You'll be able to visit her whenever. You said your mom moved to California recently, right? That's just a plane ride away." Gabrielle noticed Serena bristle at the mention of her mother. The money probably made it one hundred times worse. She changed the subject. "In other news, Rosie and Anne really enjoyed spending time with you."

"Care Bear is a character. I didn't get to spend a lot of time with their other children, but she was a doll."

"She knows she's adorable. That's the problem. She gets away with anything and everything."

Serena shrugged. "I don't blame her."

"I don't either."

Gabrielle stood when Serena stood.

"I guess I should go. My meeting is across town."

"Thanks for stopping by. I'll drop these off at my mom's on the way home. Or I'll keep it for myself, eat the brownies because they're my favorite dessert, and never tell her that you returned her favorite dish."

Serena whirled, surprising Gabrielle, who stopped short of running into her. Gabrielle watched as Serena looked down at her mouth and back up to her eyes.

"You wouldn't dare."

"You stood me up for lunch. Of course I would." Gabrielle smiled to let Serena know she was kidding.

"How about lunch Friday? Or better yet, how about dinner?"

Gabrielle stuttered for only a moment. Dinner was a different game altogether. "Sure, that's fine. Maybe by then I'll have a lot more for you to look at."

Serena shook her head. "No, no work. Just a casual dinner out to get to know one another better."

Chapter Thirteen

Did she really just ask her architect out on a date? Was it a date? What just happened? Because Faith was in class, Serena dialed Chloe to calm her down.

"You're never going to believe what just happened."

"Well, I'd say you won the lottery, but that already happened. Everything else pales in comparison." The sound of crunching followed.

"What are you eating?"

"A carrot. Don't judge." Chloe was making so much noise, Serena turned down the volume on her speakers. "What am I not going to believe?"

"I asked Gabrielle out to dinner."

Coughing ensued as Chloe choked on her carrot. "Are you kidding me?"

"Was that the wrong thing to do? I mean, I made it sound like it was just a casual dinner. She invited me to lunch but I have a meeting with my lawyer, so I asked her to dinner instead."

"You could have warned me before dropping that bomb," Chloe said between coughing fits. "And no. It's perfect. From what you and Faith have told me, she sounds great."

"Maybe she's not one to mix business and pleasure. She was kind of standoffish at the barbecue."

"She was charming and babysitting a bunch of kids and staying as far away from L.B. as she could."

"I apologized to her for L.B. and having him around a lot." Serena's heart dropped as she thought about the psychological issues Gabrielle had endured her entire life. She wondered if she'd ever been to therapy. No way was she going to ask. Therapy was too personal.

"You couldn't have known that. Gabrielle is a smart lady. She's just not ever around pets. If she wants to have a relationship, she's either going to have to be really good in bed for somebody to get rid of their pets, or she's going to have to figure out a way to be around them."

"I wouldn't dream of giving up L.B. Ever. As a matter of fact, now that I have all the furniture in the house, I'm thinking about getting another dog or a few cats. I'm pretty bored most days. I can't wait until the Pet Posh Inn is up and running. Then I can work there."

"I love the new you. I mean, I loved the old you, but the new you has something the old you didn't."

Silence. Serena smiled. "Really? A dramatic pause?"

"Hope. It's beautiful on you."

"I love you. Get back to your carrots." Serena wasn't used to hearing praise, even though Chloe and Jackie were nothing but the best support group she could have. It embarrassed her.

"I love you, too. See you tomorrow."

Serena had invited Chloe and Jackie over to see the house. They'd done a walk-through before she furnished it and knew they would be more than happy to help her decorate. She drove the rest of the way to Mason & Grant law firm with the air conditioner on high, a luxury she was thankful to have, and even turned up the music. She had it tuned to satellite radio on a hit music station. Even though she didn't know the songs, she sang the chorus as if she was in the band. Thirty minutes later, she pulled into the parking lot feeling pretty damn good about her day. She considered her impromptu meeting with Gabrielle a success and managed to get a date out of it. Today's conference with her lawyers was hopefully going to be quick and painless. She wasn't familiar with any of the laws and barely understood what her lawyers were suggesting, but since Chloe and Jackie trusted them, she did, too.

"Ms. Evans. Nice to see you again. I'll let the team know you're here." Heather smiled while she picked up the phone and softly announced her arrival. "Please have a seat. They'll be with you in just a moment."

Serena liked visiting the firm. It was spacious and welcoming. Most law firms she saw on television or in the movies screamed wealth with mahogany walls and oversized offices with large views. Mason & Grant was contemporary and bright. Serena didn't feel out of place. As a matter of fact, they treated her with a lot of respect there, but then a lot of money demanded a certain top-tier-type treatment.

"Nice to see you again."

Serena stood to shake the hand thrust in front of her. "Ms. Grant. Nice to see you as well."

"Come on, let's head to Mr. Randall's office and get started."

Serena followed her lawyer, admiring her tight form and shapely calves. As attractive as she was, she just struck Serena as being cold and direct. Beautiful smile, but the warmth didn't quite meet her blue eyes. She was one hundred percent business, which Serena appreciated, but she couldn't help compare her to Gabrielle, who was just as attractive, but treated her more like a person rather than a client.

"Ms. Evans. Good to see you again," Mr. Randall said.

Serena shook his hand, too, and sat when they did. The advisory meeting wasn't as painful as she expected, and she approved of the division of the rest of her money. She had several accounts, and even set Faith up with one. Moving to Denver wasn't going to be a huge expense, but she wanted her sister to have the best of everything.

Since paying off her mother's house and giving her a modest stipend, she hadn't heard from her since their big blowup. She wasn't going to give Diane any more money, but if Faith wanted to give her some of hers, that was her decision. She signed form after form until her hand cramped. The entire process of reading all the documents, asking questions, and signing her name took almost two hours. Serena was exhausted but happy that most of it was wrapped up. The Pet Posh Inn was going to be a well-oiled machine that would generate good, repeat business. At least, that was the goal, and she had every intention of holding her staff to the highest standards.

"That should do it. If anything comes up, just give us a call, night or day," Mr. Randall said.

Serena shook his hand and followed her lawyer out to the lobby. "Thanks so much for taking me on as a client."

"Are you kidding? You're a dream come true. I wish all of our clients were as easygoing and as trusting as you are," Ms. Grant said.

Serena stifled a slight surge of fear and a squeezing in her chest as she processed what she'd just done. She reassured herself that she'd hired this firm to work on her behalf and invest her money because they came highly recommended. She tamped down the panic that nestled in her throat and took a deep breath.

"Thanks. I'll call you if I have any questions." Serena gave a half wave on her way out the door and dropped her hand because her social awkwardness was embarrassing. With an afternoon free, she decided to roam Denver and ended up in a quaint neighborhood that had local businesses including a bicycle store, a coffee shop, a pet boutique, a donut café, and an old bookstore. She checked her watch, knowing she'd hit all the stores. She missed the peacefulness of being around books and the adventures she had with them daily. That was her first stop. She pulled open the door, smiled at the small bell that signaled her arrival, and took a deep breath. Coffee was brewing somewhere close, or the smell wafted over from Peak Brew next door. There was a distinct difference in the smell of freshly printed books to ones that had been shelved for decades, even centuries. She loved both. That meant people were reading.

"Can I help you find anything?"

A sweet elderly woman who looked like the quintessential librarian approached her.

"No, thank you. I'm just looking," Serena said.

The woman smiled and excused herself. She was nothing like Mrs. Brody, Serena thought. She walked up and down the aisles, her fingertips brushing the spines of all types of books. There was something satisfying at feeling everything from the ribbed, faded spines of classics to the new smoothness of dust jackets.

"Serena?"

As if busted, Serena stood up, instantly dropping her hands from the books. Piper, Gabrielle's friend from the barbecue, pulled her in for a quick hug. Serena tried not to tense up.

"Piper. Hi. How are you?"

"I'm great. What a nice surprise. What are you doing in Denver? And specifically, my neighborhood? You should have called."

"I had a meeting with my lawyer, who's not too far away, so I'm just killing time now."

"Would you like to grab a cup of coffee or tea? I have an hour before my next class starts," Piper said.

It was hard not to stare at Piper. She was gorgeous. Shaylie was a lucky woman.

"Yeah, sure. That would be great."

"Let me just buy this book and we can head next door. If you're finished here."

Serena nodded. "Oh, I was just looking around. I saw the little shops here and they all have things that interest me."

"You work in a bookstore, right?"

"I used to. Not anymore."

"That's right. Gabrielle is designing your project, right?" Piper asked. She paid for her book and followed Serena out.

"A pet inn. We're getting close to finishing the design part of it. Do you have any pets?" Serena asked.

"We have Clifford, the yoga cat, and a ton of fish. We're only a year out from a dog. We're just waiting for Maribelle to get a little bit bigger. Your dog is adorable." Piper held the door open for Serena and was immediately handed an iced tea. She turned to Serena and shrugged. "They know me here. What can I get you?"

"I can get it. I'll have an iced blackberry sage tea." Serena said the first tea she read on the list. If Piper wasn't standing next to her, she would have taken a solid five minutes to make a selection.

"Valeria, please put it on my tab." Piper gave a single nod to the barista. "Come on. Let's sit at that table back there."

"Thank you for the tea."

Piper put her hand on Serena's arm. "You're welcome. Now, let's get to know each other better in the next forty-five minutes until my next class."

"What do you want to know?"

"What do you do for fun?" Piper sipped on her tea and gave her undivided attention. It was unnerving, but in a pleasant way. Piper was gorgeous, nice, thoughtful, and Serena often forgot that there were good people out in the world who didn't want her for anything other than her friendship.

"My life in the last three months has been a whirlwind, so my level of fun has been shopping and working on the pet inn."

"Shopping is fun. My wife doesn't like it nearly as much as I do."

Serena wondered if Piper knew she won the lottery. She had to give props to Gabrielle for not blabbing that juicy bit of information to her friends.

"I just closed on my house, so I needed to get furniture."

"Congratulations. I love looking at houses. The views around here are gorgeous, especially in Vail." Piper softly covered her mouth with her well-manicured fingers. "I didn't mean to interrupt. I just hear a lot about real estate."

"It's okay. I love talking about it. I just furnished it and now I'm looking for artwork and general décor. I need help."

Piper's eyes lit up. "I can totally help you there. There's a local artist, Lori Stewart, whose gallery isn't far from here, and she has amazing work. She uses all types of media, but she's probably known best for her landscapes. I'll send you a link to her website." She picked up her phone, found the link, and asked Serena for her phone number. It was done so fast and smoothly that she didn't have time to process that she was giving out her new number to somebody else.

"Now how did you meet your wife? Shaylie, right?" Serena asked.

Piper leaned back in her chair and took a deep breath. "So, remember that plane wreck that happened just outside of Denver about five years ago?"

"Yes, of course. It was all over the news." Serena leaned forward and pressed her elbows down on the table, both frightened and intrigued by the story already.

"Shaylie was on the flight. My fiancée and best friend were on the flight, too, but they didn't make it."

Serena reached out and squeezed Piper's hands. "I'm so sorry. That must have been horrible. For both of you."

"Shaylie had some bad injuries, but she made it. We met at a grief counseling meeting and became friends. Five years later we're together and have a beautiful daughter and some questionable pets."

"An unfortunate beginning, but a beautiful ending," Serena said.

"Oh, don't end us yet." Piper winked to let Serena know she was joking. "We're still going strong. And we're trying for baby number two."

"I can't handle this much perfectness. You have to stop." Serena put her hand on her heart jokingly, but truthfully, Piper's story got her a little emotional.

"It's been a journey, but we're going strong and we have a large group of wonderful people in our lives, including you, so life is good," Piper said.

"I'm sad that I live in Vail because I probably know more people in Denver than I do back home." Serena didn't even think of moving before she bought the house. Vail was home to her, and with the Pet Posh Inn almost in production, she was there to stay.

"Denver is close, though. Didn't you say your sister is moving to Denver?"

"Yes. She got a job at Frederick's Restaurant but doesn't start until September first. She's a chef studying at the Vail Culinary Center."

"That's a great restaurant. Shaylie and I love it. She must be so excited. And really good to land a job there." Piper looked at her watch and stood. "Oh, my gosh. I'm almost late to my class. I hate to leave because we're having such a good talk, but hopefully we can do this soon when I have more time."

Serena stood, too. "Definitely. Go. Thank you for having tea with me. I'm going to hit a few more stores before I start my trek back." She really liked Piper and thought her and Shaylie's love story was amazing. Her phone dinged in her pocket, signaling her she had a text message. It was from Faith.

Mom needs a place to stay and my place isn't big enough.

Serena's anger spiked immediately. *Mommy Dearest has plenty of money. She can afford a hotel.*

She's paying for her own airfare. Can you just do this for me?

Fuck, Serena hated it when Faith did that. To be fair, Faith didn't know what Serena had given to Diane unless Diane told her. And Faith wasn't going to receive her money until she graduated. It was all a surprise. The only thing Serena had told her was that she needed to look for a place to live in Denver.

Baby sis, Mom has money. Let's leave it at that. I love you, but she gets nothing else from me. Trust me when I say she can afford it. There was a solid minute before Serena saw any texting activity on her phone.

Okay. See you tomorrow night.

Faith was coming to her little open house, too. Small crowd. Chloe, Jackie, Faith, and L.B. They were her family. Serena smiled when she thought about Piper, Shaylie, Rosie, and Gabrielle. Her circle now was tiny, but she had a good feeling that it was about to triple in size, and it had nothing to do with her money.

Chapter Fourteen

"Miles, I'll be out the rest of the afternoon."
"Where are you going?"
Gabrielle stopped, turned, and waited three seconds before answering. "I'm working, and I will be available by phone if anybody needs me." She lifted her eyebrow, challenging Miles to say anything else. Miles broke eye contact first.
"That's fine."
Gabrielle called Rosie on her way out to the parking lot. "It's time."
"Whatever you mean, I'm in."
Rosie always knew how to make Gabrielle feel like she had her back no matter what. "I need to hang out with Muppet. I need to start getting comfortable and facing my fears head-on."
"You're fist-pumping the air again, aren't you?"
Gabrielle never understood how Rosie always knew when she did that. She slipped into the car and waited until the phone connected to Bluetooth. "Nope. Maybe. It doesn't matter. Should I bring treats? Or a toy?"
"Honey, Muppet just loves people and attention. You show up and pat his head and he'll love you for life. Now take a deep breath, go home, change into comfortable clothes, and get over here. We're having pasta primavera."
"Want me to bring anything?"
"Just your courage."
Gabrielle said goodbye and disconnected the call. If she was going to spend time with Serena that didn't involve design work, she was going to have to familiarize herself with dogs. Muppet was as easygoing as L.B., so he was the perfect test case. Plus, several of her

friends were thinking about adopting a dog. She was going to be thrust into a world of canine companionship whether she was ready or not.

She also needed to find something to wear. Serena only knew her professional wardrobe and the one simple outfit she wore to the barbecue. She didn't have anything new to wear on a date, casual or not. That would have to be remedied this afternoon. She felt a little guilty shopping during working hours, but since she worked almost twice as many hours as most of her coworkers, the guilt was quickly forgotten. She pulled into the Cherry Creek shopping areas and boutiques and did something she hadn't done in forever. Splurged. Two hours later and a back seat full of shopping bags, she headed home to unload, change, and head over to Rosie's.

"Are you ready?" Rosie answered the door holding Kittypurrs.

Cats didn't scare her as much as dogs. She was just wary of them because of all of the horror stories she heard. They were unpredictable. And Kittypurrs had used her claws on the children a time or two.

"I guess so." Gabrielle followed Rosie into the living room, where she was instructed to sit on the couch. Rosie dumped Kittypurrs next to her. The cat looked at Gabrielle, then promptly jumped off and ignored her.

"Nothing's going to happen. I'll keep him across the room from you, and if you ignore him long enough, he'll lose interest in you." Rosie didn't sound convincing, but disappeared to retrieve him.

Gabrielle gripped the armrests of the recliner as she waited for Muppet's arrival. True to her word, Rosie commanded Muppet to stay next to her. He slowly army-crawled his way over to Gabrielle, wagging his tail the entire time. He really was cute, Gabrielle thought, even though she tensed up when he got close enough to sniff her shoes.

"Be nice, Muppet. Be sweet," Rosie said. He rolled over and offered his tummy for Gabrielle to rub. "Okay, sweet is one thing, this is something else."

Gabrielle laughed nervously.

"Now, you can reach down and pet him if you want, or I can make him sit and you can let him smell you."

"Maybe if he sat up I wouldn't worry about any sudden moves," Gabrielle said.

Rosie commanded Muppet to sit on the other side of her so that he was close enough for Gabrielle to pet if she wanted to and Rosie was directly between them if something happened that frightened her.

"He'll smell you, and might lick you, but he's very gentle. And if you get scared, you just have to say 'd-o-w-n' and he will listen. I promise, he's chill."

Gabrielle reached across Rosie's lap to let Muppet smell her. She pulled away when she felt his cold, wet nose but didn't let that deter her. She reached out again and kept her hand out while he sniffed her fingers. When he licked her palm, she shuddered and pulled back again. "Ew." She wiped her palm on her jeans but couldn't help but smile. It wasn't a big step to anyone else in the world, but it was a major one for her.

"Good job," Rosie said. She squeezed Gabrielle's knee encouragingly and nodded her approval at this monumental step. "Now maybe you want to rub his head? But don't tap it. Just kind of brush your fingertips front to back over and over."

Gabrielle pulled back when Muppet raised his snout up to her hand to kiss it. "Okay, Muppet. Let me pet you. Then maybe you can kiss me again." She reached out again, and much to her surprise, Muppet lowered his head and allowed Gabrielle to stroke the top. "He's so soft," she said.

"He just got a bath. We wanted this to be the best experience for you. He probably won't smell this good or be this clean again in a long time, so get all of your petting in now." Muppet lay down in front of their feet with his head almost resting on Gabrielle's foot. Rosie petted his side slowly from his shoulders to his ribs. He thumped his tail slowly when he felt Gabrielle's fingers on his fur. "Look at how good you're doing. He's so used to the kids climbing on him, pulling his ears or accidentally stepping on his paws. Most dogs are pretty amazing if they're around the right people. I'm sure L.B. is just as gentle as Muppet is. And if anything is going to happen with Serena, then you're going to have to get used to being around him."

Gabrielle leaned back and held up her hands. "Whoa, whoa, whoa. Hold on. Nobody said anything about something happening with Serena. We're just friends."

"That's something, right? I mean, you don't have dinner with your pharmacist at CVS, do you? Or what about that nice lady who works at the cupcake shop? Have you had lunch or dinner with her? Hmm. Let me think." Rosie put her forefinger on her chin and tilted her head up as if she was trying hard to recall a memory.

Gabrielle nudged her with her shoulder. "Okay, so it's something."

"And it's not against company policy, right? Do you even have a company policy?"

Gabrielle thought for a minute. "Not that I'm aware of. I don't even think we have a policy against fraternizing. Then again, most of the employees are male. And the assistants are old enough to be their mothers. Except for Miles, and he's engaged to a chick named Taffy."

"And let's be real. You've never had a client as attractive as Serena," Rosie said.

"You're absolutely right. She's rather attractive."

"And she's a single lesbian. Correction. She's a wealthy single lesbian." Rosie kept talking and talking, about subject after subject. They somehow went from Serena, to Rosie's opinion on snowboarding versus skiing for the children, to whether hot chocolate was better from a mix or a syrup, to whether or not Runts had changed their flavors.

"Are you drinking something and I'm not aware of it?" Gabrielle asked.

"What do you mean?" Rosie asked.

"You're all over the place with this conversation." Rosie's eyes didn't look unfocused. They were sharp and staring at Gabrielle intently.

"I just wanted to keep your mind whirling so you wouldn't be aware that you've been petting Muppet for the last few minutes without even realizing it."

Gabrielle looked down at Muppet, whose eyes were closed. His ears were back as she moved her hand from his brow to his neck over and over again. "Wow. I'm petting a dog." She pulled her hand back when Muppet flopped and gave her his belly to scratch. "I don't know if I'm at that stage yet." She pointed to his splayed-out body at her feet.

Rosie leaned down, scratched his belly, and told him to go see Anne. He scrambled up, scaring Gabrielle in the process, and tore off into the other room. She reached down and squeezed Gabrielle's hand. "I'm so proud of you. Look at what you did today."

Gabrielle squeezed Rosie's fingers back. "Big moment. Thank you. It wasn't as bad as I thought."

"I don't expect you to wrestle on the floor with him yet, but let's keep things going. I want him to be around you more, so I'd like for him to stay in during dinner if you're okay with that."

"I'm okay for now."

"And Kittypurrs won't come over until Muppet is gone. Then she'll want you all to herself."

"Cats don't seem as space invasive as dogs."

"Thankfully, Kittypurrs is also nice. You know the kids and how awkward they are. Care Bear has learned how to be gentle with her, and if she can do it, you can, too."

Gabrielle watched Kittypurrs strut into the living room and rub against all of the furniture. She smiled when she jumped on the kitty condo and climbed the platform to look out the window. That gave her an idea for Serena's project. She whipped out her phone and took a picture of Kittypurrs chilling in her space.

"You can pet her if you want. That's her safe place. The kids can't reach her there. They know when she's there, they're to leave her alone."

"Let's keep it that way for now. Baby steps." The spike of adrenaline in Gabrielle's body at making the first step with Muppet made her stand. "It wasn't bad. Muppet didn't charge at me or jump on me."

"If you're sitting, he's pretty good, but sometimes he gets overwhelmed and might jump on you. He means you no harm."

"Aunt Elle."

Gabrielle squatted and held out her hands to Carolyn. "Hello, Care Bear. Look at you. You got so big since last week."

Carolyn smiled at Gabrielle and hugged her tightly. "We're having pizza."

"Again? I thought you said we were doing pasta primavera."

"Hey, it's Thursday night. We had dance and piano. Pizza ended up being the easy choice."

"I could have brought something. I took the afternoon off."

"It's a big day. I'd have taken the day off, too. Let's grab some pizza before it's all gone. The girls are growing like weeds, which means they're eating anything and everything."

Gabrielle slid Carolyn into her booster seat and sat at the table where three giant steaming-hot pizzas were placed in the middle. They held hands and said grace and dug in. True to Rosie's word, Muppet stayed in the kitchen, head on his paws, lifting his head up whenever Gabrielle made eye contact.

"So, tell us about this date tomorrow. Where are you going?" Anne asked.

Gabrielle swallowed her mouthful of pizza, covering her mouth until she was done. "I don't know. The exchange happened so quickly that I don't think either of us was ready. I'm assuming it's in Denver, but maybe there's a place she wants to go to in Vail." She shrugged. "I'll text her later and find out. It's not a big deal. I think we're exploring friendship more than anything." Even though her voice was calm, her stomach was quivering. She was finding it more and more difficult to see Serena as just a client. She was attractive, quiet, smart, and it was nice seeing her confidence grow in just the short time she'd known her.

"And yet you bought all of the clothes for one friendship date? Hmm. I think there might be something there, and I'm happy as shit," Rosie said. Anne elbowed her when the kids giggled. "Oops. Sorry, kids. Mommy shouldn't have said that word."

"Let's not get ahead of ourselves. Maybe she's looking for friends who aren't out for her money. I get the feeling she didn't have very many before, and now it's even harder to find them because of her instant wealth. She's not tight with her mom. There were issues there. But I really like Faith." Both Anne and Rosie nodded in agreement. "And apparently Phillip's been helping Faith look for a place. Denver's pretty expensive, but not nearly as much as Vail. I know Serena's going to help her financially."

"That money's going to go faster than she realizes," Rosie said.

"The Pet Posh Inn is going to cost her quite a bit. The land alone was outrageously expensive, but most of the area we are designing is open space. The lodge is sizable, and the fence will be expensive, but I don't think it will be more than the land."

"She has a lawyer, right?" Anne asked.

"A team of them. That's what got us into this date. I invited her to lunch, but she was having a meeting with them, so it turned into an impromptu dinner that surprised both of us."

"I like her and I'm going to like having her around," Rosie said.

"Piper texted me that she had tea with her this afternoon. Guess she has time for her," Anne teased.

"Well, can you blame her? Piper's a knockout," Rosie said.

"Thankfully, happily married," Gabrielle said.

"Truer words have never been spoken," Anne chimed in, and they all sat and thought about Piper and Shaylie. "I mean, we're pretty awesome, too, but they win for best romance."

Rosie leaned over and kissed Anne. "We really are awesome."

"Stop. Both of you. Not in front of the children." As much as Gabrielle teased them, she loved that they were very affectionate.

"What are you going to wear?" Rosie asked.

"Since I bought one of everything, I think I'll find something nice and casual."

"She was looking at you a lot during the barbecue," Anne said.

"I told her the same thing," Rosie said.

Gabrielle could feel heat blossom on her cheeks. She'd noticed Serena glancing her way a few times, too. She chalked it up to intrigue rather than interest. "I'm sure it was just because she was looking for a familiar face."

Rosie rolled her eyes. "Yeah, that's it. Because we don't know anything about chemistry."

"You should be around when we discuss the project. Nothing is right. We did have a breakthrough moment today, so that was nice. And Kittypurrs gave me a great idea for the cat wing just now, so I feel better about what I'll show Serena next." Gabrielle felt inspired. All she needed was quality time here with both Muppet and Kittypurrs. She knew it would be a long time before she'd feel comfortable, but this was the first step. Petting Muppet and just watching Kittypurrs walk around the house helped so much.

"You ready for step two?" Rosie asked.

Gabrielle finished her Diet Coke and nodded. "I'm ready."

"Let's go outside and see how Muppet does."

Gabrielle followed Rosie, not too closely, and a very animated Muppet to the backyard. He had a tennis ball that he dropped at Rosie's feet and waited. She threw it four times, and every time he retrieved it, he dropped it right at her feet. "I'm going to give you the ball and you just have to throw it for him." She picked up the half-chewed ball and handed it to Gabrielle.

"Yuck. It's wet."

"Yes. It's slobber. You can wash your hands later. Now throw it over by the trees." Rosie pointed to an open area off the deck.

Gabrielle took a few steps back as Muppet danced around her, waiting for the toss.

"The longer you wait, the closer he gets."

Gabrielle threw it and moved closer to Rosie as he charged back at them. Rosie held her hand out and he stopped three feet from them and dropped the ball.

"Come here, Muppet." She held on to his collar. "Pet him."

"Right now? But he's very excited. What if he jumps on me?"

"He won't. I'm holding him." Rosie did a hand command and Muppet instantly lay down. With her hand still on his collar, she waved Gabrielle over. "Sit down next to him."

"Are you crazy?" Gabrielle stared at Muppet, whose long tongue lolled out of his mouth, his white, sharp teeth exposed while he panted.

Rosie sat on the top step of the deck and Muppet put his head on her lap. She patted the empty spot on the other side of her. Gabrielle slowly slid down until her thigh was flush with Rosie's. "Reach out and touch him."

Gabrielle carefully rubbed Muppet's head. Rosie whispered a few words to him and he didn't move the entire time. Gabrielle moved her fingers down to his ears and rubbed the floppy tips until he sighed with contentment. When he licked her hand, she didn't pull back. A look of pure disgust was on her face, but she kept rubbing his head and ears.

"He likes his neck and chin scratched."

"Too close to the teeth. Let's stick with this for now."

"I'm going to slowly move so that you end up next to him. Don't be nervous. He'll probably roll over." Rosie commanded him to stay and stepped away so he and Gabrielle were maybe a foot apart. Muppet stretched his head back and looked up at Gabrielle. "How can you resist him? He's so loving and he trusts you. Look into those magical brown chocolate eyes."

Gabrielle rubbed his shoulder until his tail wagged. He leaned up, but Gabrielle pulled back and stopped petting him.

"You're doing great. He loves you already. Remember, he's around the most precious people in my world, and I trust him implicitly."

"I know. He really is a good boy." She resumed petting him but made the mistake of looking away to ask Rosie a question. Before she even registered what was happening, Muppet leaned up and licked her from chin to eyebrow, leaving a slobbery trail on her shocked face.

Chapter Fifteen

The open house dinner turned into a "let's get Serena ready for her date" evening instead of a "welcome to my new house" party. Once Chloe, Jackie, and Faith found out Serena had asked Gabrielle out to dinner, everyone had advice.

"I'm going to show you how to apply makeup," Faith said. She pulled out a cosmetics bag that was bigger than Serena's purse and rolled out all different kinds of makeup and brushes. Jackie squawked about how she should wear her hair and decided to take her for a mani-pedi in the morning. She strongly suggested getting Serena's eyebrows waxed, too. Serena was too tired to be offended and truthfully had never had a spa date before. It sounded wonderful, even though she pretended to be put out by all of their suggestions. Now, twenty-four hours later, she stood outside North Italia waiting for Gabrielle, feeling beautiful for the first time in her life. She was polished and had allowed herself to be pampered and felt fabulous.

"You found it."

Serena turned to find Gabrielle walking up behind her. There was a tightness in her chest when Gabrielle's eyes traveled up and down her body. Gabrielle, her hair loose and flowing over her shoulders, wasn't wearing her glasses, and the transformation, like before, was breathtaking. She was beautiful at the barbecue, but this was a mature, sophisticated Gabrielle who wasn't holding a baby on her hip or handing out drinks to guests. This was dateable Gabrielle who wore a sleeveless blouse and pants that clung to her hips and thighs and gathered fashionably at her thin ankles. The three-inch heels gave her height that made Serena look up at her and instantly regret wearing flats.

"You look great," she said. She almost regretted saying it, but when Gabrielle's smile blossomed, she knew she'd said the right thing.

"Thank you. You look great as well. Have you been waiting long?" Gabrielle asked.

Serena shook her head. "I just parked. Right there." She pointed to her Jeep, which was only a few spots down from the front door.

"You're so lucky."

Serena smiled, knowing that she meant so much by that statement. "Only for the last few months."

"Come on. Let's sit down and drink wine and talk about only fun stuff," Gabrielle said.

Serena smiled when Gabrielle held the door for her. The low lights and soft music gave the place a romantic glow. She was going to kill Chloe and Jackie for recommending it. She should have let Gabrielle pick the place since she lived in Denver, but having extended the invitation, she wanted to seem mature and in control.

"This place is gorgeous." Gabrielle leaned down and spoke softly in Serena's ear as they followed the hostess to their booth. When Serena had suggested it, Gabrielle said she'd heard only good things. Apparently neither of them knew this was the hot spot for date night. "I'm surprised you were able to get a reservation."

"My friend Chloe is friends with the manager. I had no idea it was so intimate." Yep, she was definitely going to kill Chloe for setting this up.

"I think it's great. Even though it's packed, it's pretty quiet. We'll be able to have a conversation," Gabrielle said. She smiled at Serena and slid across from her in the booth near the back of the restaurant. They agreed on a bottle of pinot noir and sipped on water until the waiter returned with the bottle.

"How was your appointment with your lawyer? Did you get everything squared away?" Gabrielle asked.

Serena was seriously going to lose herself in the amber warmth of Gabrielle's eyes. The candle flickered between them and filled her head with inappropriate thoughts. "I did. Just a heads-up, if you win the lottery, the money goes fast."

"Only if you're setting yourself up for life it does. I think your business plan is actually very smart and has the longevity that a lot of businesses now don't. People love their pets, and allowing them to bring them on vacation is brilliant. A lot of wealthy people ski in Vail."

"That's exactly why I want it upscale. I know I've been a massive pain about all of this, but I do have my reasons."

"You're not a pain at all, trust me."

The sommelier returned with the bottle of wine and poured a taste into a glass. Serena nodded at Gabrielle to try it. After the single nod of approval from Gabrielle, he poured a second glass. He assured them their waiter would return shortly.

"I have news," Gabrielle said.

"Is it good news?" Serena leaned forward and put her elbows on the table for just a moment before she remembered her manners. She leaned back and kept her hands busy by playing with the stem of her glass.

"Ask me what I did yesterday."

The smirk was so damn charming Serena couldn't help but smile back. "What did you do yesterday?"

"I played ball with a dog."

Serena grabbed Gabrielle's hands. "That's the best news. How was it?"

Gabrielle looked down at their entwined fingers. "It wasn't as scary as I thought it would be, but Rosie has a very chill dog named Muppet and he was calm and gentle. I petted him and even threw the ball for him."

"That's great. I'm proud of you," Serena said. She knew Gabrielle didn't need her praise but couldn't help but want to encourage her even more. "When you're ready to meet L.B. again, then we can maybe take him for a walk." Serena softly pulled her hands away from Gabrielle's when salads arrived.

"So, I have to know. Why do you call your dog L.B.? I've heard you call him a few different things."

Serena laughed softly before she explained. "So, Chloe and Jackie went with me to the shelter. There was one scruffy dog that had brown wiry fur and was super happy and kept making eye contact with us. They didn't have a name for him yet. Chloe called him Lucky Bastard when I picked him."

"His name is really Lucky Bastard?" Gabrielle laughed at the silly name.

"No. Here's the best part. I asked the clerk there why he didn't have a name, and a little girl, who was waiting for her parents to pick out a dog, turned to me and said his name was Lucky Baxter because she misheard Chloe."

"That explains why when I first met him, you called him Baxter."

"He answers to Lucky, Baxter, Lucky Baxter, and L.B."

"And one day I'll be able to pet him, I promise."

"Wait. Are you doing this for me? Because of the project? I promise, I can put L.B. in a different space. It's no trouble at all." Serena was proud of Gabrielle for facing her demon but didn't want her doing it just for L.B.

"It's time. Most of my friends have dogs or are getting them. Even though I might never get comfortable around them, they will be around me, so Rosie is offering me Muppet anytime I need to work on it."

"I think that's incredible. And makes you brave. And if you need L.B., you can borrow him, too."

"See, I have this client and she wants me to build this corral for all kinds of animals, and I figured it's a good idea if I get used to them being around. I mean, I'm only the designer, but I usually stick around until a project is done," Gabrielle said.

Serena laughed. "A corral? That's not true."

Gabrielle put her hand over her heart. "Wait, are you making fun of my client? Because I take that personally. She's a nice young woman. She just loves animals. All of them, so I have to at least try."

"I'm glad you're trying. I'm sure she is, too." Serena smiled at Gabrielle and took a sip of the pinot noir.

"But enough about work. Tell me about you. What do you like to do? What do you do now that you didn't like to six months ago?" Gabrielle leaned forward and gave Serena all of her attention.

"You have the prettiest eyes. I can't believe you hide them behind glasses all the time." Serena covered her mouth at her outburst. "I didn't mean it like that. I'm sure you have to wear glasses to do your job. Yikes. Never mind. Anyway, I don't really know what I like to do. I've always worked."

"No hobbies? Like scrapbooking or collecting thimbles or building furniture out of matchboxes?"

"Definitely none of those. I like to read. I watch movies. I pretty much keep to myself. Chloe and Jackie are my best friends. They're a couple, but they include me in a lot of things."

"They sound really nice and I can't wait to meet them," Gabrielle said.

Serena looked over in time to see Chloe and Jackie weaving their way through the restaurant. "Son of a bitch. Looks like you'll get to meet them sooner than later. They're here." Serena rose out of her chair as Chloe and Jackie approached their table. "What are you doing here?" She hugged them both and introduced them to Gabrielle.

"We're not trying to crash, but after making reservations, we decided to grab dinner, too. Later, much later, than your reservations. We're going to have a drink at the bar. It's nice to meet you, Gabrielle." Chloe shook her hand and turned to Serena while Jackie shook hands with Gabrielle. Chloe quickly fanned herself and mouthed "wow."

"Maybe we can all meet up later for a drink when you're done," Gabrielle said.

"We might do that. Enjoy your dinner," Jackie said.

Serena watched them walk away and shook her head apologetically at Gabrielle. "They live ninety minutes away. This was planned."

"I think it's sweet that they're looking out for you. Don't be mad at them. They're your closest friends and they want to make sure I'm not a murderer or trying to take advantage of you."

"I know, but it's childish of them."

Gabrielle reached across the table and held Serena's hands. "It's okay. I'm not offended. I like them more now since they're looking out for you. That's what makes friends your family."

Serena tried to ignore the softness of Gabrielle's touch, tried not to think how strong and long her fingers were. Even in the few seconds they were physically connected, Serena felt something she hadn't felt in a long time. Safe. Even though they had very little in common, even though up until this point they had a professional relationship only, the gesture felt intimate and stirred something deep inside Serena. "It's nice to have people I can trust." When the waiter showed up with their entrées, Serena reluctantly pulled away from Gabrielle's warmth.

"Back to what do you like to do. What have you been doing since you quit your job?"

"Truth?"

Gabrielle nodded.

"I'm bored. Legit bored. Everybody works," Serena said.

"You'll just have to come up with new and exciting things to do. And once the Pet Posh Inn is up and running, you'll be so busy, you'll cry for some alone time," Gabrielle said.

Serena looked down at her serving of rigatoni with sausage and fennel. There was too much on her plate, but Gabrielle didn't seem like the kind who wanted to share an entrée. She smiled thinking about all of the meals she and Faith shared growing up. She always gave Faith an extra chicken nugget and gave her most of the fries when she could scrape together enough money for a Happy Meal at McDonald's. How long ago that was, but not really.

"What are you smiling about?" Gabrielle asked. Her dinner of the citrus Italian steak with a tomato salad smelled delicious.

"I was remembering something my sister and I used to do. It's nothing."

"I love that you two are so close. Phillip only has good things to say about her. Are you sad that she's moving away?"

"Yes and no. Denver isn't far, so I'm good with that. I'm also so proud of her for getting a job, a good job, before she even graduated."

"What are you doing for her graduation? Anything?"

Serena put her fork down and sighed. "That is a hot mess right there. I don't want to have a party at my house, and we aren't sure who's going to show up. For sure her three roommates, plus my mom and stepdad, and Faith. We're better off going to a restaurant, but we don't know if any of her classmates want to attend. I want it to be open so people can come and go as they please."

"Does she live in an apartment building? They probably have a community room you can rent. Most places do. You can host in a club room." Gabrielle shrugged when Serena looked at her.

"That's a great idea. That way we can decorate and people can come and go as they please. Thank you for the idea."

"That's why I get paid the big bucks. I solve problems. Even when it takes me a million tries."

Serena lifted her glass and clinked it with Gabrielle's. "And the Pet Posh Inn will be fabulous when it's all done."

"I have a great idea that I'll share with you next week, but tonight, no shop talk. Tonight I'm going to get to know you and you're going to get to know me."

They spent the next hour slipping into comfortable conversation about things they liked, things they disliked, music, favorite movies, and television shows that ended prematurely. They were still sitting at the table laughing and talking when Chloe and Jackie finished their meal and asked if they would join them for drinks at the bar. Serena insisted she pay the bill, since it was her invite, and the four of them found a high top at the bar.

"We've heard good things about you," Chloe said.

"And some questionable things, I'm sure." Gabrielle smiled.

"Not at all. One thing you should know about Serena is that she's never said a bad thing about anyone. She's perfect."

"Oh, stop. I'm far from perfect. I've said a few choice things about people in my past."

"Pfft. Take the compliment. You're perfect." Jackie leaned over and kissed her cheek.

Serena blushed as her friends talked her up, telling Gabrielle how nice she was when she did this, or heroic she was when she did that.

"I've raised my voice a time or two," she said. Thankfully, everyone avoided talking about her mother. That was the only time she got angry. The only time she raised her voice at someone. Now that she was an adult, she knew she was going to have to let it go and possibly find a therapist.

"She is pretty sweet," Gabrielle said.

Serena held her breath at the look Gabrielle shot her. It was sexy and flirty and Serena allowed it to flutter inside, tickle her stomach, brush her ribs softly, and explode in her chest. Chloe nudged her under the table. It was apparent to her, too.

Chloe stood and tapped Jackie on the shoulder. "Listen, we should go. I'm getting tired because I ate too much food and drank too much wine."

"What? We're leaving? But we're having such a great time."

"Yeah, busy day tomorrow."

"It's Saturday," Jackie said.

Serena saw Chloe squeeze Jackie's waist.

"Oh, oh yeah. Tomorrow is Saturday. Chore day or planting flowers day. Something like that." Jackie stood and finished her drink. She kissed Serena on the cheek and leaned over and hugged Gabrielle. "It was so nice getting to know you, and I hope we see you again soon."

"Likewise. Serena has great friends," Gabrielle said.

Serena waited until they left the bar. "Sorry about all of that. My friends are extremely protective. I had no idea they were going to show up."

Gabrielle finished her water and reached over to touch Serena's arm. "It's okay. You got to meet my friends and so I met yours. And they're really cool. I don't mind that they crashed our date at all."

It was a date. Serena smiled at the confirmation. When she'd asked Gabrielle out, it was such a spur-of-the-moment thing and Gabrielle accepted so quickly that lines weren't established.

"Come on. Let's go outside for some fresh mountain air." Gabrielle reached for Serena's hand and walked her through the throngs of people. Once they were outside, instead of dropping her hand, Gabrielle entwined their fingers. Serena smiled hard.

"What's your favorite thing about Denver?" Serena asked. "Have you lived here your entire life?"

Serena felt Gabrielle pull her close and out of the way when a couple crossed their path. Gabrielle felt warm and soft. And tall. Her skin smelled like orange blossoms and her breath had a hint of wine when she spoke.

"Born and raised. I love it. I couldn't imagine living anywhere else. Even in the winters, when I get so sick of snow and whine in May when most of the world is swimming and I'm trying to get by with a sweater and a scarf. What about you?"

"I've lived in western Kansas and Colorado most of my life. When my mom moved to Vail, I fell in love with it. It's expensive, but it's the town of my fairy tales. Plus, when it's cold, I have a legit reason to hibernate. Nobody bothers me, nobody tries to drag me out. It's perfect," Serena said.

"Western Kansas is brutally boring," Gabrielle said.

"That's true. But it was cheap and I could get a decent paying job at fourteen. I also got my learner's permit then. I worked on a farm after school every day feeding horses and cattle, so I needed to drive around to get to all the different corrals. Real corrals with horses and cows."

"Wait, you had a car at fourteen?"

"No, but I could drive the farm trucks around to get feed and deliver it to the barns. It was a good job."

"What happened?"

"Two words: my mother." Serena rolled her eyes and leaned into Gabrielle. "She met a guy who promised her the world, so we packed up and headed to Vail. The relationship lasted about a year, but he left us with a stack of bills. Let's just say the high school years were tough."

Gabrielle pulled her close again and stopped. "Tonight is only about the good. You were in a different place back then. Now you have the entire world at your disposal and there's nothing stopping you. Especially not your mother."

"You're right. Okay. No more talk about that."

Serena walked in silence, enjoying the night air and the feel of Gabrielle's hand in hers. She hated that it was getting late and she had to get home. If it wasn't for L.B., she'd have agreed to stay with Chloe and Jackie at their hotel and the night could have continued.

As they made their way back to Serena's Jeep, slowly, the butterflies queued up in her stomach and she had to squelch them down for fear of embarrassing herself at the simultaneously exciting and dreaded end-of-the-date moment.

"Do me a favor? Text me when you get home? It's eleven now, so if I don't hear from you by one, I'll send out a search party." Gabrielle walked Serena to her door and opened it. "Okay?"

With the car door between them, Serena missed their contact. She was hoping for a long hug and maybe even a kiss, but she'd take right here right now because it was as close to cloud nine as she'd ever been. "I promise." She held her breath when Gabrielle leaned down and placed a soft kiss on her cheek.

"Be careful going home."

Serena nodded only because she was afraid to say the wrong thing. She slipped into her seat and waved goodbye. On her way back to Vail, she called Chloe and Jackie and they talked the entire drive about Gabrielle and the possibility of something happening. It was the best night Serena had in a long time. She pulled up into her driveway and texted Gabrielle immediately. The text she received back and the promise of a phone call over the weekend made her smile. She slipped into the house and was warmly greeted by L.B. Faith was asleep on the couch even though she had her own room upstairs. She put a thin blanket over Faith and watched her sleep. It was amazing how much her life had changed, all for the better, and all because of a choice she made based solely on a whim.

Chapter Sixteen

Gabrielle set her phone on the coffee table for the fifth time. It was only ten in the morning, but she wanted to connect with Serena. Last night was relaxing and fun. Chloe and Jackie were hilarious, and Gabrielle appreciated that they were looking out for their friend. The only time the conversation turned serious was when they talked about Serena's ex-girlfriend Amber, who was demanding and jealous, and cheated on her not once, but three times. Gabrielle talked about her one and only long-term relationship. Even though they'd never had a deep connection, she embellished. Truth be told, she hadn't fallen in love since high school. Once her heart hit the ceiling because of a nasty breakup, she'd blocked herself off and made education her number one priority. Quick hook-ups and casual dating worked in her twenties, but now she saw life and the opportunity for love a little differently.

Her phone rang and she leapt to answer it, but it was only Rosie. "I think we should work with Muppet for a bit today. You up for it? I'll even make lunch."

Gabrielle mulled the offer and decided it was a good idea to take a step away from Serena. She'd call or text her later. "Is this a ploy to get me to talk about my date last night?"

Rosie paused five dramatic seconds before answering, "Yes. One hundred percent."

"Okay, I'll be there in twenty."

"Wear good workout shoes."

"Where the hell are you taking me?"

"To the park."

"The one with the off-leash park?"

"Maybe, but you won't go inside. I thought it might be good to be on the other side of the fence from all the dogs. You'll be safe. That way when Serena gets the vacation pet place built, you won't be so awkward or scared to visit."

"Okay." Gabrielle was still hesitant. She trusted Muppet, but didn't know about other dogs. She hung up and slipped on a T-shirt, yoga pants, and her old Adidas that she wore to wash the car and help her mother garden. She pulled her hair into a ponytail, threw on light makeup, and was out of the house in ten minutes. Even though it was already hot, she took the top down on her coupe and cranked up 98°. She slipped on her sunglasses and slid into weekend traffic. By the time she got to Rosie's, they were in the minivan waiting for her.

"What took you so long?"

"Traffic sucked."

"You should move closer to us."

"Now see? That translates to babysitter in my head and makes me want to move farther away," Gabrielle said.

"Get in here. Muppet, go in the back like a good boy." Rosie pointed her finger to the third row seats, which he promptly hopped to. "Don't look back at him because then he'll think it's okay to come up a row of seats and plant slobbery kisses on you. I mean, if that's okay with you, go ahead and look at him."

Gabrielle kept her eyes straight ahead. "No, thank you. Let's go before I lose my confidence."

Rosie gunned the minivan and peeled out once she hit the asphalt.

"This is the one thing that prevents me from nominating you for Mother of the Year," Gabrielle said. She clutched the "oh, shit" handle with her right hand and wrapped her left around the armrest. "Who drives like this in a minivan?"

"Moms do. We always have to be in five places at once."

"It's just me and Muppet."

"It's a habit at this point." Rosie slowed to the speed limit and turned into the park. Muppet made little happy dog noises once he realized where they were. "Okay, you get out first and I'll hook him up to his leash."

Gabrielle opened the door and squeezed out of the small space between the passenger door and the giant truck Rosie parked next to. "It's a good thing I'm in shape to maneuver out of this spot." She grabbed her baseball cap and waited at the front of the minivan for Rosie and Muppet. He hopped with excitement in the small space the leash afforded him. Gabrielle took a step back out of habit.

"At this point, it has nothing to do with you and everything to do with him, so he doesn't care that you're here," Rosie said. At her command, he sat, and they waited for him to settle down. Even though Muppet weighed in at forty pounds, Rosie walked him through the two-gate entrance to the big dog park where packs of large dogs romped and played together. She let him loose and leaned on the inside of the chain link fence next to Gabrielle, who was safely on the other side. They watched him get reacquainted with the big dogs before they all galloped off to smell, play, and do whatever dogs did best.

"Aren't you worried he'll get hurt on the big dog side?"

"Nah, he knows most of the dogs. Plus, there are only four dogs in the small dog park, and he would get bored. Somebody would get mad and say he's too big to play with their little chihuahua and then I'd have to get ugly." Rosie leaned closer to Gabrielle. "Anyway, now that Muppet is taken care of, tell me about last night. Most importantly, tell me about the good-night kiss."

Gabrielle playfully nudged her with her shoulder. "Our evening was really nice. Her friends showed up at the same restaurant and we all had drinks and chatted after dinner." Gabrielle smiled remembering the horrified look on Serena's face when she realized her friends, who lived almost two hours away, were at the same restaurant. "I kissed her on her cheek after I walked her to her car. It was all very innocent and nice."

"You look happy. Actually, you look fantastic." Rosie looked her up and down and nodded her approval. "Spin class has really worked well for you. You've lost weight and tightened up."

Gabrielle blushed but appreciated her best friend's compliment. "The winter was harsh, so I needed to push myself. Ten pounds is getting harder and harder to lose."

"Wait until you have three kids. Then you'll wish it was only ten pounds you have to lose every winter," Rosie said.

Even though Rosie was softer and probably twenty pounds heavier than Gabrielle, her curves were gorgeous, and Gabrielle couldn't understand why Rosie was so hard on herself. She had the vivacious body of a 1940s pin-up model. Gabrielle would give anything to have Rosie's full breasts. She sighed when she looked at her B cup. "You're perfect. Besides, you know how much I enjoy a little meat on the bone." Except for the last woman she slept with and the one she was presently pursuing. Dani was firm and trim, and based on their time together, drank most of her calories. Serena was slight but wasn't afraid to eat carbs. She was probably someone whose metabolism was sky high and she never had to worry about her weight.

"Tell me about the kiss." Rosie looked at her dreamy-eyed.

Gabrielle rolled her eyes at Rosie's overactive imagination. "It was just a sweet kiss on the cheek. It was very natural. She's my client. I need to have some boundaries."

"Any hugging?"

"No, but we did hold hands. A few times, actually. I told her about Muppet and petting him. She held my hands because she was excited about it. And then we held hands on our short walk around the block."

"You know, you think you're all business without any romantic bones in your body, but deep down, you're a softie. I've known you for a long time, and I've seen you blow through women, but I think you just haven't found the perfect match. Until now."

"One date. We had one date," Gabrielle said.

"It's a start. Have you talked to her since?"

Gabrielle groaned. "It was last night." Rosie stared at her, eyebrow lifted, until Gabrielle answered. "She texted me when she got home and I texted her that I would call her this weekend. That's it." She shrugged, indicating there wasn't more to the story.

Muppet chose that moment to race over to them, breaking up what would have been a serious moment. Even though he was on the other side of the fence, Gabrielle backed away until Muppet calmed down. Rosie whipped out a collapsible bowl from her bag and poured water into it. He happily lapped it up, spilling most of it in the process. "Are you enjoying your play time?" Rosie asked and petted the top of his head. "Maybe Auntie Gabrielle will pet you, too."

With a few more encouraging words, Gabrielle leaned over the wobbly fence to pet the top of Muppet's head. He leaned his snout up once to smell her, then happily leaned into her hand and accepted her soft pets. "Who's a good boy? Are you a good boy?" Gabrielle moved her fingers down his coat until she reached the tender spot above his tail. He wiggled into her nails, dancing side to side. "What's happening here?"

"He likes to be scratched there. It feels good. And with your nails, he's probably in heaven."

Confidently, Gabrielle scratched and petted him until five dogs who were running in the large field worked their way over to them. Gabrielle stepped back as they invaded her space. Much to Rosie and

Gabrielle's surprise, Muppet stood in front of her and growled at the other dogs. It was as if he understood the other dogs would cause her grief.

"Wow. Good job, Muppet," Rosie said as the carefree pack took off to frolic on the other side of the park.

"That was incredible," Gabrielle said. She reached down and stroked the fur on Muppet's back that had stiffened when the other dogs showed up. "Thank you, Muppet." He looked up at her and wagged his tail. It took a few minutes for all of his fur to fall flat, but after several minutes of praising and petting, he slipped back into carefree, happy Muppet and trotted off to find new friends.

"See? Not only would he not hurt you, but he wouldn't let anyone else hurt you either." Rosie puffed out her chest with pride. "Want to head over to the small dog park? They seem pretty tame. And small. Maybe you can say hi to a few of them."

After twenty minutes of meeting and carefully petting the four small dogs in the adjacent park, Gabrielle decided she'd had enough. When a pug jumped on her leg, she didn't freak out. Not completely. And the chihuahua was as nervous as she was. After much coaxing he finally sniffed her hand and let her touch him. "He's adorable, but I'm ready to get out of here."

Rosie didn't hesitate. She whistled over the fence for Muppet. He perked up and raced over to the gate. "You ready, boy?"

"Should I get out his bowl?" Gabrielle asked.

"Let's get back to the car and we'll do it there. That will give him time to calm down and chill for a bit," Rosie said. She snapped his leash to his collar and grabbed her backpack. "Look at you, making friends with a few dogs."

Gabrielle waved her off. "Let's not go that far. I petted three different dogs today. That's my limit. For a long time."

Rosie squeezed her arm. "I'm so proud of you."

"Can we go home so you can make me a delicious lunch?"

Rosie handed Gabrielle Muppet's leash. "Lead the way."

❖

Gabrielle looked at the clock for the seventh time. She bounced her phone in her hand. Why was she so nervous to call Serena? It was because Rosie put thoughts into her head. She was in complete control of their date last night from the moment she said hello to the soft kiss on the cheek. Now she was acting like a nervous teenager. She took a deep breath and hit call.

"Hi."

Serena sounded out of breath.

"Hi. How are you?"

"I'm good. Hang on just a minute."

Gabrielle heard rustling, laughing, and finally Serena's voice again.

"Okay. Hi. Sorry about that."

"Did I catch you at a bad time?"

"Oh, no. I was playing fetch with L.B. I'm throwing the ball out the window and he's returning it via the doggie door. He slid on the kitchen floor this last time, so maybe this isn't the best idea."

Gabrielle smiled at Serena's carefree voice. "Speaking of fun dog things, I took Muppet for a walk today. Sort of."

"That's great. Every time I talk to you, you surprise me with something big."

She heard pride and encouragement in Serena's voice and continued. "Rosie invited me to the dog park. Then she made meatball sandwiches for the family. It was a good afternoon. She didn't even have to put up Muppet and Kittypurrs."

"Are you still feeling adventurous? Feel like a short hike tomorrow with me and L.B.?" Serena asked.

Gabrielle had plans to work on the Pet Posh Inn, but spending one-on-one time with her client seemed like the smarter move, professionally and personally. "Sure. I mean, that sounds like fun. What should I bring?" Even though Gabrielle was in fact in the best shape of her life, she didn't get that way by hiking.

"Good hiking shoes, water, and maybe a towel. I'll bring the snacks."

Where the hell was Serena taking them? "A towel?"

"There's a waterfall trail I want to hit, and the last few times I went, I got a little wet," Serena said.

Even though it was said innocently, Gabrielle felt a rich heat spread throughout her body. When was the last time she felt a slow burn? Dani took her from a peak adrenaline rush to an explosion within minutes. This warmth laced with excitement felt new and different.

"Okay. Are you sure I can't bring anything else?" Gabrielle knew she was going to overpack, regardless of what Serena said.

"Just your courage." The happiness in her voice made Gabrielle smile.

"Easier said than done."

"We're just keeping the momentum going."

For a brief moment, Gabrielle wondered if Serena was talking about her comfort level around dogs or the fate of their blossoming relationship.

Chapter Seventeen

Serena stood at the overlook and filled her lungs with the sweet, thin mountain air. Colorado was beautiful early in the morning. Even though it was summer, there was a slight chill in the breeze that ruffled her hair and slipped inside the collar of her T-shirt. She shivered, knowing in about three hours she would beg for anything this refreshing.

"Come here, L.B." He was getting too close to the edge, and even though she kept him off-leash and he stayed close, accidents happened. If he slipped and tumbled down the steep mountain, Serena would never forgive herself. She snapped his leash on and moved away from the cliff.

Gabrielle was meeting them in ten minutes. Serena took the time to stretch and rearrange her backpack. Five waters—four for the humans and one for the dog—a towel, T-shirt, trail mix, two apples, kibble for L.B., and jerky. Her phone was completely charged. The trail to the waterfall was an easy four miles. Even though Gabrielle looked like she was in shape, Serena didn't want to assume she could do a longer, more strenuous hike. Besides, it was their second date and she wanted to take it easy, but still give L.B. a workout.

Gabrielle pulled up beside Serena's Jeep and lowered her sunglasses so her eyes, those beautiful amber eyes that made Serena swoon, sparkled in the early morning sun. "Are you taking me out here to kill me?"

Serena leaned forward so her face was only a few inches from Gabrielle's. "Now why would I do that when I still need you for so many things?" Where her brazen behavior came from, she didn't know, but Gabrielle's reaction was priceless. Most impressive was that she didn't lean back at Serena's nearness. Surprise registered on her face, but she leaned forward, pushed her glasses onto her head, and played with Serena's braid.

"Let's spend the next few hours of you telling me exactly what you need me for."

Their moment was broken up when L.B. put his front paws on Gabrielle's convertible. She shrank back, out of habit, but didn't make a sound and her eyes didn't show as much fear. It was obvious he'd startled her, but Serena was impressed with her ability to keep her control. "Get down, L.B." He immediately lowered his paws and sat next to Serena. "I'm sorry about that."

"It's okay, but I won't get out of the car until he's maybe a few feet away."

"Oh, of course. Come here, L.B. Let's get a drink before we walk." Serena opened the back of the Jeep, tapped the carpet for him to jump inside, and poured a bit of water into his bowl. While he lapped it up, Serena watched Gabrielle slip out of the car, straighten her shorts and T-shirt, and retie one of her shoelaces. She looked fantastic. She was tan and fit, and Serena couldn't stop staring at her legs. It was obvious that Gabrielle worked out with heavy emphasis on her lower body and arms. She wasn't overly muscular, but extremely fit. It made Serena's mouth dry and other body parts tingle. Gabrielle was perfect. Not too thin. Her shorts hit her mid-thigh and the T-shirt she wore was white cotton with a purple yoga studio emblem right above the curve of her left breast.

"Oh, this is Bodhi, Piper's studio. If you finish her torturous advanced class, you get a T-shirt," Gabrielle said.

Serena blushed at getting caught. She cleared her throat and exhaled before she looked at Gabrielle. "I'm impressed. Yoga is tough."

Gabrielle laughed. "Or you can buy one. In this case, I bought it. No way could I handle one of her advanced classes. Besides, I'm more into spinning." That explained her toned calves and firm thighs.

"I only recently picked up hiking. Please don't leave us behind on the trail."

"You're younger with more stamina." Gabrielle swung her small backpack over her shoulder. "Lead the way, boss."

Serena liked the sound of that. Nobody had ever called her boss before. Even playing. She blushed and locked up the Jeep. "I'm not that much younger."

"Three years? Is that right?"

Serena nodded. She had turned thirty in the midst of her mother moving, the middle of signing all the Colorado lottery forms, and a week before she hired Gabrielle's firm. It was something that came and went with very little excitement, like most milestones in her life. Chloe and Jackie knew her aversion to big celebrations, so Serena slipped into her thirties with a small dinner party, no gifts at her request, but surrounded by the people she loved most. Faith baked a small chocolate cake. She couldn't bring it by until after her shift ended at eleven, but Serena blew out the candles a few minutes before her birthday slipped into the next ordinary day.

"This trail is one of my favorites."

"I'm ready when you are," Gabrielle said.

"Do you want to say hi to L.B. or should we wait?" Serena dropped her best smile, hoping it was charming and not too dorky.

Gabrielle took a deep breath. "Let's do this."

Serena slowly walked L.B. to Gabrielle. "Be a good boy. Stay down." She patted his head and rubbed his ears while Gabrielle held her hand out for him to sniff. He smelled her fingers and licked them. The stricken look on her face made Serena intervene. "Okay, let Gabrielle pet you. She doesn't want your kisses. Yet."

"Thank you." Gabrielle reached over L.B.'s snout to touch his head. He wasn't as soft as Muppet, but he was just as gentle. When he arched into her touch, Gabrielle pulled back. "That was okay, right?"

Serena nodded. "It was perfect. Let's go before the mass of people swarm this place. At least we'll get a head start on them." They walked along the path making small talk until Serena unleashed L.B. He ran ahead of them but looked back several times to make sure he didn't go too far.

"How was the rest of your night?" Gabrielle asked.

Serena didn't want to tell her she'd spent at least an hour trying to figure out what to wear for their walk. Or how she'd tried to remember all the makeup tips Faith gave her just a few nights before. She'd even ironed her T-shirt. Who did that? Her navy shorts covered her pale legs and flattered her ass, according to Chloe and Jackie, who helped pick out her outfit. She glanced over her shoulder as if they would show up again.

"What's the matter?" Gabrielle looked over her shoulder because Serena did.

Serena laughed and reached out to touch Gabrielle's arm. "For a moment, I expected Chloe and Jackie to show up." She liked the way Gabrielle's muscles twitched under her touch.

"I think it's sweet that they're concerned for you. They seem like great ladies and very positive people in your life." Gabrielle always knew the right thing to say. She was either sincere or really smooth, and Serena, in her tiny little fairy tale, wanted to believe it came from the heart.

"I'm thankful they showed up in my life when they did. They saved me." Serena's stomach did a hard bounce when Gabrielle slid her hand down her arm and held her hand.

"You make more of an impact on people than you give yourself credit for."

"Now that I have money," Serena said. She felt a squeeze on her fingers.

"Even before you did. Faith. Chloe and Jackie. And then the people whose lives you touched that you don't even know about."

"I worked at a diner, a car wash, and a bookstore. I don't think people even knew who I was." Serena's shoulders slumped as she thought about the people who never saw her, never looked at her, and barely knew she existed.

"Hold on." Gabrielle stopped and turned Serena to face her. She tucked a piece of hair that the wind had blown across Serena's face behind her ear. "Listen to me. I know that winning the lottery was a massive improvement to your life, but if I met you, bookstore clerk Serena Evans, you still would have caught my interest." The fierceness in those amber eyes made Serena literally swoon. Needing to hold on to something to keep her grounded in this pivotal moment, she put her hands on Gabrielle's waist. A bold move on her part.

"Thank you," she said. *Thank you?* She inwardly groaned. A beautiful woman was in her personal space telling her wonderful things and she said "thank you"? She wanted to lean forward and kiss Gabrielle's full, red lips, but she was afraid. What if she didn't want to be kissed? Before she could doubt herself further, she felt Gabrielle's lips press against hers. Her eyes fluttered shut and she slid her grip down to Gabrielle's hips. This was what heaven was. This was perfection. She boldly took a step closer until she could feel the heat radiate off Gabrielle's body. Their first kiss grew into something that she had never experienced before. Flames fanned out, the burning sensation swelling her body in delicious places. Serena had been kissed before, but never this thoroughly. Gabrielle's hands were in her hair, pulling her closer, deepening the kiss. Her mouth was warm, her lips soft, but she was completely in charge. When Gabrielle released her, Serena wobbled a bit as her knees threatened to give out.

"Are you okay?" Gabrielle put her hands on Serena's waist to steady her.

Serena looked at her shoes and kicked a rock out from beneath her. "Yeah, I just came down wrong." She wasn't going to admit their kiss shook her to the core. Or that it was perfect and nothing was ever going to be the same again. "I hope we didn't lose L.B. Where are you, boy?" That was the great thing she said after a kiss like that?

"I saw him over there by the short trees." Gabrielle pointed as a small group of shrubs rustled and L.B.'s head popped up. "He's been pretty close to us."

Serena took a step back because as much as she wanted the kissing to continue, the great outdoors wasn't the ideal place to make out. There was only one trail to and from the waterfall, so the chances of people bumping into them were great. She was never a fan of public displays of affection only because she never was a part of it before. "Come here." She tapped her thigh and waited until he sprang back over to them. Gabrielle stood behind Serena and reached down to pet him quickly, but softly. "You're doing well."

"I'm trying," Gabrielle said.

Again, Serena was only inches from Gabrielle's mouth. "We should keep going."

The lopsided grin on Gabrielle's face revealed that she knew just how her nearness affected Serena. She flashed a quick smile and moved ahead on the trail. The path narrowed so only one person could fit at a time. Serena missed the warmth of Gabrielle's fingers interlocked with hers, but a surge of excitement coursed through her veins when she felt her palm on the small of her back. Thankfully she wasn't sweaty yet. By the time they reached the waterfall, Serena was more relaxed but still very much aware of Gabrielle's nearness.

"This is gorgeous. I'm so happy you brought me here," Gabrielle said.

"With all of the rain we've had and the snow melting, the waterfall is really full. It's actually more impressive than I remember." Serena led L.B. to the edge so he could drink and take a swim to cool down. He waded in, but stayed close.

"Somebody's thirsty," Gabrielle said.

"He walked twice the distance that we did. He's going to sleep well later today," Serena said. She pulled out a small pack of sanitizing wipes and offered one to Gabrielle, who gladly took it.

"I know you told me not to bring anything, but I had to bring these cookies. Rosie and the kids made the best peanut butter cookies and brought a dozen to me. I would feel guilty if I ate them all by myself." Gabrielle sat on a boulder after brushing off dirt and leaves. She opened her backpack and offered Serena the bag.

"Oh, my favorite. And crunchy, too. I like Rosie. She's really nice. Actually, all of your friends are super nice." Serena stopped short because it made her sound desperate and she felt strange going on and on about Gabrielle's friends.

"They've said nothing but nice things about you, too. It seems as if you and I have made good choices with friends."

"And they bake for you, so I say that's a win." Serena told herself she was only going to say positive things. Faith had pointed out that most of their conversations ended up on the fast track to Negativeville, and she wasn't wrong. It had been a while since she was able to relax and just be herself. But being positive was harder than she'd anticipated. She'd spent the first thirty years of her life waiting for the other shoe to drop. And it always did.

"And yours show up on dates to make sure you aren't out with a murderer or dog kicker."

Serena laughed. "Dog kicker was a concern, but now that I understand your history, I know you wouldn't kick a dog unless you had to." She winked at Gabrielle to let her know she was teasing and was rewarded with a killer smile.

"I'm getting better. I've made friends with three or four dogs now."

"I'm proud of you. And just so you know, I might pick up another pup or a few kittens at the shelter. How do you feel about cats?"

"I generally stay away from all animals, but cats are okay. They don't really like me, but they leave me alone. We have an understanding." Gabrielle quickly added, "You should do what you want to do. If you want five dogs and twelve cats, that's completely your decision."

Not sure how to take that news, Serena pushed a little bit. She didn't want to start a relationship with somebody who was never going to like animals. Then the relationship was doomed to fail. And after a kiss like that, she was having second thoughts about adding four-legged family members. "Do you think you'll ever be comfortable around dogs? L.B. is very gentle and loving."

"Do you know why he was surrendered to the shelter?" Gabrielle asked.

"They found him running around the shelter, so somebody probably dumped him. I'm sorry I don't know his history better, but I think he's sweet."

"Come here, L.B.," Gabrielle said.

Serena masked her surprise when L.B. popped up from drinking and trotted over to Gabrielle. She broke off a piece of cookie and put it on the palm of her hand for him. Serena wanted to tease her that he wasn't a horse, but this was a huge moment, so she didn't want to say anything to upset Gabrielle. And even though she didn't want him to be fed table scraps, Jackie was forever slipping him pizza crusts, so this also was a thing she was going to overlook. She smiled as Gabrielle patted his head while he crunched on the cookie. "Are you ready to see the waterfall up close and personal? Or do you want to eat lunch?"

"Oh, can we go behind it?"

"We can, but we'll get soaked. Leave your phone and keys in your bag so they don't get wet," Serena said. She tightened her laces and waited for Gabrielle to secure her bag on the tree next to hers.

"What about L.B.?"

"He'll wander around," Serena said. She thought about tying his leash to the tree, but nobody was around and he'd probably follow them anyway. Access to behind the fall was on a narrow path about fifty feet away. "We won't be gone long. It's more exciting to sniff at all the woodland creatures here than to go behind a waterfall." She led the way, motioning Gabrielle to follow. "Be careful. Here's where it gets slick." She reached to guide Gabrielle behind her. When her hand came in contact with hard abs against soft cotton instead of the arm she was aiming for, she quickly dropped her hand. The waterfall was loud once they slipped behind it, so Serena raised her voice. "Sorry about that. I just wanted to make sure you were walking behind me and not beside me or you would've fallen."

"It's so loud." Gabrielle leaned closer to Serena. "But so pretty." Her back was flat against the wet stone wall. She pushed her hand through the flow of water two feet in front of them. "That's a lot of power."

Serena liked looking at Gabrielle's lips when she talked. More so now that she knew what they were capable of. Kissing that rendered her both speechless and weak in the knees. She nodded, losing herself in the memory. Gabrielle reached out and pulled her close. Her gasp got lost in the rushing sound of the waterfall.

"You know that when you look at me like that, I can't think of anything but kissing you again." Gabrielle slipped her hand on the back of Serena's neck and leaned to kiss her. Before their lips touched, before she felt the whisper of Gabrielle's warm breath against her mouth, she heard a shout and felt Gabrielle slip out of her embrace. Serena watched helplessly as Gabrielle slid down the rock, through the waterfall, into the pool below.

Chapter Eighteen

Gabrielle had never liked swimming. She didn't like the helplessness of being underwater. There was a vulnerability the instant her head slipped below the surface, and she hated the loss of control. Her bikini and bathing suits got a workout in hot tubs, not pools. But now she understood why Serena had told her to bring clothes and wisely suggested they keep their electronics in their backpacks.

"Oh, my God. Are you okay?" Serena scrambled to the edge of the pond with her hand extended.

Gabrielle waved off Serena's offer of help. She brushed back her hair with her fingertips and looked at her clothes. She was soaked to the bone and only had a dry towel. "You should have told me we were going to swim today. I would have dressed accordingly." Her clothes, swollen with water, clung to her body. The tightness left nothing to the imagination.

"I can give you a dry T-shirt," Serena said.

Gabrielle noticed how Serena averted her eyes when she started wringing out the clothes still on her body. "That would be great." She took her towel and Serena's extra T-shirt and ducked behind a clump of bushes. She peeled off her drenched clothes and dried off the best she could. At least she'd be comfortable from the waist up. Serena's T-shirt felt soft and worn in. She tied the towel around her waist.

"I'm going to set up for lunch. We'll leave your wet clothes on the rock to dry as much as they can in the sun," Serena yelled from the path.

Gabrielle grabbed her clothes and weaved her way back to the pond. "Well, that was definitely invigorating." She draped her clothes on the warm rock, knowing it was going to suck to put them on in half an hour because they wouldn't be dry by then. She was nervous standing there in a T-shirt and a towel. Her black panties were right there on the rock next to her shorts for Serena to see. At least they were somewhat sexy. Not that Gabrielle expected anything to happen today, but she was always prepared for the unexpected.

"I'm so sorry you slipped. We shouldn't have done that. It was irresponsible." Serena looked so crestfallen that Gabrielle couldn't do anything except laugh.

"You know what? We're always going to remember this moment. I'm not sorry. It was funny. That's what I get for trying to be smooth," Gabrielle said. She liked the way Serena's cheeks pinkened and how she had a hard time looking at her. All good signs in her book. She leaned against the rock and sighed. She hated the way her toes squished in her socks with every step she took. Getting her shoes and socks off was the next priority. She kicked off her shoes and stripped off her socks. A pedicure was in her very near future. "I have a pair of dry socks in my backpack, but I don't think it's going to help much if my shoes are soaked."

"You could put them on now and add your shoes and socks to the drying rock."

"Good idea."

"I figured we can have our picnic now and wait to head back. I'm not in any hurry. You?" Serena asked.

"I have zero planned today other than time with you." That wasn't true. Gabrielle wanted to make a few changes on the plans. Serena had a meeting with her and Christopher next week, and Gabrielle wanted everything to be perfect. Her promotion was all about this single job and her ability to pull it off and make the company and the client happy.

"Great. I didn't make sandwiches or anything, but here's what I brought." Serena laid all of the food on her backpack.

Gabrielle placed her cookies and sunflower seeds beside the apples and jerky. "Looks like a good meal to me."

Serena nodded. "For me, meals are always a handful of this and a bite of that. Cooking for one is hard."

"I agree. Do you like to cook?"

"No. Yes. Sometimes, but the kitchen in the new house is huge and I plan to spend a lot of the fall and winter learning how to cook real food. I want to find a good macaroni and cheese recipe and learn how to cook meats well and steam vegetables."

"I'm with you. It's hard to cook for one. Most of the time I hit Tommy's or make breakfast for dinner." Gabrielle took a bite of an apple and reached for a piece of beef jerky. "This is perfect food for today. Until we get back to civilization where we can sit down, in dry clothes, and have a four course meal."

"That sounds like a good idea." Serena was respectfully staying on the other side of the path. She was probably as embarrassed at seeing Gabrielle's panties as Gabrielle was to have them out in the open.

"How did Faith get interested in cooking?" Gabrielle asked.

"I think she got tired of my crappy cooking and decided to learn on her own. In her teens, she was basically on her own. I worked a lot, so when she didn't come in to the diner for a free meal, she cooked something."

"Where was your mother most of the time?"

"That's a very good question. We're still trying to figure that one out."

"I know that I was lucky. Am lucky. My parents are still together and my family is close." Gabrielle mentally reminded herself to call her brothers and check in with them. She worked too hard and finally understood that not everybody had the same upbringing that she did.

Voices on the path made Serena panic. "Where's L.B.?" She whistled. "Come here, boy."

Gabrielle moved her leg as L.B. trotted past her to drop a pine cone at Serena's feet. She quickly snapped the leash to his collar just as a group of four hikers showed up.

"Hi. How's the water?" The tall twenty-something looked Gabrielle up and down.

"I kind of fell in. If you go behind the waterfall, be careful. The rocks are slick," Gabrielle said.

"Good to know." He dropped his bag, kicked off his shoes, stripped down to his boxers, and dove into the water. His friends followed his lead.

"Oh, sure. It's fun when they do it."

Serena snickered. "Look, it was a bummer, but it's like you said, we won't ever forget today, and I will always think of you in this place."

Gabrielle flipped her clothes over on the rock. "I'd say we've got about thirty more years before I can put these on again."

"Unless you want to hike in a towel."

"Knowing the luck I've had today, I don't think that would be a great idea," Gabrielle said. The towel wasn't staying around her waist as tightly as it had when it was dry. She was afraid to move and decided just to put the clothes back on and get the hell out of there. The new hikers ruined the moment anyway. "I'm going to put these on so we can go." They weren't making her uncomfortable, but she could tell her mood was fouling.

"Are you sure? I don't mind hanging out."

Gabrielle nodded at the foursome in the natural pool. "There's nothing wrong with them, but they're ruining my mojo. Besides, I'd like to put on something dry."

Serena nodded and gathered up their food. Gabrielle grabbed her damp clothes and walked gingerly behind the bush. She was wearing her dry socks but stepped on everything sharp along the way from pine needles to rocks to things she didn't want to think about. She cursed under her breath, low enough that Serena couldn't hear, and slipped into the damp clothes. Even though the shorts and panties had been in the sun, they were cold and she shivered. She stepped into wet shoes, pasted a smile on her face, and joined Serena and L.B. on the trail. "Ready?"

"We'll hurry back. That way you can get into dry clothes," Serena said.

The walk back was a bit more rushed and the conversation sporadic. The sun felt good on Gabrielle's body, so she slowed whenever they hit a long patch of full sun. Serena was sweating, but she never complained. When they got back to the cars, Gabrielle found an old blanket in the trunk and put it on the driver's seat before she sat down.

"I'm sorry today turned into a bust. I know you probably want to get home and change into some warm clothes, but we'd like it if you came over for a bit and saw the new house. I have clean clothes you can wear." Serena's soulful eyes almost made Gabrielle cave, but she was too miserable. Besides, she needed her hair products and cosmetics, which she doubted Serena had.

"How about we separate and get cleaned up, and I come over for a visit tonight? If you're up for it." Gabrielle held her breath as she waited for Serena to answer. Judging by the audible exhale, Serena had been holding her breath, too.

"I think that would be great. I'll text you my address. Go home and get dry." Serena tapped the door and stepped away.

"I'll see you later. Bye, L.B." Gabrielle waved and drove off. Her car displayed a new text message from Serena before she even hit the highway.

How about seven? I'll even cook. Serena's follow-up text was her address.

Gabrielle smiled and mentally added a short trip to her day before heading to Vail. After all, she couldn't show up empty-handed. She also decided to leave a bag in the trunk of her car with product and fresh clothes in case she ever fell into a pool again. She refused to call it an overnight bag, but deep down, she was kind of hoping for the opportunity tonight.

❖

After a long, hot shower, and a two-hour power nap, Gabrielle threw her emergency bag of clean clothes but not technically an overnight bag into the trunk of her car. She put up the top because her hair was styled perfectly and she didn't want it windblown. Before leaving Denver, she made a quick stop at the grocery store for a bottle of her favorite red wine and a squeaky toy for L.B. The stop at Unique, an off-the-beaten-path specialty shop that offered different and unusual gifts, took a bit longer. She found the cutest herb garden with six different herbs in marble planters. It was perfect given their talk earlier about learning how to cook adult meals. Her phone rang as she pulled onto I-70 on her way to Vail.

"What's up?"

"Nothing. Just checking in," Rosie said.

"It's like you know when I have a weird day."

"Tell me everything. You know I live vicariously through you. Does this have anything to do with Serena?"

"It has everything to do with Serena," Gabrielle said smugly. She knew full well Rosie was dying to know everything about their budding romantic relationship. "I'm headed to her place now."

"Oh, late night for you, then?"

"I was with her this morning already."

"Define with her."

Gabrielle laughed. "Definitely not what you're thinking. We went on a hike at a halfway point between us. I tried to kiss her behind a waterfall but failed when I fell into the water."

"How far up were you?" Rosie's voice was a combination of concern and excitement.

"Maybe ten or fifteen feet. Not too high. I managed to ruin the moment, though," Gabrielle said. She looked over her shoulder and zipped into traffic. Saturday traffic was always hellish in the Denver area, especially the closer it got to evening.

"That must have been miserable." Rosie knew Gabrielle didn't like to swim. Whenever the kids played in the pool, Gabrielle sat under the umbrella and drank margaritas with Anne while Rosie swam with the kids.

"I couldn't wait to get home and shower. Aside from falling in, it's a really cool place. You should take the fam. They would love it."

"Send me the info. In the meantime, what's happening tonight? Dinner? Movie? An evening in?"

"I'm going to see her new house. She said she's going to cook dinner. After all of the excitement this morning, I'm hoping for something low key," Gabrielle said.

"What are you wearing?"

"Remember that sundress we found at Nordstrom? It finally fits. That and simple sandals." Gabrielle looked at her reflection in the rearview mirror and was pleased with how her hair held up and how she needed very little makeup after getting sun from their hike today. Just a little bit of lip gloss and a quick swipe of mascara.

"I want all the details tomorrow. If you can sneak pictures of her house, that would be great, too. I've always wondered how the other half lived."

"She told me it wasn't over the top, but I imagine it's nice. And paid for," Gabrielle said.

"The best kind. Okay, I have to go. Have fun and don't behave."

Gabrielle said goodbye and disconnected the call. Her GPS gave the arrival time of one hour and thirty-six minutes. She cued up her latest audio book and decided to get lost in a romance for the next hour and a half, and if she was lucky, perhaps even several hours after that.

Chapter Nineteen

Under pressure from Chloe, Serena had agreed to have a cleaning crew come in once a week to straighten up the place, blow out the dust bunnies and piles of fur that settled under the furniture, and return L.B.'s toys to his basket by the fireplace. Today was their day, so the house was spotless and the only thing Serena had to do was get ready. There wasn't enough time to go for a walk with L.B. or even a quick workout. Just enough to slip into a much-needed nap. Her alarm jarred her awake. So did L.B. who, even though he knew how to use the doggie door, preferred to have Serena go out with him. She dragged her body off the couch and opened the door to let him out. She loved her backyard. The previous owners had plugged a lot of money into the landscaping. She thought about a pool, but that would limit L.B.'s play space, and she never took to swimming like Faith did. She checked her watch. She had an hour before Gabrielle arrived.

"It's all yours, L.B. You don't have to mark every part of your territory. Come in when you're ready."

She closed the door and thought about what to wear. She could afford anything she wanted, but her closet was still sparse. Standing in the doorway, she smiled sadly as she realized the one time she had her own bedroom growing up, it was a lot smaller than her current walk-in closet. She stared at her clothes for a solid ten minutes before deciding on a skirt and a sleeveless blouse. Casual, yet cute and flirty. After spending twenty minutes messing with her hair, she went with a simple, loose braid that hung over her shoulder. Her cheeks were sunburned from the hike, but she added mascara and touch of lipstick. She jumped when the doorbell rang at exactly seven. Her heart dropped, twirled in her stomach, and ended up somewhere in her throat. She swallowed her excitement and casually walked to the door as if beautiful women visited her home often.

"Hi." Serena barely remembered her manners when she opened the door. Gabrielle took her breath away. Not in the typical romance book way where the main character sees hearts and rainbows when their love interest appears, but in a way that scared her. Her knees locked and a pressure built in her chest like a steam engine gathering too much energy. She placed her hand against her chest, hoping it wouldn't burst open. Just when she thought she was going to pass out, her body remembered how to breathe. She tried not to gulp the air that filled her lungs. "Don't worry about L.B. He's still in the backyard sniffing and doing dog things." That was what she said to the gorgeous woman standing two feet from her?

"I really love your house. It's very secluded. I missed it the first time I drove by," Gabrielle said. She handed Serena a bottle of wine and a gift bag and lingered in the doorway. "Um, can I come in?"

There was something different about Gabrielle tonight. The energy radiating off her made Serena take a small step back. Not because she was frightened of her, but because she was scared of her own reaction. To say Gabrielle was sexy was an unjust description.

"You look wonderful. A lot different than you did earlier today. Please, come in." Serena swallowed hard as she watched Gabrielle walk confidently into the living room. The sway of her hips was hard to miss. That dress, tight around her waist and breasts and loose around her hips and thighs, only pointed out to Serena how easy it would be to touch her intimately. Her legs went on forever. The hem of her sundress hit her knees, which meant when she sat down, it would show even more soft skin.

"Thank you. I feel a lot different and a lot drier than I did this morning." Gabrielle ran her hand along the back cushions of the sofa while her eyes scanned the room. "I love the vaulted ceilings and all of the windows. And that fireplace. This place is gorgeous, Serena. Are you going to give me a full tour?"

Serena beamed with pride. Not that she had anything to do with the design of the house, but praise from Gabrielle, her architect, made her heart skip at least two beats. It surprised her how much she'd missed Gabrielle in the short time they were apart. She took a deep breath and walked over to her, focused on getting that elusive kiss, the one she'd been thinking about since Gabrielle slipped out of her arms earlier that day.

She stopped when she heard the soft thump of the rubber flap of the doggie door hit the frame and the clicking of nails on the hardwood floors. "L.B.'s coming." She made her way to intercept him, knowing he would make a beeline to Gabrielle out of curiosity and excitement. "Stay down. I know you like her, so do I, but you have to stay down." She held his collar and watched Gabrielle. As much as she loved her dog, his timing sucked. "I can put him in the other room if you want, but if you ignore him, he will leave you alone. Do you trust me?" Amber eyes met hers and she lost herself in the depth of what she saw. A hint of doubt, a flicker of panic, but a steady trust.

Gabrielle nodded. "I don't want you to put him away. The rules are simple enough. I just don't make eye contact unless I want to pet him, right? And there's no chance of that."

A small frown pulled at Serena's mouth. She had to remind herself that Gabrielle had different experiences than she did. She hadn't spent a lot of time with dogs, but she was trying. The least Serena could do was keep L.B. away until Gabrielle was ready. She nodded. "He thrives off attention. Just keep talking to me and he'll settle down." When she let L.B. go, he walked over to Gabrielle and sniffed her dress, waiting for her to pet him. When she didn't, he circled her once, then trotted off.

"Phew."

Serena held up her hands. "See? No big deal. I know my doggo pretty well." She watched Gabrielle's shoulders relax. "Ready to see the rest of the house?" In a move that surprised both of them, she reached for Gabrielle's hand and guided her through the downstairs, fingers entwined. "The master bedroom is on this floor, but I normally sleep upstairs. The large bedroom up there has a skylight and it's beautiful to see the stars right before I fall asleep."

"You're such a romantic," Gabrielle said.

"Are you telling me you don't like to look up at the stars and daydream about things?"

"I live in the heart of the city. Too many lights." Gabrielle shrugged. "But I bet you can see them all from any window in your house. I really like it."

"Thank you. Let me show you the upstairs." Serena was very aware of Gabrielle one step behind her. She could feel her body heat, smell her vanilla and lavender soap and something else. Something sweet and spicy that she couldn't identify. Pepper and grapefruit maybe? Whatever it was, it made Serena want to turn and lean up against her and inhale her scent. "There are three bedrooms, three bathrooms, and a loft I'm going to use as my reading nook."

"I would never leave this place." Gabrielle sat in the oversized, overstuffed chair that faced the windows. As predicted, her dress slipped up to three inches above her knee, and Serena fought the urge to touch the soft skin that was exposed. "I love the built-in bookshelves. Did you buy all of these books from the bookstore you worked in?"

Serena laughed. "Absolutely not. I went directly to the publisher's website and bought most. Some I bought off Amazon. I will never give Mrs. Brody a piece of my business."

Gabrielle lifted her eyebrows. "That bad a boss?"

"You have no idea. She was awful. Is awful." Serena leaned against the railing and stared at Gabrielle. Her bright eyes were darting everywhere and her smile was illuminating. She truly seemed to appreciate the nuances in the architecture and the lighting of the house. As much as Chloe and Jackie loved her house, they didn't get it like Gabrielle did.

"Then I'm glad you didn't give her any business. You have a vast array of genres here."

"Books have always been my best friends. I would go to the library every weekend and check out five books, all very different, and read them during the week. It was only natural that I would gravitate toward books as an adult," Serena said.

She didn't bring up that she only took the job at the Hooked Bookworm after she got fired from the diner for missing too much work when Faith was in high school. Every time Faith ditched school or got sent to the principal's office, they called Serena instead of Diane. Once Faith graduated, Serena made it clear that she was going to have to be responsible. Faith surprised her by signing up for culinary school and sticking with it. The bookstore job ended up not being as fulfilling as Serena hoped, but she settled into a life that was stuck on an endless loop of work, sleep, laundry, and reading. Every day was the same, but it was comforting.

"I should read more, but if I had a special place like this, I would read every day," Gabrielle said. She stood and slowly crossed to Serena. Serena didn't move. She held her breath at her nearness.

Gabrielle leaned down and brushed her lips across Serena's. It was more of a whisper of a kiss, but it shook Serena to her core. "Are you going to show me the rest of the house?"

Serena bit her bottom lip, still reeling. "Yes. Um, just the bedrooms are up here."

"Show me yours," Gabrielle said. She grabbed Serena's hand, entwined their fingers, and playfully tugged her along. "I'm guessing it's this first one."

"Actually, mine is at the end of the hall."

"Let's take a peek."

Heat spread quickly in Serena's body and settled in sensual spots that made her squirm. "It's probably a mess." She knew that it wasn't, but she didn't want to seem too eager.

"I have to believe it's as spotless as the rest of the house. You can't dangle something this beautiful in front of me and not show me all of it."

Serena blushed again. She couldn't help but read into the innuendo. She ducked her head and walked to the first bedroom. "This is the room Faith usually stays in. That or she crashes on the couch." The spacious room boasted floor-to-ceiling windows and its own en suite bathroom.

"I love it. I can't believe this one isn't your bedroom. I can't believe Faith doesn't stay in this room all the time." Gabrielle looked out at the window and audibly sighed. "I really love Colorado. It's so majestic."

"Wait until you see my room."

Gabrielle walked across the room and stood in front of her, hands on her hips, smirk lifting up the corner of her mouth. "I can't wait." Gabrielle slid her hand down Serena's arm and entwined their fingers before gently tugging her back down the hallway to her room.

Serena held her breath when she opened her door and stepped aside to let Gabrielle in.

"Wow. No wonder you picked this room."

It was a corner bedroom with two floor-to-ceiling windows and a glass door that led out to a covered balcony. Serena had added outdoor furniture, but truthfully never felt as lonely as she did on that deck. It was a romantic hideaway, but her life lacked romance. She was hopeful, though, and willing to wait. L.B. kept her company, but she wanted the fairy tale. "It's not as big as the master downstairs, but it's completely private. And with the press of a button, I can be shrouded in darkness." She pointed to a remote on a nightstand.

Gabrielle gave a low whistle. "I love it. It's perfect. Can I go out on the deck?"

"Of course." Serena unlocked the door and followed Gabrielle out. "It faces east, so sometimes I get up early and watch the sunrise."

"You even have a Keurig out here. And a wine bar. You never have to leave this beautiful house. And you're so secluded, but not too far from neighbors in case there was ever a problem. Have you thought about a gate for your driveway?"

"It's such a dangerous driveway, I'd hate to have people wait on that street and get nailed trying to make a turn, especially if there's a gate."

Gabrielle lit up. "Oh, you can put the gate about fifteen feet up on the driveway so they can turn but have to be buzzed in. I'd feel better about you here all alone if you had that added protection."

"That's actually a very good idea."

"I know people. I can give you a few numbers. Let's finish the tour. I can't tell you how much I love this house, Serena."

"Thank you." Her friends oohed and aaahed about it, but it was different because Gabrielle had a true appreciation for how a house was built. And maybe Serena was trying hard to impress her, so her reaction was more important than her friends'. "Let's head downstairs. Then you can see the basement, which is a game room really."

"Oh, that sounds fun."

"If you like it, you can thank Faith."

"How is she doing? I know she and Phillip were out last night."

Serena turned to face Gabrielle. "Really? She didn't say anything to me."

Gabrielle shrugged. "Maybe she didn't want you to know? Maybe she wants you to focus on you."

The tour was interrupted halfway through the game room when the doorbell rang. Serena looked at her doorbell app and excused herself even though she didn't want to miss any of Gabrielle's reactions. "Dinner's here. I know I said I would cook, but I was too tired," Serena said.

"I'll come with you."

L.B. was at the door barking at the delivery service. "Good boy. Sit down." Serena repeated herself before L.B. complied and she was able to open the door. The delivery person recited everything she'd ordered and handed her two bags of food. Gabrielle took the bags to the kitchen while she signed the receipt. Before she was able to say thank you, another car pulled up the driveway. Chloe and Jackie jumped out and passed the delivery guy on their way to the door.

"We brought wine. We want to hear all about your hiking date with your sexy architect." Chloe kissed Serena's cheek and walked inside before Serena had time to react.

"I can't believe you wouldn't tell us immediately. I had to find out in a text." Jackie followed Chloe in and also kissed Serena on the cheek, but ran into Chloe, who had stopped in the foyer. "What's wrong?"

"Hi, Gabrielle. We brought wine, but perhaps we should do this another time. Our dear, sweet friend didn't tell us she had company tonight." Chloe tried to sound chill, but looked at Serena and raised her eyebrow.

"Oh, please stay. There is plenty of food here. Way more than the two of us could eat," Gabrielle said.

"Is this your first time to Serena's house? Isn't it fantastic?" Jackie said. She clearly didn't pick up on the awkwardness of crashing their date. She dug around in a kitchen drawer for a wine opener and expertly pulled out the cork. "Voilà. A delicious red. Hopefully it goes with the food. If not, we can drink it after."

"Babe? Maybe we should go." Chloe gave her a wide-eyed look and nodded at Serena.

Serena, although frazzled by their sudden appearance, spoke up quickly. "Gabrielle's right. There's plenty of food for all of us."

"Okay, but we won't stay long," Chloe said. She spoke low when Serena walked by, "I'm so sorry."

Serena squeezed her forearm. "It's not a problem. Really." She grabbed four plates instead of two, and bowls for salad. "Let's do this buffet style."

There was more than enough vegetable lasagna, garlic bread, and salad to go around. Serena had stopped at a bakery and picked up a tiramisu. By the time they consumed it and a pot of coffee, it was almost eleven. So much for not staying long, Serena thought. She was happy they approved of Gabrielle but really wanted some downtime with her since she lived far away.

"You're not going to drive home tonight, are you? It's starting to rain." Chloe pointed outside where fat raindrops started hitting the windows.

"Oh, a little bit of rain doesn't scare me." Gabrielle scoffed. "I have to work tomorrow anyway."

"You should stay the night. Go in late tomorrow. Tell them you were with your number one client. Besides, I have plenty of space,"

Serena said. She didn't regret saying it, but after the words escaped her lips, she thought she could have said it more diplomatically. Having Gabrielle alone in her house during a storm was a scenario directly from her fantasies. She swallowed hard and waited for the answer.

Gabrielle pulled up Doppler on her phone. "That's probably a good idea. It looks like this will be a whopper."

"I don't know that I trust your little sports car in this weather," Serena said.

"And we should go because I don't want to fight traffic. It's like everybody forgets how to drive whenever there's rain or snow." Chloe stood and hugged Serena. "I'm sorry we crashed your date," she whispered.

The evening had turned out nice, and it was kind of a relief that they were there to ease the tension. Serena had no idea what to expect, but now that it was determined that Gabrielle would be spending the night, her anxiety revved up several gears. "Be safe going home."

"How far away do you live?" Gabrielle asked.

"About ten minutes away. No biggie," Jackie said. She pulled the door open and raced out in the rain to the car. "We'll text you when we get home."

Serena gave her a thumbs-up and watched them drive away. She could feel Gabrielle standing behind her. "I love them, but they really do have the worst timing."

Gabrielle laughed. "Are you sure they don't have your phone tapped so they can tell when we're getting together? Come on. Let's close the door before everything gets drenched."

"You're probably tired of wet clothes, aren't you?"

Gabrielle groaned. "I now have a bag of dry clothes in my car because of this morning's fiasco."

"Do you have pajamas in your car?"

Gabrielle laughed and shook her head. "Jeans, a T-shirt, socks, shoes. Basically, something to wear tomorrow, but not to bed."

"You can wear something of mine. I have tons of pajamas and boxers and T-shirts. Nothing fancy, though." Serena shrugged like it wasn't a big deal, but inside she was a mess. Her stomach quivered and her heart thumped in her chest so hard she wondered if Gabrielle could see it. She splayed her fingers across her chest to calm the beat.

"I'll wear whatever you have. I'm not picky in the least."

Serena did a quick inventory of her wardrobe. She would just gather up a stack of clothes and let Gabrielle have her pick. "I'll put you in the first bedroom that you liked so much. And I'll keep L.B. with me so you won't have to worry about him all night."

"I really appreciate that. Thank you."

Serena nodded and motioned for L.B. to follow her upstairs. "I'll just be a minute." She dug up her two favorite T-shirts, a pair of boxers, a pair of lounge pants, and socks. And then added a sweatshirt when she wasn't sure the selection was enough. She placed the clothes, fresh towels, and a new toothbrush in Faith's bathroom and returned downstairs to find Gabrielle tucked in a corner of the couch looking at her phone. She could tell by the green and red on the screen that she was looking at the weather. "What's Doppler like?"

"Pretty shitty. There's a lull for the next ten minutes, then it's on for the next six hours."

"I'd better throw L.B. out one last time. I put a pile of clothing options in your bathroom for whenever you're ready."

Gabrielle stood. "Thank you. I'm sure it's fine." She pointed upstairs. "Good night, Serena."

Serena felt sweat on her brow at the thought of being alone with Gabrielle in her house, wearing her clothes, sleeping in her bed. Well, technically Faith's bed, but still. "You, too." She gave Gabrielle a weak smile and called L.B., who was hesitant to go outside. With a little bit of encouragement, he raced out, but stayed close to the house. Serena grabbed the towel she brought down with her and waited for him. He sprinted inside and shook as he skidded into the kitchen. "Come here. Don't get everything wet." He stood still as Serena dried him off. "Are you ready for bed?" L.B. understood the word "bed." He waited for her at the bottom of the stairs as she turned off the lights and set the alarm. As she passed Faith's room, she ran her hand along the door, hoping to hear something inside, but the lights were off and it was quiet except for the storm raging outside and the pounding of her heart.

Chapter Twenty

The smell of coffee wafted from somewhere. Gabrielle stirred and wondered how that was possible since she lived alone. And why was it so dark? What time was it? A sliver of panic shot through her body as she realized she wasn't in her bed. Everything smelled different and felt different. And it was quiet. No traffic, no voices, just quiet. A few barks outside brought the memories back. She was at Serena's. She glanced at her phone. It was almost seven. She checked her in-box quickly and sent Miles an email that she'd be in the office after lunch. That gave her enough time to maybe have a cup of coffee with Serena and change into her own clothes. She hit the remote and smiled when the room-darkening curtains pulled back and revealed a very sunny, very peaceful morning. She slipped on the sweatshirt and pajama bottoms, which were too short for her, and opened the door.

Serena was downstairs leaning against the kitchen island, flipping through a magazine and sipping coffee. "Good morning. It's a beautiful day outside. A little bit muddy, but sunny and not hot." She looked refreshed, very comfortable, and very beautiful. She was wearing dark ankle jeans and a sleeveless top that brought out the green in her blue-green eyes. Her hair was down and brushed her bare arms.

"Hi. I can't believe it's so late. I sent the office an email telling them that I'd be in after lunch." Gabrielle felt very self-conscious.

"I wasn't sure if I should wake you or not," Serena said. She closed the magazine and offered Gabrielle a cup of coffee, which she graciously accepted. "Sugar? Creamer? Milk?"

Gabrielle waved off any additives. She loved black coffee. She inhaled the steam and took a satisfying sip. "It's perfect the way it is."

"I wasn't sure if you ate breakfast or even had time for food. I can cook us something or we can go into town and grab a quick meal." Serena's voice sounded hopeful, and it pained Gabrielle to have to disappoint her.

"I need to meet with Christopher over a few projects. And we have our meeting with him to see how things are progressing, so I need to make sure I have everything in order," Gabrielle said. Her voice had a clip to it, and she quickly softened. "So, unfortunately, I have to go. I had a really nice time yesterday. Even though I had to wear a towel for an hour." She smiled until Serena smiled, too. Gabrielle knew when she slipped into professional mode, she was all business. "I'm going to grab my bag and change into casual clothes, but after I finish this coffee." Small talk wasn't her thing. Her relationships, if one wanted to call them that, were quick, to the point, and she was out the door before dawn. Serena was so nice, and sweet, and what the fuck was she doing with her? She took another sip and sat at the counter. "What are your plans for today?"

Serena shrugged. "I have none. I'll probably take L.B. for a walk, go grocery shopping, maybe watch a movie. I know once we get started on Pet Posh, I'll never sleep or have time to eat breakfast and read a book at a coffee shop."

"I will make sure you don't forget to have a good time. I promise." Gabrielle looked over the rim of her cup to meet Serena's eyes. Was that surprise she saw or anticipation? Either way, it was sexy. Gabrielle liked the control Serena gave her. Fuck. She was doing it again. The internal struggle she had about this woman was driving her crazy. If she wasn't her client, would she date her? Or would Serena be a fling? Definitely not a one-night stand. Serena was the kind of woman who deserved a top-notch romance. She appreciated flowers, chocolate, and the attention people gave L.B. Gabrielle had brought the flowers and even remembered a toy for L.B., but could she be everything that Serena wanted?

"I actually believe you," Serena said. She rinsed her cup and opened the dishwasher to place the cup upside down on the top shelf. Gabrielle noticed how graceful she was, how careful she treated her things. She melted a bit on the inside and felt guilty for taking so much for granted.

"Okay, I guess I'll go get my clothes and get out of here. Thank you for coming to my rescue not once but twice yesterday."

"Anytime. It's nice to have company," Serena said.

Gabrielle grabbed her bag out of the trunk and changed into her casual clothes. For some reason, she felt an incredible need to get out of there. If she stayed, it could get messy, or it could be the best thing ever. That was the part that scared her. She could still work with Serena, but if she started touching her now, that might jeopardize their working relationship, and right now that was more important. This week was the big meeting with Christopher and Serena to review the plans. According to the schedule she'd tentatively mapped out, construction was to begin in a matter of weeks, and the design phase wasn't even finished. The meeting would either go really well or she would crash and burn. Not to mention she still had to send the drawings out for bids. Serena had asked the firm to help her find a builder. Gabrielle gave her top three a heads-up that she would need bids back quickly. The first snow was always early, and the foundation needed to get poured and set sooner rather than later. Gabrielle rolled last night's clothes in a ball and shoved them into her overnight bag. She quickly stripped the bed and left the linens in a neat pile in the bathroom. She wasn't sure what the etiquette was since she never stayed over at anyone's house except Rosie's, and most of the time she crashed on the couch. She was lucky to get a flat sheet and a blanket. She trotted down the stairs with her bag in hand. "Thank you again for coming to my rescue yesterday."

"I'll walk you out. Don't worry about L.B. He's outside getting muddy," Serena said.

"I was wondering where he was this morning."

"He loves hanging out in the backyard."

Gabrielle threw her bag in the trunk and reached for Serena. "Thank you for everything." She pulled her close and hugged her. She wanted to kiss her but refrained. "I'll call you later." She slipped behind the steering wheel and looked at Serena, who took a few steps back.

"Have a good day."

Gabrielle smiled and backed out of the driveway. She knew Serena wanted a kiss just from her slightly parted lips and the way she kept looking down at Gabrielle's mouth. The overwhelming need to feel her lips against Serena's was the reason she had to make a quick getaway. Regardless of their hand holding and few kisses they'd shared, Serena was still a client. Never mind that every single person in her life told her Serena was the girl for her. Too much was at stake. She had to pull back for the sake of her professional life. It was the one true thing that never disappointed her.

❖

Dani was in the row ahead of her, two bikes over, spinning and sweating hard. Gabrielle didn't mind one bit that she was in second place. The view was spectacular.

"Dani's in first place. Nobody wants to beat her? Okay, I'll buy whoever beats Dani a recovery shake after class. You all know how expensive those are." Blaine made eye contact with Gabrielle and nodded.

She nodded back and kicked it up. Today was an easy day. She got to work at noon, worked on the Pet Posh Inn all afternoon, and by seven, decided to go to the gym. She needed release, and the only way that would happen was at the gym, with or without Dani. When she saw Dani's blond hair and tight form on the bike, she smiled as her body hummed with anticipation. Her heart pinched in her chest as she thought about Serena. What was their relationship? A few kisses, two dates, and hand holding. That didn't make them exclusive, but she felt guilty for wanting a quick fuck with Dani. She pushed herself harder, faster, knowing she had more energy since she got a good night's sleep and had a light morning. It didn't take her long to tie Dani. In the last thirty seconds, she squeaked out a win. She held her hands up victoriously.

Dani folded her arms in front of her chest and gave Gabrielle an eye roll and a smirk. Gabrielle took a long pull from her water bottle, wiped her face, and winked at Dani. She turned and made her way to the locker room, hoping that Dani would follow. She grabbed her shower caddy and slipped into one of showers. She shut the door but didn't lock it. The water was a step above lukewarm but felt wonderful cascading down her body. She stood under the flow and wiped down her body. She heard the click of the door turning and almost smiled. She shrank back a little when fingertips flitted across her stomach.

"Surprised?" Dani whispered.

Gabrielle shook her head and moved so Dani was under the flow. Even though she was thin, her muscle tone was admirable, as were her full breasts that were probably purchased at a high price. Gabrielle kissed Dani hard and their passion ignited immediately. Gabrielle reminded herself to be quiet. She tensed up as Dani entered her, two fingers first, followed quickly by a third. She leaned back against the shower, her hands pressed against the sides for leverage. Dani pumped in and out of her, but instead of feeling wonderfully wanton, guilt washed over her and flooded every sensitive part. "We have to stop." Dani's fingers stilled inside her. Gabrielle gasped for breath.

"What?" Dani whispered.

"I can't do this. We have to stop." Gabrielle leaned her head back and sighed as she felt Dani's warmth leave her body. Of all the times for Serena's face to fill her mind, now was not ideal. Fuck. Her body was on fire and begged for release, but her brain, or maybe it was her heart, forbade it. For the first time, a quick hook-up didn't feel right.

"Any particular reason why? Your body seems to like this just fine." Dani kissed her again, but respected her wishes and kept her hands off Gabrielle.

"It feels wonderful, but I just can't." Gabrielle hated that she pictured Serena instead. She felt dirty standing in the shower with someone she didn't even know that well. She shut off the water and rubbed her face. This wasn't her. Wham, bam, thank you ma'am and she was the first one gone. What was happening?

"No worries." Dani reached for her towel. "Congratulations on beating me today. I'll see you soon." She dropped a quick kiss on Gabrielle's lips and slipped out of the shower room.

Gabrielle slapped the wall in frustration. Somewhere between her last encounter with Dani and this morning with Serena, she'd slipped and started to care about Serena. Her friends were to blame. And her mother. Gabrielle only lived in the moment. Maybe if she'd never mentioned Serena to her circle of friends, she'd be coming right now instead of standing in a semiprivate gym shower near tears.

She dried off and wrapped the towel around her body. She headed to her locker, not caring if Dani was still around, and quickly pulled on a pair of shorts and a T-shirt. She slicked her hair back in a ponytail, skipped makeup, and left the gym. She needed a reboot. And a glass of wine. Maybe she would even dig into her red velvet box of dildos and finish herself off. She ignored her missed calls from Rosie and her mom and drove straight home. It was getting late and she was exhausted. She sent them both a text explaining she was at the gym and would talk to them tomorrow. She poured a glass of Doña Paula Malbec and plopped on the couch.

What a fucking day. And it was only Monday. She would have to finish the final touches on Aaron's gas station job and send the drawings off to their builder. She was only a week late, which was fine because the customers were pleased with everything. A week didn't screw up their schedule, as they had allowed for the architect switch. She wondered how Tom was doing on his hotel. He was two months in and had acquired help, so she figured he was probably back on track.

The Pet Posh Inn was moving along, but she knew Christopher wasn't going to be happy at Wednesday's meeting. In the real world, dealing with people who put one hundred percent of their faith in an architect was a lot easier than dealing with an indecisive one. Wait. Not indecisive, just extremely picky. Gabrielle sighed. She couldn't fault Serena for wanting everything to be perfect. She came from nothing and suddenly could have anything she ever wanted. Most people blew through their money. It was risky plugging so much of her winnings into her new business, but Gabrielle believed Serena's business plan was solid and had potential. There were doggie daycares around, but this daycare was for all pets, and really rich people had unique pets, not just dogs. And posh? That was the problem. Gabrielle couldn't understand posh for pets. She didn't know what that meant for animals.

How was the rest of your day?

Gabrielle looked at her phone and groaned. Why was Serena everywhere? She woke up with Serena on her mind, spent five solid hours on her project, stopped having sex in the gym shower because she couldn't stop thinking about her, and now she was invading her wine time with a text.

It was a crazy day. How was yours?

I went to the animal shelter today. Probably shouldn't have, but I did.

Oh no. How many more Evanses did we add to the family? Gabrielle's stomach tightened as she waited for the answer. Her biggest fear was a puppy, or worse, two. Serena had warned her that now that she was in her house, she was ready to fill it with all the pets.

Surprisingly zero. But I wanted them all. I'm going to volunteer there for a bit and see how they take care of the animals.

Of course she was volunteering. Gabrielle felt even worse about what happened at the gym tonight. Serena was perfect, and for some reason, that upset Gabrielle. Her own flaws were even more pronounced around Serena, and it made her realize that her life lacked feeling. She loved her friends and her family, but she had put work first for so long that she sacrificed her heart, the romantic one, for what? Success? Money?

That's a great idea. I'm sure you'll learn a lot. Gabrielle didn't know what else to say, so she put her phone down and refilled her wine glass. Realizing that she was successful at everything else in her life except for what her heart needed, what it wanted, she brought the glass up to her lips and muttered "fuck" before draining its entire contents in one swallow.

Chapter Twenty-one

Serena noticed that Christopher, a man of precision if his perfectly pressed shirt and full Windsor tie were any indication, wasn't happy with Gabrielle's progress on the Pet Posh Inn. He leaned forward, his elbows on the table and his forefingers meeting to form an upside-down V on his bottom lip as he studied the plans. As if he'd forgotten that she, the client, was in the room, he asked a thousand questions. Gabrielle answered each one professionally, without emotion, and as rapidly as he was asking.

"Is this enough space for the canine area?"

Christopher turned to Serena and pointed to the section that Gabrielle had worked on yesterday. It was everything she'd asked for, yet his question threw her off. She cleared her throat and straightened in her chair.

"Do you think it's not enough?" Serena didn't miss Gabrielle's eye roll. "This is everything I asked for, but what do you think?" Why was this so hard for her? Why couldn't she make up her mind about it?

"I think it depends on how many dogs you think you will have. Most animal daycares are going to have dogs because they're the most popular and require the most attention. Do you think you're going to have a lot of birds? Because if not, you can take away from this room and add to the canine section so their indoor activity room is larger. Not all dogs are going to like to be outside in the snow. Maybe you can increase the nature room with real grass and real trees or bushes that can be maintained in the winter."

Serena didn't dare look at Gabrielle. Gabrielle had made the same suggestion a few weeks ago and Serena had shot it down because she wanted more outdoor space for the dogs, but Christopher made a good point. The chances were slim that birds would need boarding and the natural inside area was a good idea, especially in the winter. Dogs would love grass in January.

"I think that's a good idea," Serena said.

Gabrielle shuffled in her chair and took a drink of water. It was obvious that she was upset. Serena decided to do some damage control before she completely blew her relationship with Gabrielle.

"Gabrielle suggested that, but I didn't really think, at the time, that it was a good assessment of the area." Serena looked at the table, unable to meet Gabrielle's eyes.

"We could actually change the layout a bit and keep these two trees as part of the architecture." Gabrielle pointed to an area on the screen, typed in a few commands, and the nature area shifted to include two existing trees. "See? This doesn't compromise the bird area and we can make other adjustments."

"How much time do you think you'll need to map out all the changes for civil?" Chris turned to Gabrielle and waited for her answer.

"I can get this done by the end of the week."

"Good. We need to start thinking about getting plans to a builder and get the foundation down before the weather changes or this will have to wait until spring. I'd like to avoid that, and I'm sure Ms. Evans would as well." Christopher smiled at Serena and nodded. He stood, shook Serena's hand, and excused himself from the conference room.

Serena had never been more nervous than right now. She knew Gabrielle was upset with her and had every reason to be. "Look, I'm sorry that happened. You've more than done everything I've asked."

Gabrielle finally looked at her, and her stare was cold. Serena looked away.

"I'm going to really think about this space and I'm going to cover everything. My boss is right. We need to finalize the plans and get them to the builder so we get as much done as possible before the cold weather hits. I'm going to send the plans to builders who do great work and are fast. If you want, I can offer a financial incentive for completion before the time frame they quote us."

Serena nodded. "Whatever you think."

Gabrielle smirked. "Well, that's not true, but let me work on this and we'll see where I am at the end of the week."

The chill between them was unsettling. Serena had no idea what to say or how to fix it. She understood Gabrielle was upset. She was embarrassed in front of her boss and Serena had no idea how to fix it or even what to say.

"I guess I'll go." She grabbed her messenger bag at Gabrielle's curt nod. As she passed Gabrielle, she reached out and touched her arm. "I'm sorry that was uncomfortable. I didn't mean to belittle your hard work in front of your boss." When Gabrielle didn't respond, Serena took that as a fuck off and walked out of the room. The one thing Serena was good at was walking away, shutting down and leaving her emotions right there on the battlefield. She wasn't a fighter, she was a survivor. But this? This was new to her. Gabrielle had broken through so many of her walls that it was hard to just shut down.

Serena wasn't sure of Piper's schedule, but she thought she'd at least try. She was probably in class, but on the second ring, Piper answered.

"I could use a friend right now," Serena said.

"I can meet you in twenty minutes. Peak Brew?" Piper's voice was soothing and made Serena take a slow, deep breath.

"Thanks. I'll see you in a bit." She ended the call and her heart felt a little better. If anyone could help, it would be Piper. She knew Gabrielle and had a big sister vibe. She was strong and quiet, and seemed to understand feelings. Ten minutes later, she was parked at Peak Brew.

Piper knocked on the Jeep window. "Hi." She followed up with a small wave.

"Hi, yourself." Piper's smile was so genuine that Serena instantly forgave her for scaring the shit out of her. "Come on. Let's grab a cup of tea and talk."

Serena locked the Jeep and followed Piper inside, where Piper was immediately greeted with a warm cup of Earl Grey tea. Serena ordered a mint tea and they sat at a small booth in back, away from the other patrons.

"I'm sorry to just call you out of the blue like this."

Piper waved her off. "Oh, stop. We're friends, and this is what friends do. We drink tea and solve problems. Tell me what's going on in your world."

Serena leaned back in her chair. "It was a bad meeting with Gabrielle today and I'm afraid I screwed up."

Piper squeezed Serena's hands. "It can't be that bad. You both are sweet women and you have really good chemistry, whether it's friendship or something else."

Serena's shoulders slumped. "I screwed up today."

"I doubt that, but tell me what happened."

Serena told Piper everything from their dinner date and hiking trip, to all of the back and forth on the design of the Pet Posh Inn, to today's fiasco meeting with Gabrielle's boss. Piper was attentive, interrupting only when she needed more information.

"Let me just say a few things."

"Okay, hit me."

"I've known Gabrielle for years, and she's a workaholic. Every time we all got together, she'd show up in a business suit because she came straight from work. The only time I saw her in normal clothes was if we had a barbecue on a weekend. She prides herself on her work."

Serena dropped her head in her hands and groaned. "And I just embarrassed her in front of her boss."

"Gabrielle has always been the best. At everything really."

"She's made all these great suggestions and I kept pushing back. No, that's not big enough, no, that's not right. Dogs need more space. I just couldn't make up my mind." Serena slumped back in her chair. "Her boss attends the meeting today and makes the same suggestions, and for some stupid reason, when he says them, they sound like a good idea."

"Oh," Piper said.

"Yeah, so that's the problem. At least one of them."

Piper nodded and squeezed Serena's hand. "She's a strong lady. I'm sure she'll get through this. Trust me when I say she's had some very difficult clients over the years. This? Today? Wasn't a big thing. She'll bounce back. I promise."

"She was just so cold and professional when I left. I feel like I just ruined the relationship we were developing," Serena said. Her voice lowered. "And it's always been hard for me to make friends. I don't open up to people very well."

"Well, that's news to me. You've always been sweet and kind, but I understand," Piper said.

Serena was sure by now Piper had heard about her upbringing. It wasn't a secret anymore. People from her past talked to the news. Neighbors told reporters how quiet she was and how her mom wouldn't come home sometimes. Students from her middle and high schools who claimed they were friends said Serena would stay with them because she was scared of her mother. Not once had Serena stayed the night at a friend's house. She didn't have any friends. She knew the dangers of people getting too close.

Since the articles brought light to her upbringing, people who thought they were close to Serena, like the butcher at her grocery store and her pharmacist, offered her their condolences. Hanging out in Denver was nice because the people she knew in Denver were friends. Nobody in Denver knew she won the lottery. "Thank you. I've met some really good friends because of Gabrielle. I'd hate to lose everybody because I've upset her. But more importantly, I hate to think I hurt my relationship with Gabrielle, even if all we have is a friendship. What should I do?"

Piper smiled sympathetically. "First of all, take a deep breath. I'm sure it's going to blow over. Gabrielle isn't one to hold a grudge. She'll get your project done and everything will be fine."

"Piper, you didn't see the look she gave me. It was as if she didn't even see me at all."

"That's just Gabrielle shutting down. I've known her for quite some time. I've never met anybody she was dating because she doesn't date. I watched her at the barbecue and she only had eyes for you. This will blow over."

"I hope so." Serena sighed. "How are you doing? I've been crying over my own life and haven't even asked how you're doing."

"No complaints. Shaylie's great. Maribelle is starting preschool in a few days and she's very excited about it."

"What do you do for daycare now?"

"Shaylie has her in the morning, then she drops her off at Bodhi. I have class until noon, then we go out and do fun things like ballet and tumbling. If we need additional help, my mom is available. Some of my instructors like to babysit. There's always Rosie if I'm desperate."

"I like Rosie and Anne. Very sweet family. And their children are very well behaved. I love watching families interact."

"Then I have the best idea. Come over for dinner on Saturday night. We'll host and I'll invite them over. Bring L.B. and Faith if she's not working."

Visions of Gabrielle filled Serena's head. She didn't want to be rude and ask if Piper was going to ask her to the party, too. "That sounds great. What do you want me to bring?"

"How about I text you and we can finalize food and time and all that good stuff?" Piper looked at her watch. "Crap. I have to go. It's my turn with munchkin, but thank you for reaching out. I really believe things will work out with Gabrielle. She just needs time, okay?"

Serena nodded. "I hope you're right. Thanks for taking time out to visit."

Piper pulled her into a hug. "Anytime. Be careful going home."

Serena finished her tea and thought about everything Piper said. Piper knew Gabrielle better than Serena did, and she was just going to have to trust that Piper was right. It still made her heart heavy thinking about this morning and the flash of anger she saw in those beautiful amber eyes.

❖

"We got the club house for my graduation." Faith was out of breath, but laughing.

"What's going on?" Serena had a moment of panic, but the words finally clicked into place. "I mean, good. When can we get in and decorate?"

"I only got it for twenty-four hours. We can go in that morning. I was thinking of having the open house from three to seven. What do you think?"

"Sounds good to me. Have you picked a caterer yet?" Serena wasn't about to make that decision on her own. Faith was a foodie and she could work that all out. It wasn't going to be a big thing. Their family and friends were a small group, but she wasn't sure how many students from the culinary center would show up.

"Yes, it's all done. I'll send evites out this week. I count at least ten with our family, my roommates, and Chloe and Jackie. Probably half a dozen from the school, and Phillip, his friend Tyler, and Tyler's girlfriend. I'm guessing about twenty-five total."

"That's great, Faith. When can we look at the space?"

"Anytime. It's mostly used on the weekends. Are you around today?"

"I had a meeting in Denver, but I'm on my way back to Vail. Give me an hour?" Serena wanted to pick up L.B. first. Her house was on the way to Faith's apartment complex, so it wasn't out of the way.

"Sure. See you then."

Serena wondered what plans Faith made with her mother. Ever since she told Faith she wasn't putting her mother and Paul up in a hotel, she hadn't heard a peep from Faith. She was curious, though. Hell, knowing her mother, she'd probably reached out to Jackie and asked for the Presidential Suite at Waterfall Lodge and expected it for free. Serena wasn't going to ask her friends to stop being nice people. If they wanted to put Diane and Paul up for a few days, that was up to them. She just made it perfectly clear that she wasn't paying any bills they accrued and they were under no obligation to support them either.

Being tough felt liberating, but it also had its drawbacks. The situation she was in with Gabrielle was because she stuck to her guns even though, looking back, Gabrielle was right about almost everything. She decided to send Gabrielle a text message after work. After the dust settled. She had a feeling Gabrielle would be working late. The rescheduled meeting was for Friday afternoon. That only gave her a few days to get it all done.

Serena pulled into her driveway to find a smiling L.B. looking out the window and happily barking at her. She typed in the alarm code and took him out to the backyard. She wondered if he ever used the doggie door when she was gone. When he was finally done marking everything out back, she whistled and he raced back to her. "You want to go for a drive?" He twirled and barked his answer. "We're going to go see Auntie Faith. You ready?" More barking. She grabbed his leash and opened the front door. He bolted to the Jeep and pranced until she opened the back door. With all of the recent rain, Serena decided to limit him to the back seat only after putting down a weatherproof blanket to catch the mud. He didn't complain. She rolled the window down enough for him to stick his snout out and smell the fresh air.

Faith met them as they pulled into the parking lot. "The manager is going to meet us in five minutes." Serena loved looking at her younger sister's sweet, innocent face. They'd been through a lot together and Serena was so proud of her. She was on the fast track to a solid career that she wanted. She reached out to touch her sister's cheek, but Faith slapped her hand away. "Weirdo, stop that."

Serena laughed, opened the door, and accepted Faith's hug instead. "You're such a brat."

"People can see us." Faith wasn't one for public displays of affection. It was almost considered a weakness with them. They grew up bracing for disappointment.

Serena rolled her eyes and opened the back door so L.B. could say hello to Faith, too. She sat on the sidewalk and allowed him to kiss her and try to curl up in her lap.

"Be careful. He might be dirty. The backyard is still sketchy."

Faith brushed off a partial muddy paw print. "A little mud is the least of my laundry problems. You should see my aprons. They're a hot mess."

Serena squelched the urge to buy her sister one hundred new

aprons. She had one week off between the end of school and the start of her new job. Serena was surprised that she took time off, but Faith was turning twenty-one and wanted to go to Vegas. She had already been saving for it. When Serena won the lottery, she offered to pay for the flight and the hotel for Faith and her best friend Becca as her graduation present to Faith. They had already picked the hotel and both girls were pestering Serena into going with them, but gambling wasn't her thing. She still had a hard time throwing money away, and since she knew nothing about gambling, she would be doing exactly that.

"Hi, Leo. You remember my sister, Serena, right?" Faith did a quick introduction.

Leo mumbled hello back and motioned for them to follow. The clubhouse was near the pool, nestled in a cluster of fir trees. The trees provided nice shade, which they would need since the unit didn't have air-conditioning. He unlocked the door, flipped on the lights, and stepped back for them to enter. It wasn't musty, but the air was stale and the place needed airing out. The large room, albeit dated, boasted a built-in bar, two long countertops for food, a refrigerator with ice maker, and several round tables and chairs that were folded up and tucked into a slotted metal structure that kept them out of the way and organized. It wasn't a bad space, it was just boring, but when Serena turned to Faith, her eyes were wide with excitement and possibilities.

"I think it's great," Serena said. She was ignoring the dark stains on the carpet, which were probably soda spills and not blood. She really needed to stop watching slasher movies.

Faith squeezed her hand. "I think so, too. Okay, Leo. I'll get the key from you next weekend at nine so we can start decorating."

He nodded and waved them back out. "I need to get back to the office, but I'll write you down."

"What color decorations do you want?" Serena turned to Faith after Leo left them on the sidewalk by their cars.

"I love teal. Or black. Or whatever really."

Serena remembered when Faith's favorite color was pink. Of course, she was eight then and she also liked mermaids. The one time Faith got to trick-or-treat she'd dressed up like a mermaid and almost froze to death. Serena was working at the diner and Diane was nowhere to be found. Faith decided she wasn't going to miss out on the free candy and festivities, so she got dressed, grabbed her pumpkin basket, and headed out. At least she'd put on boots. She got about five doors down before Serena got a call from a concerned neighbor.

Serena blinked at Faith. "I've got this, baby sis. Just get the key next weekend."

"Can I have a chocolate cake? With vanilla icing?"

"Your wish is my command. We're going to go. Call me if you need anything." Serena opened the back door for L.B. and climbed into the driver's seat.

"Thanks for everything," Faith said. She reached inside the Jeep and squeezed Serena's cheeks like she was an eighty-year-old grandma saying goodbye to a baby.

Serena slapped at her hands, but laughed. "Weirdo."

Chapter Twenty-Two

It was ten at night and Gabrielle had been working on the Pet Posh Inn since after the meeting the day before. She could finally see the finished product and was wondering why she didn't see it before. Once she moved the layout to include three aspen trees for the indoor portion of the playroom area, everything else just clicked. She was struggling to fit everything on one level. She and Serena had argued back and forth over land space when it was so obvious to go up. Literally.

She put the offices upstairs, along with the feline floor. To avoid the whole cats and dogs together, the offices were directly over the canine condos. The cat cottages were on the other side above the quieter, smaller pets. Serena finished the canine section with everything Serena wanted including individual heaters and air conditioners, fans and free-flowing fountains. She playfully named each condo for dogs in movies, literature, and television shows after googling a list of the most famous canines. Those were only suggested names, but they made Gabrielle smile. Lassie, Toto, Rin-Tin-Tin, Odie, Snoopy, Benji, Pluto, Muttley, Scooby-Doo, Scrappy-Doo, Clifford, and Winn-Dixie. She deleted Cujo because this was a serious job and she wanted to please Serena. Shit.

She picked up her phone and looked over her messages. Serena had sent her an apologetic text that she barely read because she was in the groove. She decided to take a minute to breathe. And eat something. The sandwich Miles had picked up from the deli was soaked in pickle juice and barely edible, but she was hungry, so she ate around the soggy side of the croissant.

Are you alive?

Gabrielle smiled at Rosie's text and fired one back at her. *Barely. I'm still at work.*

Shut the fuck up. Go home! Her message was followed up with stern emojis.

I'm finishing up the Pet Posh Inn. Meeting tomorrow. Gotta finish. I'll get home before midnight. The meeting is at one. I have time.

You know that for every hour you work overtime, you gain a wrinkle, right? Rosie asked.

Shit. I'd be dead by now.

Seriously. Go home. You can't possibly be accomplishing a lot.

Au contraire! I've been on a roll. Had a breakthrough. I'll call you tomorrow.

Rosie responded with a gif of a sheep holding its thumbs up.

In the middle of designing the outdoor space, Gabrielle came up with a brilliant idea for the cats. She designed a giant tree wrapped in sisal they could access from catwalks from their own cottages. There was a communal area inside the tree if they could all get along. She actually liked it more than the dog space. And why didn't she think to use the loft space before? It solved all their problems.

She would run this by civil in the morning since now there was a bathroom upstairs for the employees, but she didn't make too many changes other than utilizing the trees, which would need a watering system. It took her a couple more hours to polish it all. It was perfect. All of this time it just took a swift kick in her ass to get past her ego and put her crush on Serena on hold to get this project done. She saved her project, then fired off a quick email to Miles that she would be late in the morning, and would he make five copies with a note that civil needed to stamp them before final approval.

Gabrielle got home and snarfed down two handfuls of pretzels and a chocolate bar. By then, it was one in the morning. She took a shower before bed and slept until ten. She refused to look at her phone until she was damn well good and ready.

She put on slim gray slacks with a matching jacket. She chose a white tailored shirt and left the top button undone. Sensible heels since she'd be standing for most of the presentation. In a spontaneous decision, she left her hair down. In the ten years she'd worked at Arnest & Max, there was only one other time she left her hair down. Her first day. The men had looked at her wolfishly and she decided she wasn't going to be sexualized at work. She always pulled her hair back and wore her glasses most days. She wanted to be taken seriously, not looked at like a conquest they felt the need to master. Today she demanded attention from her boss and, more importantly, from Serena. She tamped down her excitement at showing her the new plans. If Serena hated it, Gabrielle would hand the project over to Christopher, quit her job, and go work at her parents' nursery where she could take out her anger on bags of dirt and mulch. This project, for all of its ups and downs, ended up being something she was extremely proud of.

On her way out, Miles had called to let her know he'd made the copies and set up the conference room with a coffee bar, bottles of sparkling water on ice, cookies, brownies, and trail mixes in biodegradable pouches he'd purchased from Denver's famous nut store a few blocks from the office. It wasn't necessary because Gabrielle knew Serena would be too nervous to eat. Hopefully Miles didn't go overboard. He had Gabrielle's credit card and wasn't afraid to use it. He often ordered excessive amounts of everything and took the leftovers home. Gabrielle decided any leftovers would go with her to Piper and Shaylie's informal gathering this Saturday. She got the evite last night while she was shoveling pretzels in her mouth and quickly checking her emails. She'd confirmed and barely remembered it until just this moment.

Gabrielle parked and grabbed her bag. Serena was due in fifteen minutes, and she wanted to review everything before she presented. Christopher was waiting when she got to her office.

"I hope you don't mind, but I looked at your plans this morning."

Gabrielle bristled but kept her cool. Christopher was her boss and was on her side. "Oh? What did you think?" She continued her routine as though his presence didn't rattle her. She hung her messenger bag on the coat rack, undid her suit jacket, and sat to answer a few emails from this morning. She didn't take her eyes off her computer although she was dying to read Christopher's expression.

"I think the changes are great. I can't imagine your customer not liking this new layout."

Gabrielle finally looked at him. He was at ease with a hint of a smile perched on his lips. "I already told myself if she doesn't like this one, I'm quitting and working for the family business."

Christopher broke the threshold and sat down. He waved her off. "If she doesn't like this one, I'll quit, too."

Gabrielle smiled. For her boss to tell her this and so casually meant only one thing: She'd nailed it. This meeting was either going to go extremely well or she seriously was going to hand it off. She could deal with Serena after the drawings were in the hands of the builder. This was her make or break job, and a possible relationship couldn't jeopardize her future.

"When Serena gets here, please escort her to the conference room." Gabrielle hung up the receiver after Miles confirmed. An instant message flashed from Christopher.

Heads up. Lawrence and John will be in the meeting.

Fuck, Gabrielle thought. Two partners were going to see her plans before they were finalized. That didn't happen very often, so either they were concerned, checking up on her, or Christopher told them to be there because he approved.

Thanks. See you in there.

She really wanted to panic. She paced the front of her desk, reviewing her speech, all the major points she wanted to hit, in order to please both Serena and the partners. Keep it professional, Gabrielle, she repeated. Keep it professional.

Miles called her again. "Serena's in the conference room. So are Mr. Anderson and Mr. Lacy. Oh, and Serena brought somebody with her."

That got Gabrielle's attention. Keeping the surprise out of her voice, she said thank you crisply and hung up. She took a deep breath, ran her hands over her suit to smooth the wrinkles, buttoned the top button of her jacket, and headed to the conference room.

"Gabrielle," Christopher said. She turned to find him behind her. "Don't worry about the partners. I told them you were presenting the final before you finalized it, and they want to see how the client receives it. They did the same with Tom. Don't worry. It's a great, creative design."

She offered him a quick smile. "Thanks, boss. Your support means a lot."

"Go get 'em." He followed her into the conference room.

Her steps stuttered when she saw Serena. *Wow* was all she could think. Serena was wearing a sleeveless cream-colored blouse, black slacks, and black peep toe heels. Her hair was styled and her makeup looked amazing. She looked amazing. Gabrielle smiled when she recognized Serena's guest. Chloe stood close to Serena, perusing the available sparkling waters.

When Gabrielle's eyes met Serena's, the room stilled. Gabrielle heard the whoosh of air leave her lungs, then nothing but silence. The look Serena gave her made Gabrielle's knees weak. There was a flash of uncertainty, but the thing that made the room drift away, the part that made her lungs take a breath again, was the heat she saw in Serena's eyes. Maybe it was the makeup, maybe it was that for a split second her guard was down and Gabrielle saw desire. A small, hesitant smile appeared at the corner of Serena's mouth, as if she wasn't sure she should smile at the meeting or not. Gabrielle hitched her brow, gave a curt nod, and winked. Serena blushed.

"Hello, everyone. Thank you for coming into the city, Ms. Evans. I think you will be pleased with the revisions. Please, take a seat." Gabrielle reached across the table and shook Chloe's hand. "I'm Gabrielle Barnes, Ms. Evans's architect. It's nice to meet you." Confusion, then a soft, barely noticeable kick from Serena spurred Chloe to introduce herself.

"I'm Chloe, Serena's friend, and I'm just here to see the revisions. I know it's getting close to being done, and Serena asked for a fresh set of eyes."

"Next to me are Christopher Morrow, Lawrence Anderson, and John Lacy, all partners of Arnest & Max. Thank you to everyone for coming. Should we get started?" Gabrielle asked. She turned on her laptop and synced it with a large screen that lowered in front of the conference room. A video cued up and a 3D image of the Pet Posh Inn filled the screen. Gabrielle described each section as the video took them from room to room. She refused to look at anyone, too afraid of their reactions. She wanted them to like it—no, love it, and if there was a hiccup in their reaction, it would throw off her semi-prepared speech. When it was over, Gabrielle left the mock-up of the front of the Pet Posh Inn and turned to face her audience.

"I think we covered everything you wanted, Ms. Evans." She turned and looked at Serena for the first time.

"Gabrielle, it's…well, it's perfect. It really is." Serena stared up at the screen and smiled. "How did you do all of this since Wednesday?"

Christopher spoke up. "That's why Gabrielle is one of our best. Does anybody have any questions or concerns?"

"I love it, too," Chloe said.

"The loft is brilliant. Can you go back to it?" Serena asked.

"Certainly. You can get a closer look at the drawings in front of you, too." Gabrielle flipped through her slides and found the loft. "I thought it might be fun to have a few cats walking about upstairs while you work. That's why your offices have toys and small kitty trees and scratching posts."

"Not once did I even consider a second level. It's great."

Gabrielle watched Serena flip through the drawings, point and even laugh with Chloe. She heard the name "Scooby" and smiled. She looked at the prints, jotted a few notes about nothing just to look busy while her client and the partners asked questions.

"We're headed off to another meeting, but thank you for letting us sit in on the reveal. Ms. Evans, I'm sure Gabrielle will answer any questions you have." Lawrence rose and buttoned his jacket. He shook Serena's hand, then Chloe's while John politely nodded and followed him out. Christopher shot Gabrielle a look that she took as positive reinforcement.

"Do you have any questions?" Gabrielle asked.

Serena looked up from the prints with a giant smile. "I still can't get over how incredible this is. This is everything I want and more."

"You did a great job, Gabrielle," Chloe said.

"Looks like you've got this," Christopher said. He scooped up his iPad and his drink and excused himself.

"Where's the restroom?" Chloe asked.

"Down the hall on the right," Gabrielle said without breaking eye contact with Serena. They remained quiet until Chloe closed the door behind her.

"I sent you a message apologizing to you. I'm really sorry I put you in a bad spot on Wednesday."

Serena's voice wasn't accusatory but laced with sadness that stung Gabrielle's heart. She bit her bottom lip as she thought of an appropriate response.

"I'm sorry, but I got on a roll and didn't want to step away or have any distractions. And you, Serena Evans, are a distraction."

Gabrielle watched Serena nervously cap and uncap the pen in her hand. Serena's hands were slender and her long fingers were void of any jewelry. She waited patiently for a response.

"Oh?" Serena's voice cracked. She cleared her throat and repeated herself, her voice stronger with confidence. "Oh?"

"There were a lot of reasons why this job wasn't clicking for me. At the beginning it was that I didn't have an inkling about pets and I was scared of L.B." Gabrielle stood and slowly worked her way to the side of the table where Serena was sitting. She kept her distance, though, partly for her own sanity, but also to tease Serena a bit. "But then I got to know you and wanted to get to know you better. Then the job wasn't important. You were all I could think about, so in order for me to get this done, and really understand what you needed, I had to close myself off."

Serena scooted her chair back a bit so she could look up at Gabrielle. "That would have been nice to know. I was worried I upset you in the last meeting."

Gabrielle leaned down. "Oh, you pissed me off, all right, but that meeting kicked my ass in gear. I needed that to happen." She looked at Serena's mouth, wanting to kiss those full lips, but took a small step back. "Now you got exactly what you wanted." She pointed down at the set of drawings. "Take these home, study them, and we can get together next week to discuss any changes."

Chloe walked into the room, breaking their moment. Gabrielle turned and faced her. "I'm glad you came to support Serena. I'm sorry about introducing myself to you. I don't want any suggestion of impropriety."

"I get it." Chloe shrugged and waved her off. She looked from Serena to Gabrielle. "What happens now?"

"I've asked Serena to take the drawings home and look them over and see if there are any changes. Since we're against the clock, I'll send these off for bids today so they can get started. Hopefully. we'll get numbers back by next week." Gabrielle returned to the other side of the table and sat, ready to take any notes. "Any changes you make won't affect bidding that much unless it's a major thing." She already knew who she was going to send the bids to. There were a few favors she intended to call in to get a rush on the project. At this point, it wasn't because of the promotion, but getting Serena's dream business up and running. Getting the foundation down would be tricky. Concrete took time to cure, and the lot still had to be excavated.

"How long do you think this will take?" Serena asked.

"The good news is that you already filed for permits, so that will help out immensely. Your lawyer is a keeper. If everything goes according to schedule, which it never does, but in a best case scenario, the Pet Posh Inn will be up and running by next summer, maybe late spring."

Serena's shoulders slumped. "That's great."

"Not fast enough?"

"I trust you. I'm just impatient," Serena said.

"The good news is that once the foundation is up and the framework begins, you will be more involved. You'll have to pick out paint colors, window treatments, toys and beds for the rooms. So technically you'll be bored only for the first two to three months. By Christmas, you and the builder will be best friends."

"It'll be fine. You'll have plenty of things to keep you busy," Chloe said. She put her arm around Serena's shoulder.

"Do you want to meet next week to follow up? I can meet you in Vail since the last two times you had to come here." Gabrielle wondered if Serena heard the desperation in her voice. From Chloe's quirked eyebrow, she guessed it was obvious. "If you have time."

Serena nodded. "Sure. I have three months where I'm going to binge-watch all the cable shows I missed."

"Then I'll know where to find you." Gabrielle stood when Chloe and Serena stood. She hated that their meeting was over because she wanted to clear things up with Serena on a personal level, but she didn't feel comfortable with Chloe standing there.

"Thank you so much for designing the perfect place for me. It's everything I ever dreamed of," Serena said.

If it was just the two of them in the conference room, Gabrielle would have pulled her into a hug. Since she had an audience, she shook Serena's hand instead. "Thank you for not giving up on me."

Chloe picked up the drawings and rolled them up. "We should get going. Jackie's waiting. It was nice to see you again, Gabrielle."

"Thanks for coming, Chloe."

"Bye, Gabrielle."

Gabrielle walked them out, her fingertips barely brushing the small of Serena's back as she opened the door for them. "Call me. You know, if you need me."

Serena turned and squeezed Gabrielle's hand. "I will." Her gaze dropped to Gabrielle's lips and then back up to meet her eyes. "I definitely will."

Chapter Twenty-three

"I'm so glad you made it." Piper greeted Serena with a hug. "And you brought your friends. Hi, I'm Piper. It's so nice to finally meet Serena's friends."

Serena almost laughed at Chloe and Jackie's reaction to Piper. They were smitten.

"Thank you so much for inviting us. You have a beautiful home," Chloe said. Jackie nodded.

"Make yourself at home. I have a wardrobe emergency to take care of, so excuse me for a moment." Piper leaned in closer. "Somebody spilled juice all over the front of her new unicorn shirt, and Shaylie is trying to prevent the inevitable meltdown." She laughed and headed up the stairs.

"Wow. Maybe we all should move to Denver," Chloe whispered.

"I'm not even going to give you a hard time for staring at Piper because you're totally right," Jackie said.

"Come on. Let's find the kitchen and drop off our food. Then we can mingle and meet people," Serena said. She'd made an artichoke and black truffle dip. It took her three tries to get it perfect, but she wasn't going to bring something average that nobody would want to eat. Jackie made pineapple cheesecake bars. Faith had given her the recipe her first year in culinary school. Serena could easily eat three in one sitting. But here at Piper's house, she was almost too nervous to eat. The minute they found the kitchen and all of the delicious food, her grumbling stomach reminded her she needed to eat.

"It sounds like everyone is outside. Let's go mingle."

Chloe loved to meet new people. Jackie was more reserved, like Serena, but they followed Chloe outside to a deck full of women.

Serena quickly scanned the deck and felt her heart sink because she didn't see Gabrielle there.

"Hi, I'm Chloe and this is my wife, Jackie, and our best friend, Serena."

Chloe made the rounds and introduced them to every person there. It was overwhelming, but Serena followed their lead. Two people who were in the yard setting up cornhole and ladder toss games waved hello to them.

"Jenga's ready." A cute brunette named Shelly waved them over. Chloe and Jackie, always competitive, jumped at the opportunity. Serena grabbed a longneck from a cooler and waved them off. She found an empty chair nearby and sat to cheer them on. She was too awkward to participate and too nervous to even try. This many people made her uncomfortable, but she was resolved to stay put and make more friends.

"I'm so glad you came." Piper sat next to Serena with Maribelle on her lap.

"Hi, there. I'm Serena."

Maribelle leaned close to Piper but smiled at Serena. Piper whispered in Maribelle's ear.

"Hi." Her tiny voice sounded shy, but happy. Apparently, the meltdown was averted or had happened and she was spent.

"She's being shy tonight. This is Maribelle."

"Hi, Maribelle. Are you enjoying the party?"

"I spilled juice."

"Oh."

Maribelle nodded. "Yeah. All on my shirt. I put a new one on. This is a raccoon." She pointed her little finger to her belly, where a cartoon raccoon was playing hockey.

"Your shirt is better than mine." Serena looked down at her fitted button-down black shirt with the sleeves rolled up. "Mine is boring."

"Hi, Serena. It's good to see you again." Shaylie leaned and kissed her on her cheek. The gesture surprised Serena.

"You, too. I see the wardrobe crisis was averted."

Shaylie wiped her brow. "In the nick of time."

"You have a beautiful home."

"I heard your new house is very nice, too."

"It's amazing how expensive real estate is here in Colorado," Serena said. She'd never get used to the idea that she had money.

Shaylie laughed. "I sell real estate."

"No way. Just in the Denver area?"

She nodded and reached for Maribelle, who crawled over to her lap by way of Serena, who had the seat between them.

"Sorry about that." Piper wiped the bit of dirt Maribelle's shoe left on Serena's dark jeans.

"Oh, don't worry about it." She secretly wanted to hold Maribelle because she was adorable. Serena sighed at the perfect family surrounding her. She wanted this. When she was a teenager and had to take care of Faith every day, she swore she'd never have kids. But now, seeing how supportive and loving Shaylie and Piper were, hope started blossoming inside. Maybe she could have a family. She'd be fierce and love them and never leave them. "My sister is going to move here. I was thinking a nice apartment and not a condo since who knows where she'll end up in the long run."

"I can certainly tell you good ones close to her job. What restaurant?" Shaylie asked.

"Frederick's."

"Nice. We'll have to go there to support her. I can email you a list of some apartments close by that she would probably like."

"That would be so helpful. Her job starts in a few weeks and she hasn't picked a place yet." Serena rolled her eyes and shook her head.

"I wouldn't worry. There are several places that have apartments available at the beginning of the month. Plus if she can't make up her mind, she can stay with us for a few weeks until something opens up."

Serena stared at Shaylie, her mouth dropped open. How were these people so damn nice? It was one thing for people like Chloe and Jackie to offer up their place. They'd known Faith since she was ten. "That's entirely too nice. I can put her up in a hotel for a few weeks."

Piper waved her off. "Nope. We have plenty of space and we're only about fifteen minutes from the restaurant."

Their generosity was too much for Serena. "I'm so glad I met you. Thank you."

"We are, too." Shaylie playfully tickled Maribelle, who squealed for a bit and then relaxed against her. "Since this bug is stuck to me, how about you show Serena how to play cornhole? I noticed she avoided it like the plague at Gabrielle's barbecue."

"Oh, no. I'm so not good at anything athletic." Serena waved them off.

Piper stood next to her. "I'm not taking no for an answer. Come on. You can be my partner."

Serena playfully groaned and stood. "Okay, okay. Just know I'm going to be horrible and you'll regret making me a partner."

"You'll be fine." Piper grabbed the bean bags and handed Serena three. "Get a feel for their weight and just aim for the hole."

"That's so far away."

"From top to top, it's twenty-seven feet. You can throw from the bottom of the board so you only have to throw it about twenty-four feet. That's easy. Go ahead and try one."

Serena looked around to make sure nobody was watching and then tossed the first bag. It hit the very bottom of the board and slid off.

"That's a great first toss. Just give it a little more oomph and make it stick," Piper said.

Serena took a deep breath and threw the second bag. She overshot and cringed in embarrassment. "That was horrible."

Piper laughed and pointed to the other team. "It wasn't bad. Watch this team. They'll be playing for hours."

Serena noticed none of the bean bags were on the boards. They were scattered around. "So this is harder than it looks." She took the last bag and tossed it. It slid up the board but stayed. She gave a little victory dance. "How many points?"

"One. If you hit it in the hole, that's three points. Here, throw these, too." Piper handed her the red bags and she got another point after throwing three. "See? You're good at it."

Serena smiled. "I wouldn't say good, but at least now I'm not embarrassed."

Piper wrangled two others, Meagan and Cheryl, to play a quick game. It was right in the middle of their second game, right as she was celebrating because she sank a bean bag into the hole for a solid three points, that she saw Gabrielle. Her heart kicked up and she held her breath as she watched her step onto the deck and hug two women.

"Serena. Serena, hello?" Cheryl nudged her.

She turned to her and stared at her trying to figure out what was happening. Gabrielle's presence wrecked her. "What? I'm sorry. What did I miss?"

"You're up."

How did she miss an entire round? "What's the score?"

"Your team is still ahead."

Serena was beyond nervous and missed the board completely on her first toss.

"Come on, Serena. You've got this," Piper yelled from the other side of the game.

She nervously looked over at Gabrielle who, at that moment, looked at her. Serena held her breath and stared. Gabrielle looked beautiful. She was wearing a summer dress that hit above her knee and a small front open sweater to ward off the evening chill. Her hair was pulled away from her face in a loose braid, and Serena couldn't take her eyes off her. Gabrielle smiled at her and Serena knew things were good with them. She tamped down a squelch of excitement and tried to focus on the game. The second bag landed on the board for a point, and the third made a loud thud before sliding into the hole. Piper threw her hands up in the air victoriously. She ran over to Serena and hugged her.

"We won! You did it."

Serena and Piper congratulated their opponents and wished the new teams waiting to play good luck. She tried to be casual on her way up to the deck, but the goofy smile on her face was a dead giveaway. She was excited to see Gabrielle.

"Hey, you." Gabrielle leaned over the railing and smiled at Serena.

That smile was still there and Serena couldn't do anything about it. She put her hand up to shade her eyes from the setting sun. "Hi."

"It's good to see you. And Chloe and Jackie." Gabrielle nodded at the Jenga game where they were still playing. "Piper said she invited you. Come on up and talk to me. We can talk about anything but work," Gabrielle said.

Without hesitation, Serena walked into Gabrielle's hug. She smelled like jasmine and vanilla and felt soft in Serena's arms. Although their hug lasted longer than most, Serena didn't care. They'd had quite the week.

"So, you don't want me to go on and on about how much I love the changes you made?" Serena stepped back to look at Gabrielle. She cocked her head to the side and waited.

"Well, if you are going to say great things and there isn't anything you want to change, then I say go on."

Serena placed her hand on Gabrielle's forearm. "It's perfect. I really love it."

"After you left, I sent the files to three builders. I'm sure we'll hear something back by next week."

"What happens to you? Will you get the next big project?"

Gabrielle shrugged. "As of right now, I only have a few projects on my desk."

"Do most clients pay you by the hour or by the project?" Serena asked.

"Hey, I thought we weren't talking about work unless you were going to compliment me over and over again."

"You're right. Have you eaten?"

"No. Do you want to go grab a plate and sit down somewhere a little less crowded?"

Serena nodded and followed Gabrielle into the dining room. The spread ranged from dips to baked goods to cheeseburgers, and different salads. It wasn't that different from Meredith's spread a few weeks ago. "Hey, are those the brownies and cookies from our meeting?"

"Good eye. My assistant likes to overindulge with my credit card. Much to his surprise, I took home the leftovers for the party. I knew I was going to be too busy to pick anything up, so I planned ahead."

"Why was your day so busy? I mean, only if you want to answer. It's not my business," Serena asked. She busied herself by fixing a plate.

"My mom needed my help on a project. Did you know they run a nursery?"

"No. That's really cool."

"They retired early and decided to stay active by running a nursery. I told Rosie that if the Pet Posh Inn went south, I was going to quit designing and help them with the family business," Gabrielle said.

"Oh, stop. It's perfect," Serena said. She was very aware that they were the only ones in the dining room and that Gabrielle was standing close. "But that does give me an idea. Next spring maybe I can give your parents business, because the Pet Posh Inn is going to need massive curb appeal. Pretty flowers, nice shrubs."

"I'm sure they would love it." Gabrielle turned to face Serena. "What would you like to drink? We've got wine, soda, or water."

Serena turned and perused the labels. She wasn't a wine drinker but thought a nice white wine spritzer sounded like it could take the edge off. To say she was nervous with Gabrielle inches away from her was a massive understatement. Her palms were sweaty, her stomach bobbed up and down, and she had no idea how she was going to be able to eat the massive pile of food she'd put on her plate out of sheer nervousness. She watched as Gabrielle poured two wine spritzers.

"Here's to new friends and success to both of us." Gabrielle lifted her glass and clinked it with Serena's.

Serena nodded and took a sip, her eyes never leaving Gabrielle's. She licked her lips when Gabrielle set her glass down, reached for Serena's, and set it next to hers. Without looking around to see who was in the room, she pulled Gabrielle into her arms and kissed her. It was soft for about two seconds, but a need inside Serena bubbled up and she moved closer to Gabrielle and deepened the kiss. Her tongue skimmed over Gabrielle's bottom lip and slipped inside. They both moaned as Gabrielle pulled her closer until their bodies were flush against one another.

"Oh, shit. I'm sorry."

Serena broke the kiss and stepped back at the intrusion, but her hands were still on Gabrielle's waist. She was afraid to lose the connection. It was raw and powerful, and lifted her to a level she never before felt. For the first time in her life, she felt wanted. She felt sexy and desired. "Who was that?"

Gabrielle shook her head. "No clue. And I don't care."

Serena's stomach fluttered at the look in Gabrielle's eyes. She was pretty sure that if they were alone, she'd be pressed up against the wall, her clothes already loose and her hands somewhere on Gabrielle's skin. She had zero reservations. She wanted Gabrielle. She wanted this woman to take control and make love to her, and it didn't matter where they were. Here in this dining room, back at her place, even at Gabrielle's place. Gabrielle slowly walked her back into the kitchen where there was a little bit more privacy.

"We probably shouldn't do this here." Serena's attempt to defuse their passion was feeble.

"Do you want me to stop?" Gabrielle brushed her thumb across Serena's bottom lip.

Serena shook her head. Her voice was low and cracked at the one word she said. "No."

Gabrielle didn't hesitate. She leaned down and kissed her again. That it was even better than the last kiss seemed impossible, but it made Serena's knees weak. Gabrielle interlocked their fingers and slid Serena's hands up over her head. Serena pressed against Gabrielle's body, desperate to feel her warmth and closeness.

"Oops. Sorry again."

Serena peeked around Gabrielle to see Meagan grabbing a bottle of wine.

"If I don't bring this out, they will all come in here and you'll have a larger audience than one." She smiled knowingly and slipped out of the kitchen.

Serena leaned back. "Maybe this isn't the time or place."

"I'm going to say it's definitely the time, but we need to work on the place." Gabrielle stepped away from Serena, but kept holding her hands. "Let's be social for a little bit longer."

Serena wasn't sure what that meant. Would they pick this up later tonight somewhere else? When embarrassment finally seeped in, Serena blushed. Meagan had seen her, seen them, in a very passionate embrace. Something that wasn't meant for other people to see. She picked up her overloaded plate and wine spritzer and followed Gabrielle out to the deck.

"There you are." Chloe waved them over to a table. "Hi, Gabrielle. Nice to see you again."

"You, too. Hi, Jackie."

"How many games of giant Jenga did you play?"

Chloe finished the bite of her cheeseburger before answering. "We were top dogs until Piper and Shaylie dethroned us. They make our competitiveness look tame."

Gabrielle laughed. "Yes, our entire group is full of very, let's say, ambitious women. We don't like to lose."

"I'm not falling prey to any more pretty faces in this crowd. From here on out, you all are the enemy," Chloe said. She dipped her cheeseburger in extra ketchup. "What?"

"Eat like a normal person. We are representing Serena here." Jackie shook her head at Chloe, who shrugged.

Rosie and Anne appeared behind Chloe and Jackie. "Hi, I'm Rosie and this is my wife Anne." Both sat next to Gabrielle after the introductions. "Good to see you again, Serena."

"Where are the kids?" Serena asked.

"We needed adult time," Rosie said. She ate a chip. "And from what I've heard, there have been a few adult moments already." She bumped her elbow against Gabrielle's.

Serena blushed and took a sip of her spritzer. She'd kill for a cold water to ice down her steamy memory from just a few short minutes ago. How did everybody already know? She almost jumped when she felt Gabrielle's hand squeeze her leg. It was a supportive squeeze, not a sexual one, but Gabrielle's hands on her body took her to a different level.

"Who made this dip? It's delicious." Rosie scooped the rest of the dip on her plate with a pita chip and moaned her pleasure.

"Serena did," Chloe said.

Gabrielle turned to her. "So, you do cook."

Serena shook her head. "It took three times to get it right. I can barely follow a recipe."

"It's delicious."

As expected, Chloe and Jackie became fast friends with Rosie and Anne. Gabrielle's friends were more laid back, but Serena figured it was because of the environment. Rosie and Anne knew everyone already. Their conversation attracted two more couples, and eventually their table was the center of attention the rest of the evening. Serena was excited to be a part of something that felt sincere and genuine, but what she really wanted was alone time with Gabrielle. By ten, she was getting antsy. She needed to either go home or figure out what was happening with Gabrielle and stay. She was the kind of girl who never asked or assumed, so she sat there not knowing how to ask for what she wanted.

Gabrielle leaned over. "Who's taking care of L.B.?"

Serena turned to answer. Her lips were only inches away from Gabrielle's. "Faith."

"Is she going to be there all night?"

"I could ask her to." Serena looked down at Gabrielle's mouth and back up to her eyes, which had darkened during their private exchange.

"Would you like to come over?" Gabrielle's voice was low and sexy.

Just the thought of being alone with her was enough to make her want to stand, say her goodbyes, and spend the rest of the night and a good portion of the morning making love to Gabrielle. She wasn't one to take charge, but this newfound confidence was exciting. She nodded. "Definitely."

Gabrielle stood. "Thank you for having us, but we're going to leave."

She reached for Serena's hand and pulled her up.

Serena should have been embarrassed, but she didn't care. Chloe and Jackie had the biggest smiles on their faces, and the squeeze that Piper gave Shaylie didn't go unnoticed.

"Have a good night. I'll talk to you tomorrow," Chloe said.

Serena knew that it was Chloe's way of telling her to call her immediately after her night with Gabrielle. She hugged Piper and Shaylie and thanked them for the invitation.

Gabrielle reached for her hand. "Ready?"

"Definitely."

Chapter Twenty-four

When was the last time Gabrielle had a woman at her loft? It was always clean because she was never there, but she was still nervous when she opened the front door. She wanted to play it cool and offer Serena a drink, but she was tired of getting interrupted at the most inopportune moments. Instead she shut the door and pulled Serena to her. They both knew why they were there, but Gabrielle wanted to do the right thing. "Are you okay with this?" She rubbed her thumb across Serena's bottom lip.

Serena gently pushed Gabrielle's hand away from her mouth and kissed her. Gabrielle moaned when she felt the tip of Serena's tongue stroke her bottom lip and suck the fullness into her mouth. She took that as a yes and pulled her gently to her bedroom. As much as she wanted to rip Serena's clothes off, Gabrielle didn't see Serena as that kind of woman. She was going to take her time and appreciate every inch of bare skin. At the foot of the bed, Gabrielle slowly unbuttoned Serena's shirt and gently peeled it off her shoulders.

"You're so beautiful," she said. Serena's skin was pale, unblemished, and softer than she imagined. She outlined the black lace that rested along the swell of Serena's breasts with her fingertip and smiled to herself as chill bumps exploded along Serena's skin. Serena shivered when Gabrielle's touch moved to the button on her jeans. She sped up the process by stepping closer and searching for the zipper on the back of Gabrielle's dress. By the time Gabrielle's zipper was down, Serena's jeans were already past her hips. Gabrielle wasn't wearing a bra or panties, so when she stepped out of her dress, she was completely and confidently naked. She unbraided her hair and stood in front of Serena.

"You're the beautiful one," Serena said. She looked her up and down and smiled again when their eyes met. "I've been waiting for this night for a very long time."

For the first time ever, Gabrielle didn't want to rush. She felt beautiful and cherished and finally understood why people took their time during sex. She took a step back as Serena slipped out of her jeans. As much as Gabrielle loved seeing Serena in a matching bra and panty set, she wanted her naked so she could feel Serena's skin against hers.

"I have, too." Gabrielle meant it. She'd wanted to have sex with Serena a long time ago. Not wanting to waste another moment, Gabrielle kissed Serena and pulled her slowly onto the bed with her. Her body was on fire, and judging from the blush that tinted Serena's alabaster skin, she knew this moment affected her as well. She slid on top of Serena and started a trail of featherlight kisses that started at her neck and ended when her lips brushed the black lace of her bra. "Can I take this off?"

Serena leaned up with Gabrielle and unhooked it, tossing it off the bed. Gabrielle cupped her breast and ran her tongue across Serena's already hardened nipple. Serena's moans encouraged her to suck harder. When she felt Serena's hands on the back of her head, keeping her in place, she unleashed more of the passion she felt. Serena fell back on the pillow and let Gabrielle take full control of the moment. Gabrielle crawled between her legs until her hips rested against Serena's. She should have pulled Serena's panties off first, but the need to be close to her was so great at that exact moment that she didn't care that a thin strip of material kept their cores from touching. She gently pressed into Serena and kissed her again and again until Serena's hips pressed back, lifting off the mattress for more friction. Gabrielle rewarded her by pushing harder and moving her hips in a circle.

"I need these off." Serena's voice was almost a growl as she pushed at her panties.

Gabrielle brushed Serena's hands away, sat up, and not too gently tugged the soaked panties off. She returned to her position between Serena's legs.

Serena hissed under her breath. "Fuck, yes."

Gabrielle almost smiled, but in the moment, knew exactly what Serena was feeling. She slipped her hand between their bodies until her fingers found Serena's soaked slit. She ran her fingers up and down. Within seconds, Serena's body starting quivering. As much as Gabrielle wanted to give her immediate release, she slowed her movements. She wanted this to last. For the first time in her life, she wasn't racing against a clock to fuck fast and leave. She wanted to build Serena up and wait until the perfect moment for her orgasm to crest. She moved her hand away and planted kisses on Serena's neck, over her extremely sensitive collarbone. Serena moaned and tossed her head side to side. Gabrielle kissed over both breasts and stopped right before she reached her slit. She inhaled the wet scent and moaned her appreciation. Even in the dimly lit room, Gabrielle could see how swollen and wet Serena was.

"Please don't stop." Serena's voice cracked.

"I'm not stopping. I just want to look at you—all of you—for just a moment."

Serena surprised Gabrielle by spreading her legs wider and slipping her hand down to touch herself.

Gabrielle watched in awe for about five seconds before she ran her tongue over Serena's fingers until she allowed Gabrielle to take over. Without hesitation, she opened her mouth and greedily licked and sucked every swollen part. Serena cried out when Gabrielle's tongue flicked across her clit. Gabrielle slipped two fingers deep into Serena's wet pussy and moaned. Serena was slick and tight, and pulsed around her fingers. She wasn't sure if it was an impending orgasm or Serena's rapid heartbeat. Either way, it was sexy as hell and made Gabrielle speed up her movements. Serena clawed at Gabrielle's shoulders, her back, even clutched the sheets as she approached her orgasm.

"Don't come yet." Gabrielle didn't realize she said it out loud until Serena relaxed her body and whimpered. She didn't want this to end. Everything about this moment was perfect and would forever be etched in her mind. The sight of Serena unabashedly naked and spread out for her, the sweet tangy taste of her essence, and the way she gave herself so selflessly. Nobody had ever trusted her this much. She felt the sting of tears in the back of her throat and wondered why she was so emotional. This was the time when she shined and took everything that was offered. Something was squeezing her heart. Some unknown force was swirling inside her, making her doubt everything yet feel so safe. What was happening to her?

Serena touched Gabrielle's face. "Is everything okay? Did I do something wrong?"

Gabrielle placed a soft kiss on Serena's thigh. She could feel small tremors but didn't know if they were coming from her or Serena. She looked up and smiled. "Everything is perfect. It's actually better than that. I've just wanted this for so long that I don't want it to end."

"We have all night. I don't have to go home until tomorrow. I mean, later today. Much later."

Gabrielle watched the quick rise and fall of Serena's chest and decided Serena was right. They had time. She put her hands on the inside of Serena's thighs and spread them far apart. She wasn't gentle, and the appreciative moan told her it was welcomed. She ran her tongue up and down Serena's slit and slipped two fingers back inside. Instead of building her up like before, she kept her movements steady and fast while her tongue lavished Serena's sweet, swollen clit. In virtually no time at all, Serena cried out and came hard against Gabrielle's mouth. Right here, right now was the best moment of Gabrielle's life. There was never any doubt that she would bring Serena to orgasm, but she wasn't ready for such a beautiful release.

"I don't even know what to say right now." Gabrielle rubbed Serena's stomach and watched as she rode out the waves of her climax. When Serena opened her eyes, Gabrielle was taken aback by what she saw. Raw emotion, total release, and something that made her heart swell. She saw love. It was brief and Serena reeled it in once her body relaxed, but Gabrielle saw it. The only part that frightened her was how calm she was about it. She wasn't afraid. For years she'd run from it, and the minute it caught up to her, she didn't have a desire to leave.

Serena gave a half laugh and half moan. "I have no words either."

Gabrielle reached down and pulled the covers over them. She rested her head next to Serena's on the pillow. "I do have words. You're incredible." She kissed Serena's cheek and slid her arm across her waist. As revved up as she was to come, holding Serena felt right.

"So worth the wait." Serena turned so she faced Gabrielle. "But I couldn't have waited any longer."

Gabrielle brought Serena's fingers to her mouth and kissed them. "I know what you mean. I didn't care that we were in Piper and Shaylie's kitchen. I was going to kiss you."

Serena ran her fingertips over Gabrielle's full lips. They were soft and slightly swollen. "You have the best lips. They're full and kissable and magical."

"Magical, huh?" Gabrielle chuckled. She kissed Serena again and slipped between her legs. She slid her arms above her head. "Keep your hands up here."

"They're tired," Serena said. She kissed Gabrielle. "And I want to touch you."

Her pout was adorable. Gabrielle almost let her get her way but at the last second decided she wasn't done with Serena.

"Turn over," Gabrielle said.

Surprise registered on Serena's face. "What?"

Gabrielle repeated herself and sat up. She twirled her finger in a circle. "Turn over."

Serena smiled and did what Gabrielle wanted. "Now what?"

Gabrielle covered Serena's body with her own. She scraped her teeth on the soft muscle that rested between her neck and shoulder. She bit down hard enough for Serena to feel it, appreciate it, but not enough to leave a mark.

"Okay, I approve," Serena said.

Her breathy affirmation made Gabrielle smile. "Yeah? So, this is okay?"

Serena nodded.

"What about this?" Gabrielle spread Serena's legs with hers and pushed her hips into Serena's ass.

Another nod.

"And this?" She reached down between Serena's legs and stroked her swollen folds.

"Oh, God."

The angle wasn't the best, but Gabrielle pushed her thumb inside Serena and stroked her clit with her forefinger.

Serena's moans only fueled Gabrielle's desire to fuck her again and again. When Serena lifted her hips and pushed into Gabrielle's hand, the need to please her was overwhelming. Gabrielle got on her knees and slipped two fingers inside Serena. She was able to go deeper at this angle, but stilled when Serena cried out. Serena pushed back against her hand instead of forward to get away, and she knew it was a cry of ecstasy. She filled Serena with her fingers, marveling at how brazen she was in bed. How much she wanted this, wanted Gabrielle to do this. It was empowering. Nobody had ever been so trusting with her. She kissed Serena's back, moving lower and lower. She pulled out and ran her tongue over Serena's quivering opening. Serena gasped when she slipped her tongue inside her, tasting her. It was a hard angle and Gabrielle wanted her to come again. She stilled Serena's gyrating hips, lay so her mouth was right below Serena's pussy, and not so gently lowered her onto her mouth. It took Serena less than a minute to come again. And a third time. Gabrielle let her go when she felt Serena's legs shake and knew she'd had enough.

"Okay, I'm not complaining at all, but I need a few minutes."

Serena rolled onto her back and reached for Gabrielle's hand. It was a tender gesture, one that made Gabrielle smile with smugness. She considered herself an above average lover, but being with Serena made her feel like she was the best. She pulled Serena into her arms and waited until they both caught their breath.

"Do you need anything? Water? A thicker blanket?" Gabrielle brushed a piece of hair off Serena's cheek.

"No, thanks. I don't want you to go anywhere. I finally got you right where I want you."

Gabrielle gave Serena a little squeeze and glanced at the clock. It was one in the morning and her adrenaline rush was still strong. She was dying to go to the bathroom and grab a water to hydrate, but she understood the need to be there for Serena. When she heard steady breathing and discovered Serena had fallen asleep, she carefully slipped out of her embrace. She gulped an entire bottle of water, smiled at all of the text messages from Rosie, Piper, and Shaylie, and ate a protein bar.

Warm arms draped around Gabrielle's waist. "I can't believe I fell asleep."

She turned in the embrace and placed a soft kiss on Serena's lips. "No worries. Did I wake you?"

Serena rubbed her eyes. "Not really. I am the worst girlfriend for falling asleep." Her eyes widened. "Not that I'm saying I'm your girlfriend. I just meant that—What I mean is—Well, you know."

Gabrielle got a kick out of how embarrassed Serena was. She didn't mind the idea of having a girlfriend. "Don't worry about it. Are you hungry? I can make a quick snack."

Serena averted her eyes. "No, thanks. I ate enough tonight. Can I please have a water?"

Gabrielle pulled one from the refrigerator. "You look good in my T-shirt." She hadn't bothered putting anything on.

"I found it on the chair in your room. I promise I didn't go through your things."

"Whatever you need, you help yourself to it. I mean, what kind of girlfriend would I be if you couldn't go through my closet to find a T-shirt?" Gabrielle playfully wrapped her fist in the shirt and pulled

Serena toward her. She kissed her hard and fast before Serena had a moment to react. It was a kiss that meant everything to both of them. Passionate and promising. And just like that, in the span it took to say those words, Gabrielle committed herself to a relationship for the first time in years.

Chapter Twenty-five

Serena kicked at the curing foundation, surprised at how fast the Pet Posh Inn was moving along. Gabrielle had given her three proposals, and while Trust & Company wasn't the cheapest, their lead time was the fastest. Jake Trust met with Serena and Arnest & Max and promised to have the external plumbing, foundation, and framework completed by the first hard freeze. Gabrielle told her that was pushing it, but Jake had two crews dedicated to the project and he ran a tight ship. His projects were almost always perfect, but perfection came at a cost.

"This is amazing," Serena said. She turned slowly and looked at the framework, trying to see what Gabrielle was explaining.

"The main staircase will be here. The other staircase is on the other end where that guy is standing. I know it's hard to picture it, but everything looks great," Gabrielle said.

Serena didn't like having to maintain the professional aspect of their relationship. She wanted to press into Gabrielle and kiss her and pull up the collar of her jacket as the wind picked up around them. But she respected Gabrielle and agreed to keep their personal and professional relationships separate. Technically, Gabrielle wasn't in charge of the project anymore, but she had thrown Jake a lot of business over the years, so she was always welcome at the sites she had a hand in. "Okay, I trust you. You've done this for a million years now."

Gabrielle took a step closer. "I'm not that old."

Serena melted at Gabrielle's look. She was a sucker for those amber eyes. "You know what I mean."

"Quit looking at me like that. I can't concentrate," Gabrielle said.

"What are you concentrating on?" Serena leaned closer.

"Not having my way with you right here, right now."

"Oh, I'm sure we could go for a walk in the woods or maybe go for a drive," Serena said. The last six weeks had been full of really incredible but sporadic sex. Gabrielle still worked her sixty- to seventy-hour weeks, so time during the week was impossible. She was also gone one weekend for a work retreat. It stung Serena a bit that she wasn't invited, but she had to give Gabrielle space. To be fair, one weekend Serena was also unavailable because she was helping Faith move into her new condo. This past weekend was the first time they were able to spend a weekend uninterrupted, so they'd holed up and ignored all calls and texts from their friends. It was almost perfect. The only thing missing was L.B. Faith had offered to watch him while Serena was in town. Gabrielle said he could stay with them, but Serena didn't feel the offer was sincere.

"Tempting, but L.B. might not like that." Gabrielle pointed to the Jeep where L.B. had his head hanging out the window staring at them.

"I'm sad he can't walk around," Serena said.

"He'll step on a nail or something else just as sharp. That's why we're wearing boots and hard hats. It's too easy to get hurt on job sites."

"I probably should get home anyway. I've been gone too long. Jake asked me to pick out paint colors and schemes, although it seems a bit premature," Serena said.

"This will go up fast. They're trying to get as much done on the outside as they can before it's too cold to work. I bet by the end of the week, they'll have most of the framework done. Then they'll work on drywall and mudding. Then it'll be paint time."

"That's incredible. I really like Jake. His crew is doing an incredible job. Call me later?"

Gabrielle nodded. "I'll call you when I get out of here."

Serena wanted to hug her but refrained. She turned when she got to the Jeep and waved instead. L.B. greeted her with sloppy kisses and hard tail wags.

"Okay, okay. I love you, too. Now get in the back." Serena pointed to the back seat. L.B. jumped back but continued to kiss her from there. Serena laughed at his enthusiasm. "I just petted you twenty minutes ago. And you saw me the entire time I was on the site. Come on. Let's get out of here and hit the park. Pretty soon you'll have a very large place to run and a ton of new friends." Serena secured her seat belt and drove them to town. The new dog park wasn't anything spectacular, but it was appreciated by the dog lovers in Vail. Serena had donated money for the waste disposal stations that were always stocked with bags. She pulled into the parking lot, secured L.B.'s leash, and took him over to the big dog park. There were only a few dogs lumbering about, their noses pressed to the grass, stopping at trees to either mark them or find out who was there before them. "Go be a boy dog," she told L.B. He pranced away and made friends with the other dogs instantly.

"Serena?"

Serena turned and froze. Amber stood in front of her, holding a leash that tethered a small poodle. "Amber. Hi." She didn't know what to say, so she forced a fake smile and clutched L.B.'s leash tighter in her hand.

"Fancy running into you here. How are you?" Amber reached down and picked up her dog. "This is Princess. I've had her about five months now. You can pet her if you want."

Princess was super cute. Serena could never resist the urge to pet a dog regardless of their owner. She tentatively took a step forward. "She's a doll."

"She's very lovable and has been a godsend this summer. You look great."

Serena wondered how long it would take Amber to bring up the lottery, so she kept her answers generic. "Thanks. How was your summer besides becoming a fur mama to this precious girl?" Serena stroked Princess's silky, curly fur and avoided eye contact with Amber.

"It was lonely. I miss you. I went to your place, but Mrs. Rhoads said you moved." She shrugged like she didn't have a clue, but Serena knew she knew everything.

"I moved a few months ago. I finally bought a house."

"Oh? I'd love to see it sometime." Amber flashed Serena her winning smile.

Serena mentally berated herself for falling for somebody like Amber. She was attractive, but her heart was ugly. She used people to get what she wanted, and Serena thanked her lucky stars she got out of the relationship before she won the lottery. Amber was too much like her mother and would have talked her into doing stupid things with her winnings. "I don't think that's a good idea. My girlfriend probably wouldn't like it."

Amber seemed stunned. "You're dating again. Congratulations. Anyone I know?"

"No. She's not from here. She lives in Denver." No way was Serena going to divulge Gabrielle's name or anything about her to this snake of a woman. "Well, have fun with Princess. She really is a sweetheart." Serena turned and walked the length of the chain link fence to where L.B. was playing with a sheepdog named Joe. She cringed when Amber followed her.

"Is that your dog? He's so cute. I remember you wanted to get one, but you always held off." Amber wasn't giving up that easily.

"That's L.B. I got him this spring, too. He's perfect."

"He's super cute."

They stood there in awkward silence. Out of the corner of her eye, she saw Amber looking her over a few times as if finally seeing her, or her designer clothes, for the first time.

"What's different about you?"

"What do you mean?"

"You're just different. For the better, I mean. Confidence looks good on you."

"My life improved. And I have a girlfriend who is good for me."

"Ouch."

"Oh, come on. Our relationship was poisonous. You didn't care about me. You cared that you got attention when you wanted it. How many times did you cheat on me? Three times that I know of. We won't even go into the ones I don't."

Amber placed her hand over her heart in a ridiculously dramatic way. "You were emotionally unavailable all the time. I liked being your girlfriend, but I couldn't get inside you. Inside your heart. You were so worried about Faith and your mother."

There was truth to that, but Serena had backed off after Amber's first affair. It was worse after the second. By the third, Chloe and Jackie intervened. "They're my only family. Of course I'm going to worry about them."

"How's Faith doing? Did she graduate culinary school?"

Serena turned to watch L.B. "Yes." The less Amber knew of her life now, the better everyone was. Faith hated Amber, but Serena chalked it up to siblings and girlfriends not meshing well. Both vied for her attention. Faith got more of it because she needed it more.

"That's good. What about your mom? Is she doing well?"

Serena took a deep breath and reminded herself to relax. Amber was her past and Gabrielle was her future. The days of Amber ruining her spirit were over. "My mom is fine. She moved to California a few months ago."

Amber took a step closer. "A lot of big changes happened in your life."

Serena looked her in the eye and nodded. "I'm pretty happy. I can finally focus on me for a change." She winced when Amber reached out and touched her forearm.

"I can tell you're definitely stronger and you look great. Healthier. And as much as it pains me to say, happier."

Serena smiled for the first time since running into Amber. She knew it was a big step for Amber to admit any kind of fault. Unless it was a different ruse to get closer. "Thank you for saying that." She turned her attention back to the dog park. "Okay, L.B. let's go." She rattled his leash to get his attention. He returned to her, tongue out, his signature sideways gait telling her he was happy and carefree.

"He's very sweet." Amber reached down and scratched behind his ears. "And very lovable."

"He's my true love."

"That probably doesn't make your girlfriend happy to hear. I'm sure she doesn't like coming in second."

Her words had bite because they held an element of truth. "Oh, she's fine with second place." She knew Gabrielle tolerated her dog, but only because her fear prevented her from loving him as much as Serena did. She did try, though, and that was important. It worked with him from time to time. At least that's what she told herself.

They had a weekends-only romance. Serena was bored during the week while Gabrielle worked. It wasn't fair on her part. That was Gabrielle's dream and she had no right to interfere. She frowned as her future flashed before her. She loved having L.B. and couldn't wait for future animals. She'd almost rescued two kittens, Nicole and Waverly, but decided against it. Because of Gabrielle. Even though she knew she had fallen in love with Gabrielle, they were on completely opposite ends of the relationship spectrum. The sex was amazing and everything she could have asked for, but there was a disconnect somewhere.

Amber laughed. "Even as cute as he is, I doubt that."

Serena shrugged. "Listen, it was good seeing you, but we have to get going."

"No time for lunch?" The Amber bottom lip pout was out in full force.

"No time." Serena snapped the leash on L.B. She thought about going to the lawyer's office today. There were a few investments she was considering, plus she had some personal paperwork to discuss, including an ironclad will. She was determined to make sure her mother couldn't touch her money.

When her mother flew back for Faith's graduation party, she'd been cordial and charming until the subject of money came up. Even though Faith was twenty-one, they kept the party dry because of their mother. Serena didn't want to tempt Diane. Nobody questioned it because everyone there knew there were issues. Other than her mother demanding more money and embarrassing the shit out of Paul, the party was a success. Serena had waited until her mother was back in California to give Faith her monetary present. What Faith did with it was up to her.

"I love this park. Do you come here a lot? I heard they're building some type of animal sanctuary not too far from here," Amber said.

Serena studied Amber closely. She wasn't fishing for information. She didn't have a clue that it was the Pet Posh Inn. She corrected her. "If you're talking about the one on Bear Camp Road, it's actually a pet hotel."

"Really? That's pretty cool. I filed the copy and blueprints, but I didn't pay attention to the specifics."

Serena had forgotten Amber worked at the courthouse. Since it was technically under Evans & L.B., LLC, she figured Amber didn't connect the dots. Now that she knew L.B., she might make the connection quicker. "Okay, we're leaving. Have a good day. Nice to meet you, Princess." She patted Amber's dog one last time and headed to the Jeep.

"Serena, wait. Here. Take my business card. I'm working part-time at Vail Vacations. If you and your girlfriend or Faith want to go somewhere, just give me a call. Or call me if you want to hang out." She held her hands up after Serena reluctantly took the card. "Strictly business or friendship. It's nice to see you again."

"Thanks. I'll keep you in mind." Serena slipped the card in her back pocket and walked to her Jeep. She wanted to get as far away from Amber as she possibly could. Not because she was worried about falling for her again, but because she was desperate to put her past behind her, and that included everyone who had ever caused her pain.

❖

"How was the rest of your day?"

Serena couldn't help but smile when Gabrielle called. It was later than she'd hoped, but the new project she was heading up was complex, but well deserved. Her bosses had praised her work on the Pet Posh Inn, so Gabrielle said partnership was looking good.

"It was good. We're picking out paint and watching *Jeopardy*. How was your afternoon?"

"I'm bringing home some work, but it's not too bad."

"Liar." Serena knew when Gabrielle brought home work, it was because something was bothering her. Even though Gabrielle promised no more ridiculously late nights at the office, it didn't stop her from working at home.

"I still have a few months to prove my worth," Gabrielle said.

"You're perfect. Quit stressing."

"The more I think that, the easier it will be for Tom to sneak in under the radar and steal the partnership from me."

Serena admired Gabrielle's confidence. She wasn't cocky, but extremely sure of her decisions. It was sexy. She couldn't wait until the firm made a decision. She wanted her girlfriend more than on the weekends. And with winter approaching, their weekends were already in jeopardy because of snow. Gabrielle's tiny sports car was no match for Colorado snow storms, and Serena with her four wheel drive Jeep would have to drive to Denver more than the even split they had compromised on presently. She didn't want to always leave L.B. behind or with Faith. "If I have to attend the secret 'let's vote for the new partner meeting' to talk about how much I love the design, I will."

Gabrielle chuckled. "You're adorable. It's only for a little while longer."

"How's the hotel? Have you checked lately?"

"With the additional help, Tom did a pretty decent job, but came in over budget and over the time frame. At least that's what I've heard. It will be next fall before they finish construction."

Serena figured most jobs came in over budget. She'd added a few things after the start, but they were all easy fixes. She thought the project would cost about the same as the land, but it was only a fraction of it. Even though she wanted to pay cash for it all, her lawyers recommended financing because the interest rate was lower than what she could earn on investing that money. It didn't really make sense, but they seemed to know what they were doing and she had blindly trusted them so far. "So, why don't they just make you partner?"

"As much as you love the Pet Posh Inn and I do, too, the design is relatively simple. Hotels are more intricate, and you have to remember so much. It's quite a project."

"Okay, I'll drop it for now. I'll tell you what. When you come over this weekend, I will make you forget about work."

"Oh, yeah?"

"How about a nice hot bath, a movie, and a weekend in bed?" Serena was still nervous about sex with Gabrielle. She was very trusting when she gave herself to Gabrielle but wasn't sure that she was doing all the right things to please her. She needed a confidence boost before the weekend. "I'll do all of the cooking or have it delivered."

"Delivery because if we are having a weekend in bed, I'm going to need you in bed, by my side," Gabrielle said.

"Anything you want." As Serena said the words, she knew she meant them. They hadn't spoken of love, but Serena knew that what she felt was more than hope, more than happiness. She felt love and for the first time, knowing how vulnerable it made her feel, wasn't scared of it.

Chapter Twenty-six

Gabrielle opened the door to the bedroom and smiled when she saw flickering candlelight and a bottle of wine with two glasses on the nightstand. "Ooh, what's going on here?"

Serena wrapped her arms around Gabrielle from behind. "I wanted to do something special for you."

Gabrielle turned in her arms. "Thank you. I love it." She kissed Serena, who pressed her body against her so completely, so trustingly, it made Gabrielle feel vulnerable and empowered at the same time.

"Have a seat. I'll be right out." Serena pointed to the bed and closed the bedroom door so L.B. wouldn't venture in, then went into the bathroom.

Gabrielle quickly peeled off her clothes and slipped into a robe that hung on a hook in the closet. She quickly sat back down when she heard the doorknob twist open. "Wow." Serena walked into the bedroom wearing the sexiest, silkiest, shortest nightgown she'd ever seen. Gabrielle didn't breathe until Serena straddled her lap.

"You weren't supposed to move from this spot." She barely brushed her lips against Gabrielle's mouth.

"I wanted to make it easier for both of us," Gabrielle said. She slid her hands up Serena's bare thighs and gently pulled her closer. She squeezed Serena's ass until she squirmed and moaned. Serena flicked her tongue over Gabrielle's lips and leaned back when she tried to deepen the kiss. "You're teasing me."

"That's the point," Serena said.

"You have about five minutes to do what you want before I take over." Since committing to this relationship, Gabrielle couldn't help but want to take control during sex. She wanted to please Serena all of the time, never worrying about her own gratification. She smiled when

Serena slid off her lap and knelt at the side of the bed. She untied the robe and lay back on the mattress. Serena pushed the robe away from Gabrielle's body and nudged her legs apart. Pleasure rippled across Gabrielle and settled in her core at Serena's touch. "Okay, maybe more than five minutes."

"I'm going to take as long as I want," Serena said.

Gabrielle's retort fell away the second Serena ran her tongue along the inside of her thigh, over her already wet pussy, and back down the other thigh. Gabrielle frowned when Serena's warm mouth left her body, and squirmed until she felt her warm breath caress her wet pussy. "Yes, oh yes." When Serena slowly massaged the swollen clit with her tongue, Gabrielle almost came on the spot. She hissed out a sharp breath and tried to pulled away. She didn't want to come this fast. Serena held her hips down.

"Where are you going?"

"I'm going to come too fast this way."

"You can come more than once. I know this about you."

Gabrielle relaxed and gave a pained laugh. Once she felt Serena enter her she gasped and moaned and lifted her hips to meet each thrust until Serena drilled her and she couldn't keep the pace. She braced her legs against the mattress and came hard and fast. "Oh, my God," she repeated over and over. Serena didn't stop. She slid another finger inside, stretching Gabrielle. Gabrielle had never felt anything so incredible before. She had used dildos that had more girth than Serena's fingers, but there was something so sexy about the fact that it was her girlfriend who was fucking her, who was inside her. "I can't tell you how good that feels."

"Oh, I know," Serena said.

"Oh, God." Gabrielle relaxed as Serena moved deeper. When she felt Serena's mouth on her clit, she cried out. It was too much pleasure to handle. Her entire body shook as the orgasm made its way from her core to every other part of her body. It was the most explosive one she'd ever had. Something happened. Something shifted inside her heart. Walls that she had unknowingly built started crumbling. She was overwhelmed and she didn't know if she should hide her emotions or embrace them. With Serena right there with her, she wasn't scared, though. "You're amazing. I hope you know that. If you don't, I'm going to tell you every single day."

"I want you to always feel as special as you make me feel," Serena said.

Gabrielle placed a small kiss on Serena's temple. "I do. I really do."

❖

"Is this the Amber who broke your heart? Why do you still have her business card?"

Gabrielle wasn't snooping. She was in the bedroom waiting for Serena to finish getting ready and wasn't going to leave the room with L.B. loose. She wandered aimlessly around the room, and the red business card on the dresser caught her eye.

"I ran into her the other day at the dog park."

"Oh." Was the sharp tug in Gabrielle's chest jealousy? It wasn't as if she knew Amber, but she knew what Amber did to Serena.

"It was nothing. I had to take her card because she wouldn't leave me alone until I did."

Gabrielle watched Serena for guilty body language, but there was nothing. It was as if Amber had never hurt her. Serena seemed unaffected by everything.

"Okay."

"She got a cute little poodle. That's how we ran into one another." Serena slipped on a bracelet and fluffed her hair in the mirror by the dresser. "I'm ready." She turned around to walk into Gabrielle's arms. "Are you ready?"

Gabrielle rested her hands on Serena's waist. She looked into her eyes and saw only happiness, no guilt, no deceit.

"You know, I could have driven to Denver last night instead of you coming here. Since the party is there, it just would have made more sense for me to visit you this weekend."

"But I know you don't like leaving L.B. alone every other weekend, and it's not fair to ask," Gabrielle said.

"Trust me, Chloe and Jackie love dog-sitting him." Gabrielle saw the quick flash of sadness on Serena's face before she replaced it with a smile. "Let me go round him up and we can take him to visit his aunts."

Gabrielle stopped her. "Hold on. We don't have to go to this party. We can hang out here like you planned."

"No. You need to be there to show that you're partnership-worthy. Plus, I want to see the people you work with and see what all the fuss is about with Tom."

Gabrielle had been so engrossed with her projects that she almost forgot about the end of the fiscal year party. It wasn't a big to-do, but it was an afternoon affair at Lawrence's very large house. She broke the news to Serena Thursday when the mass company email reminder pinged in her in-box. Gabrielle loathed going because she always felt like an outsider, but every year she pasted on a smile and joked with all of them whether she wanted to or not. Being so busy at work and spending her spare time with Serena made her forget other things, like this massive party.

"You look wonderful." Having Serena with her was either going to make or break her career. People would recognize her as a client, but she wasn't sure if they would appreciate her as Gabrielle's girlfriend. And honestly, she wasn't sure she was ready to reveal that part.

"Then let's go." Serena opened the bedroom door and almost tripped over L.B. She squatted and rubbed his ears. "I'm so sorry, buddy. Are you ready to go see Auntie Chloe and Auntie Jackie?" He rolled over and offered up his belly. She gave him a few rubs and pointed at the stairs. "Let's go."

Gabrielle took a step back when L.B. rolled up quickly and raced ahead of them. Serena reached back and grabbed her hand. "He's too excited to pay you any attention right now. Come on. We'll drop him off and go be social for the afternoon."

❖

"Wow. Apparently, you don't have to win the lottery to live well. So, this is what's it's like to be a partner?"

Gabrielle smiled at Serena's reaction to Lawrence's house. It was rather impressive, but Lawrence also came from money, so he was already wealthy when he helped start Arnest & Max. "Not really. I mean, the money is good, but not this good. Lawrence was born this way." She gave her keys to the valet service. "Shall we?"

Serena nodded nervously.

As luck would have it, Tom was the first person they met walking in. "Gabrielle. So nice to see you. Who's your plus one?" Tom took a sip of his drink and smiled at them. She could tell it wasn't water by the hint of alcohol on his breath and his completely relaxed body language. This was not his first drink of the day.

"This is Serena Evans. I designed the Pet Posh Inn for her," Gabrielle said. "Serena, this is Tom Gehrhart."

Serena shook his hand. He held on to it a little longer than normal. "I heard your project was a success. Congrats to both of you," he said.

"I love it. Gabrielle gave me everything I wanted. It'll be such a gorgeous place."

Tom tipped his glass at Gabrielle. "I can't wait to see it when it's completed."

"Thanks, Tom. We're going to mingle for a bit. Make an appearance. How's the temperature?"

"Surprisingly okay. Nobody's drunk yet. Everyone's behaving."

"Okay, have fun." Gabrielle put her hand on the small of Serena's back and guided her away from almost drunk Tom. She leaned over and whispered in Serena's ear. "One down, about fifty more to go. Plus, a bunch of new people I don't even know."

Serena took a deep breath. "It's okay. I can be social for one day as long as it helps you."

Gabrielle kissed her cheek. "You're wonderful. Come on. Looks like most of the people are outside. I can't believe the weather is so cooperative." She opened the door to the outside, where people mingled in small groups over high top tables and near heaters that burned low.

"This place is gorgeous. Remind me to order a few of those heaters. Then we can have after-dinner drinks outside," Serena said.

"Gabrielle. Serena. Hi." Christopher was there with his wife, Jenna. He took the initiative and made the introductions. Gabrielle had always liked Jenna. She was reserved, but friendly. They had two children who Gabrielle had only met once, but she had seen them grow up from the photos in Christopher's office. Their son was a football player at University of Colorado, and their daughter was a junior in high school.

"I heard that Gabrielle designed quite the place for animals," Jenna said.

"Yes, the Pet Posh Inn. It's perfect. A lot of people visit Vail, and I want to give them a place where their pets can have just as much fun on vacation as they're having. Plus it will be great for locals who feel guilty for going on vacation and leaving their fur babies," Serena said.

"It's a great idea. I know there are doggie daycares around, but from what Christopher was telling me, this goes beyond what they offer."

"Posh," Gabrielle said. Everyone laughed. "And it accommodates more than just dogs. The cat section is phenomenal. There's even a

small animal room for ferrets, rabbits, and anything else the wealthy like to have as pets."
Christopher leaned in and whispered to their foursome. "Mrs. Anderson has chinchillas, and she hates to leave them when they go on vacation. Chinchillas."
"She only has chinchillas because she wants a fur coat," Gabrielle said.
The group laughed even though Gabrielle instantly regretted saying it. Lawrence's wife was over the top on everything. She didn't care if it was socially acceptable if she wore fur coats or flashed tens of thousands of dollars' worth of jewelry when attending low income housing assistance meetings for one of Arnest & Max's charity programs.
"We should probably mingle," Gabrielle said.
"Good idea. The sooner everyone sees us, the sooner we can take our leave." Christopher and Jenna grabbed their drinks and wandered off to the next table.
"I think your boss is nice. He obviously respects you."
Gabrielle liked how delicately Serena held a wine glass. Like it could slip out of her fingers at any time, but never did. The slim bracelet she'd slipped on before they left her house had settled halfway down her arm. The tiny paw print charm rested against the soft skin that Gabrielle enjoyed kissing. "I like him because he's fair. He's not always overly friendly at work, but it's probably better this way. I think we all respect him more because of it."
"How many partners are there at the firm?"
"There are eight partners. Tons of associates. Seems like a lot, right? I think the firm has approximately a hundred employees."
"Is Denver your only location?" Serena asked.
Gabrielle's eyes traveled back to the charm that dangled as Serena sipped her wine. "No. We have offices in San Francisco, Albuquerque, Las Vegas, and Kansas City."
"So, if you make partner, will you stay here? Or would they expect you to move?"
The concern on Serena's face was precious. Gabrielle wanted to reach out, touch her cheek and kiss her. "No, babe. I'll stay here. Denver is my home."
The crushed look didn't go unnoticed. That probably wasn't the best thing to say, Gabrielle thought. To Serena, that just meant their

relationship would be long distance forever. "I'm going to go to the bathroom and then find something else to drink. Will you be okay for a few minutes?"

Serena nodded. "I'll be fine." She placed her hand on Gabrielle's and squeezed. Gabrielle squeezed back.

"See you in a bit, then."

Gabrielle weaved her way through several small groups of people, stopping only long enough to say hello. She found the restroom, then worked her way over to the kitchen to find something non-alcoholic and very cold to drink. When she walked in, she nearly ran into Lawrence Anderson.

"Mr. Anderson, great party as always." Gabrielle held her breath for a moment.

"Gabrielle. So glad you could make it. This is always my favorite party of the year."

She smiled, knowing it was because he was celebrating making even more money. Their office was killing it, but the Kansas City office was experiencing growing pains. The kind all businesses wanted. "It's been a very good year for the firm."

"You've done some outstanding work. Your last project was quite impressive. I heard the client was a bit difficult, though."

Gabrielle stifled the urge to wipe the rich, smug look off his face. She blinked several times before answering him. "Thank you, and she wasn't too bad. She's actually here today."

"That's great. Maybe we can do more projects for her. She's the big lottery winner, isn't she? That means she has money to spend."

"Oh, I don't know. This project is probably a one and done." For the first time, Gabrielle was offended by what he said. Before she'd have joined in and even thought the same way, but meeting Serena had changed so much inside her. She refrained from standing up to him, though. She still needed her job, needed the money, and was desperate to make partner.

"Well, it will be good to see her again. Have a good time."

He took his tumbler of scotch and left the kitchen. Gabrielle found a bottle of water and took a long pull followed by a deep breath. The last twenty-four hours had been pretty emotional. She had a few of her walls knocked down and wasn't sure how to process. She wasn't a crier. Hell, she wasn't even an emotional person, something her mother often pointed out.

"Well, I'm sure happy to see a familiar face."

Gabrielle turned to find Dani standing behind her, her hip pressed against the countertop, a glass of wine that had maybe one more sip left dangling from her hand.

"Dani. Hi. What are you doing here?"

She shrugged and took a few steps toward her. "Apparently our firm now represents yours. That means I'm going to see a lot of you."

"Now we know a little bit more about each other." Gabrielle watched as Dani moved closer. She looked around the room and found they were the only ones there. When Dani put her hands on the counter on either side of Gabrielle's hips, she grew uncomfortable. "This shouldn't happen here." Gabrielle inwardly groaned when she said the word "here." It was a hopeful word that didn't need to be said. That shouldn't have been said.

Dani quirked her eyebrow. "Well, this is a mansion and I'm pretty sure there are rooms galore. We can just find an empty one. From what I remember, it doesn't take either of us long." She ran her fingertip along Gabrielle's jawbone and tapped her lips. "Oh, yes. I remember these sexy lips. All over my body."

"What's going on?"

Gabrielle didn't have to look to know Serena had entered the kitchen.

Dani slowly turned. "Serena Evans. How delightful to see you," she said.

"Ms. Grant?" Serena asked. Gabrielle sneaked a peek over Dani's shoulder. Serena looked very upset. How did she know Dani?

"What brings you to the party?" Dani asked.

"Gabrielle is my—" She paused when Gabrielle didn't answer. "She's my architect. How do you know Gabrielle?"

Dani turned to face Gabrielle. "Oh, we're old friends." She didn't look back at Serena but kept her focus on Gabrielle's face. Gabrielle refused to give any kind of reaction. She was too stunned.

"You look like more than friends right now."

"Sometimes we like to play at the gym. You know, work off steam and tension from our jobs." Dani ran her fingertip along Gabrielle's neck.

Gabrielle leaned back to let her know she wasn't interested. She was in a sticky predicament. She didn't want to be rude to Dani since she wasn't doing anything wrong, but she didn't want to upset Serena either. "A few things have changed."

"Since last month?" Dani asked.

Serena gasped and Gabrielle shook her head. "I'm with Serena now."

Dani turned to Serena. "I had no idea. Well, congratulations, then. You have yourself quite the woman." She casually poured herself another glass of wine, smiled at both of them, and walked out of the room.

"What the hell, Gabrielle?"

Gabrielle walked to Serena and put her hands on Serena's upper arms. "Look, she meant nothing to me at all. What happened was just two consenting adults blowing off steam." The crushed look on Serena's face made Gabrielle's guilt pound inside her. The foreign ache in her heart migrated up to her head. This was not going to end well.

"When was the last time you blew off steam with her?" Serena used air quote marks to emphasize Gabrielle's words.

"I don't remember exactly." That was true. She could have tried harder to remember, but deep down she knew their relationship lines crossed.

"Was it when we were seeing one another?"

Gabrielle could barely look Serena in the eye, but knew she had to come clean. "Sort of, but I stopped her. I told her I was seeing someone."

"Was this before or after she fucked you?" Serena asked.

Gabrielle knew Serena was trying very hard to keep it together. "She didn't fuck me. She sneaked into my shower at the gym, but I asked her to leave. Nothing really happened."

Serena swallowed several times, blinked back tears, and balled her hands into fists. "Oh, nothing really happened, huh? Why did she feel really comfortable touching you at your boss's house when anyone could see? You know, like your girlfriend?"

"Please keep your voice down."

"You don't get to tell me what to do."

"Let's talk about this somewhere more private."

Serena broke free from Gabrielle's grasp. "Find your own way home."

Chapter Twenty-seven

How Serena made it home was a mystery to her. She remembered getting into the Jeep and driving away, Gabrielle fading into a dot in her rearview mirror. But the drive from Denver to Vail was a blur. When she pulled into her driveway, she remembered that L.B. was with Chloe and Jackie. The one thing who loved her unconditionally, who would have made her feel better and curled up with her as she cried out her sorrows, wasn't even there. She smacked the steering wheel in anger but decided she wasn't in the best frame of mind to drive to pick him up.

Can you bring L.B. over? I'm home but I don't think I should be driving.

She shot the text off to Chloe and slowly slipped out of the Jeep. Every step felt heavy, every breath she took seemed labored. It didn't feel like this when Amber cheated on her. She'd felt betrayed before, but the pain wasn't soul crushing. She answered her phone when it became obvious Chloe wasn't going to stop calling. "Hi."

"I'll load up L.B. and we'll be right over."

"Thanks."

She turned off her phone and sat numbly on the couch. She knew it was too good to be true. Or maybe she was just the kind of person that people cheated on. Like her mother. Fuck. When did she turn into her mother? That made her cry harder. She wiped her tears away when she heard a car door shut and the beep of the alarm turning off. She didn't even remember setting the alarm. L.B. raced to her. He jumped on the couch and kissed her all over her face. It was hard not to smile at his happiness at seeing her and being home.

Chloe sat next to her. "Are you going to tell me what happened?"

Serena took a deep breath. Her voice was shaky. "I've turned into my mother."

"First of all, no, that's impossible. And secondly, what the hell happened?" She held Serena's hand, giving it a supportive squeeze.

"So, we had this work party to go to, right?"

"Right."

"And Gabrielle excused herself to go to the bathroom and get something else to drink. Well, she was gone forever, so I decided to find her. I felt weird just standing there by myself."

"Okay." Chloe nodded.

"I go into the kitchen and guess who's there and is all over Gabrielle?"

"I have absolutely no idea. Amber?"

"No, but there's a story there, too. Remind me to tell you about that."

"Christ. Okay. Back to the kitchen. Who was all over Gabrielle?"

"My lawyer."

Chloe blinked. "Which one?"

"Ms. Grant. The hot one. Apparently, they had a thing."

"So?"

"While we were dating." Serena's voice caught in the stage right before breaking into sobs and getting louder out of anger. She felt the gentle squeeze of Chloe anchoring her.

"Like when you first started dating or like after you slept together or when?"

"I don't know for sure, but Dani said something about last month." Serena blew her nose.

"Let's do the math. You kissed when? Or had sex when? Did you talk about being exclusive at all?"

"No, but if I have sex with someone, I sure as hell don't want her to sleep with other people."

"Take a deep breath," Chloe said. She rubbed Serena's back until her breathing returned to normal. "Chances are, it happened before you slept together. I just don't see Gabrielle as the kind of woman who would do something so callous."

"She admitted it, though. She said Dani joined her in the shower at the gym, but she kicked her out. She said nothing really happened. Not 'nothing happened,' but 'nothing really happened.' That plus two naked people in a shower equals cheating."

"You owe it to yourself to hear her side of the story. And you owe it to you as well. A relationship isn't easy. It takes a lot of effort. Not to change the subject, but why is her car here?"

"We took my Jeep to Denver because it's supposed to rain later tonight and she knows I don't like to ride in her matchbox death trap of a car when it rains." Serena stroked L.B.'s ears and ran her hand over his wiry hair. He really relaxed her. "Thank you for bringing him home. I need him so much." Serena hugged him until he grunted. They sat there in silence. She was happy it was just Chloe. She loved Jackie, but she had the kind of relationship with Chloe where silence spoke volumes. It was comforting. Neither one needed to talk. Chloe never pressed her beyond speaking her mind. She always gave her time to mull over whatever they talked about.

"Do you want me to fix dinner?"

The thought of food made Serena's stomach lurch. She shook her head.

"How about some soup?"

Knowing that Chloe was probably hungry, Serena agreed to something simple. "Okay."

Chloe got off the couch and dug around in the kitchen, yelling out possibilities.

"Just fix whatever you want. I'll eat whatever."

When lights turned into the driveway, Serena sat up. Very few people knew the code to her new gate. Faith, Chloe, Jackie, and Gabrielle. Faith was working, Chloe was in the kitchen, Jackie didn't drive a minivan, so it had to be Gabrielle. L.B. raced to the door and happily barked. Serena looked at Chloe, who stood frozen in the kitchen doorway.

"I can leave if you want me to," she said.

"No, Gabrielle won't be here long."

She waited for Gabrielle to get out of the car and approach the door. Their eyes met through the side window that was as tall as the door, but only a foot wide.

Gabrielle looked determined. "Let me in, Serena. We need to talk about this."

Serena shook her head. "No."

Gabrielle crossed her arms in front of her chest. Her weight shifted to one hip. "If you don't want to talk about it right now, I can come back tomorrow when things cool down, but we are going to talk about it."

"I don't know that I want to talk about it then either."

"I made a mistake, but it's not what you think. I really wish you would listen to my side of the story," Gabrielle said.

"There is nothing you can say that's going to make me be okay with what you did." Serena's heart twitched in her chest. She was so used to just shutting down and walking away, but that way of life was getting old. She recognized that she was angry, but deep down she didn't want to lose Gabrielle. Her ego was taking a stance and wouldn't allow her to accept things so easily like her mother did, but her heart pulled her toward Gabrielle.

"I need my keys. Can I at least get them? They're on the island in the kitchen."

Chloe greeted Serena halfway through the living room with a key fob. "Is this it? I can give it to her if you want."

Right now she wanted to be mad. "If you don't mind." She headed into the kitchen, not wanting to see the exchange between Chloe and Gabrielle. The three minutes she waited for Chloe to return felt like a lifetime. She stirred the soup that Chloe had put on the stove, opened and closed the refrigerator a dozen times, and gave L.B. more dog biscuits than she ever did in a single day. She opened the door to let him out into the backyard.

"She's gone."

Serena's heart crashed inside her chest. She swallowed hard to extinguish the angry flames of betrayal. "Good. I'm glad."

Chloe remained quiet and resumed her duty as chef. She placed two bowls of steaming potato soup on the table, and a plate of crackers and cheese that she quickly cut while the soup cooled. "If you can't eat the soup, at least eat a few crackers. That'll help your stomach."

"So, did she say anything?"

"Yes, she did."

Serena waited for Chloe to elaborate. "And? What did she say?" She pressed after it was apparent that Chloe wasn't going to divulge the conversation.

"I really think you need to talk to her. I think you're making a mistake." She held her hands up when Serena started getting worked up again. "We know she made a mistake and she acknowledged it right away. She said it took place after the first date you had. She stopped it because she wanted something real with you."

"She's had several hours to come up with a lie."

"I don't think she was lying. She's not that good a liar. She knows it wasn't the ideal situation to be in, but she made a choice. She committed herself to you in that moment. I want you to listen to me closely right now. You know I love you, right?"

Serena put her spoon down and looked at Chloe. She knew something heavy was coming. Chloe didn't bring up the word "love" lightly. Not with her. Not with the way she was raised. "I know you do."

"How many relationships have you had in your life? Adult relationships? I've known you ten years. In that time, you dated two women more than a handful of times. I'm not being mean, but your experiences haven't been the best."

"I don't think my history has anything to do with this."

"See? Now that's where you're wrong. You have to communicate. I know you think Jackie and I are perfect, which we are, but we talk about everything. You had one date. She kissed your cheek. It didn't solidify a relationship. It just meant you both were interested."

"But why did she even try to hook up with her? That's what I don't understand."

Chloe reached out and held Serena's hand. "She didn't. You would know that if you talked to her, but you ran away. And she tried again here."

"I just can't deal with my girlfriend and my lawyer hooking up."

Chloe threw up her hands. "Then pick one and get rid of the other, but make damn sure you make the right choice."

❖

The framework was done and Jake Trust's workers were working on finishing the first floor. The second-story skeleton frame was too open for Serena to visualize it. She didn't understand how Gabrielle could see past the Tinker Toy outline. She sighed. Gabrielle. It had been a month since she talked to her. Gabrielle had called and texted several times, but Serena ignored her every time. She kept her texts to Piper vague even though Piper tried hard to open up a line of communication. She avoided their fall party because she knew Gabrielle would be there. Not only had she lost Gabrielle, she'd lost all of the wonderful people she met through her.

"I love how fast this is moving." Faith ran her hand along one of the large wooden pillars on the inside of the Pet Posh Inn.

"Yeah, it's pretty amazing." Serena snapped back to reality and looked at the progress.

"Poor L.B. Stuck in the Jeep. He wants to be a part of this so bad," Faith said.

Serena dug her hands deeper into her pockets and looked back at the Jeep. L.B. was staring at them, his nose pressed flat against the window. She loved him so much.

Fall was here and even though they were wearing thick jackets, the morning air whipped around the mountain, taking her breath away. She turned her head from the wind.

"I want to wait until they're done with construction before I let him loose. Too many nails, and I don't want him to step on anything that will hurt him."

"He'll know this place as home away from home soon. When is opening day again?"

Serena shrugged. "May first, but Gabrielle warned me that it could be pushed out because of weather."

"It looks like they could get everything done before Christmas."

"Jake Trust told me they would wait to put the fencing up last, and they can't do that until the ground thaws."

"That sucks. I was hoping to decorate for the holidays," Faith said. She walked to one of the window frames and looked out. "And why don't they have the windows in? It would be a lot warmer for the workers."

"That's the last thing they'll do in case they break them. I'm sure they also do it so people don't come up here to vandalize the building." Even though there was a chain link fence and plenty of cameras around the construction, Serena had been warned that people still did dumb things.

"I love everything about it. I love the cat section the most. I mean, once it's all put together, I'm sure it will all be amazing."

"Thanks. Come on. Let's get out of here before L.B. has a coronary." Serena took one last look around. It was coming together. Her big dream was finally shaping up. It was too bad that the one person who appreciated everything that went into it wasn't here to see how happy she was with it. She just wasn't sure whose fault that was anymore.

Chapter Twenty-eight

"Look, everyone. It's our long-lost daughter, Gabrielle." Meredith made a big production when Gabrielle walked into the house.

"I know, I know. It's been a long time." Gabrielle walked into her mother's embrace and, much to her chagrin, started crying. She felt her mother wave her hands and heard the rest of her family scatter.

"It's okay." Meredith stroked Gabrielle's hair.

"I don't know why I'm crying." She pulled back and let her mom wipe away her tears.

"You have a lot going on with work and all the things in your heart." Meredith tugged Gabrielle over to the kitchen and sat her in a chair. "The good news is that Arnest & Max will hopefully come to a decision soon. With all of your new projects, I can't imagine you won't get it, but I'm worried about you."

Gabrielle teared up again. "I'm just so sad."

"Love hurts. And I wish you weren't going through this. I hope Serena gives you a second chance."

Gabrielle looked up at her mom after a few moments of resting her head on the kitchen table. "I wish she would, too."

"You know her upbringing was hard. She told you she knew how to shut down because her mother always left them. Is there anything you can do to let her know you care? Honey, have you even told her that you love her?" Meredith let go of Gabrielle's hand long enough to pour them both a cup of coffee.

"Thanks." Gabrielle immediately wrapped her hands around the steaming mug. Home was comfort, and she needed comfort now more than anything. "And no, I never told her because I haven't been in love in a long time. I barely know what it's like."

Meredith reached over and cupped Gabrielle's chin. "I always knew that once it happened to you, really sank in, it was either going to destroy you or complete you. I didn't think it would do both."

"This is horrible, Mom. I'm so happy you found Dad so early in life and made it work."

Meredith laughed and leaned back in her chair. "Do you really think I've never had a broken heart?"

"You married Dad when you were in college. How many guys did you date before him?"

"You know what first loves are like. Your father wasn't my first."

Gabrielle groaned and put her head back down on the table. "No. I can't possibly hear this right now. It's always been the fairy tale with you both. You met in Political Science 101 your freshman year and fell in love immediately. That's the story."

"All of that is true, but my first love happened when I was a junior in high school. His name was Scott Mayfield. He was a tennis player and the perfect boyfriend. Very sweet, very smart. We were going to change the world together." Meredith looked off in the distance.

Gabrielle saw a flash of sadness and a frown that pinched the corners of her mother's usually upturned mouth. She squeezed her mother's hand. "What happened to him?"

"He and his father died in a plane crash. A small twin engine plane. I always hated when they went up. His father wasn't the best flyer. Did it as a hobby, but Scott wanted to learn and his father wanted him to be the best at everything."

"That is the worst story ever. I'm so sorry." She sat there quietly giving her mother time to fall back into her memories.

"It really destroyed me. He was the kind of guy who you just knew was going to be great. At everything," Meredith said.

"I'm sure he was great, Mom. You've always been an excellent judge of character." She squeezed her mom's hands. "I love Dad and the life you've given me, but I'm sorry you had so much pain so early in your life."

Meredith gave a slight shrug and looked at Gabrielle. "This is why you should never take any relationship for granted. Don't let Serena forget you. You have to fight for her. Yes, she's upset, and to a certain degree, deservedly so, but life is too precious and love is too scarce to just walk away from it. If Serena is who you're meant to be with, then fight for her. With everything you have. And if she still rejects you, then know that you did everything possible. Then you make peace with her in your heart. You can't make people love you, but you sure as hell can fight for it when there's hope."

"Mom, I don't know if there's even hope."

"Gabrielle Samantha Barnes. You're not a quitter, and I've never seen you fold so quickly. Relationships take effort. What can you do to make Serena believe you? What is the one thing that you have with her that will make her believe in you again?"

Shaking her head, she finally looked up at Meredith. "I don't know. I've been racking my brain trying to figure out a way to reach her. Her walls are fortified with steel rebar and barbed wire."

"You got through before. I have a feeling your relationship isn't over. You just need to find one another again."

Gabrielle never felt so alone before. Throwing herself into work only made her feel worse. When everyone left for the day, she was alone with her thoughts. Ninety-nine percent of them were about Serena. The one percent was over the partnership. How ridiculous it all seemed. Working so hard for a job that she didn't love. The design work she enjoyed, but the politics that went on behind closed doors wasn't who she really was. Did she really want to schmooze, wine and dine, and flirt to get business? Before she would have considered that part of the job, but now she just wanted a life. The life where she still worked too much, but freed up her weekends and spent time with a beautiful and smart and loving woman who looked at her like she was her everything. She sat up straight. "I have an idea. Thank you for this talk. It really helped."

Meredith sat up straighter, too. "Well now you have to tell me."

"I will, but let me work out some things first. I'll let you know if it works."

"That's my girl." She leaned over and kissed her temple. "Now that we have that solved, are we ready to plan Thanksgiving? Because I'm sure the people huddled downstairs are waiting to get started."

"Can you give me a minute? I need to regain some composure."

"Let's finish our coffee. I rarely get alone time with you."

Gabrielle smiled for the first time in weeks. "Too many sons."

"I love you all equally, but my fondness and love for my daughter is different."

"I'm thankful we're close. You get me. I'm just sad not everybody has a relationship like we do." She gave her mother a long hug before yelling down that it was safe. Everyone cautiously entered the living room, giving Gabrielle a wide berth. "Stop it. I'm fine. I'm sorry I lost it back there. Let's talk about Thanksgiving."

Gabrielle stayed at her parents' house until after the evening news. She missed hanging out and being a part of something bigger than herself. She missed her family. After knowing Serena and Faith's struggles, she'd tried a little harder. Well, not in the last month. Staying busy was the way to survive. She was tired of her family and friends asking about Serena and having to explain what happened. She wasn't proud that she'd slept with Serena's lawyer, but she wasn't going to lie about it either. Rosie took the news the hardest. She told Gabrielle everything she needed to hear and things she didn't want to. Hopefully, her idea to win Serena back would erase the last few weeks of Rosie's attitude and the tension between them, as well as her own sadness that only one woman could erase.

❖

"Are you sure you want to do this? I mean, I'm all for it, but you need to make sure because that kind of commitment is forever, and I know how you are," Rosie said.

"Can you just be excited for me? Support me like a true best friend?" Gabrielle needed Rosie now more than anything. She didn't need scolding or reminding that her decisions in the past weren't always the best.

"Definitely. Of course. I'll even drive you there and help you pick it out. You want to make sure you get something that fits. Something she's going to love."

Gabrielle took a deep breath. "I'm finally ready to do this. I never thought I would be."

Rosie grabbed Gabrielle's hands. "I know you're ready."

"Without a doubt. Let's do this."

Rosie squeezed Gabrielle's hands and grabbed her keys. "I'm driving, though."

"Oh, fuck. Go slow. I'm already nauseous."

Chapter Twenty-nine

The stillness after a fresh snowfall was when Serena was at peace with herself and the world. It was Sunday morning and traffic around Vail was minimal. Sleep was fleeting, and after tossing and turning in bed for an hour, she finally gave up, showered, and decided to check on the progress of the Pet Posh Inn. Jake Trust gave her weekly updates and said the loft was done, the stairs were up, and the windows were finally in. May first was five and a half months away, but from the outside, the structure looked almost complete.

"Who's that, L.B.?"

Serena eyed a large black SUV that was parked just outside the chain link fence. She didn't recognize it and cautiously looked around for the owner. "Okay, boy. You're coming with me." She grabbed her pepper spray from the glove box and slipped it into her coat pocket. L.B. was beyond excited when she opened the back door to let him out of the Jeep. This was his first time on the property since they'd started building. "Stay by me." She unlocked the gate and slipped through, deciding to keep it unlocked in case she had to make a quick getaway. Two sets of footprints were in the fresh snow ahead of her. She smiled at the tiny prints she recognized as a dog. The other prints weren't much larger than her own. She unlocked the front door with the key that Jake gave her and cleared her throat softly before calling out. "Hello? Is anyone here?"

She didn't expect a pudgy white puppy to race around the corner, slip, and crash into the wall before popping up and continuing its trek straight for her. Serena automatically knelt with her arms outstretched. "Come here, you. Where did you come from?" The puppy, a French bulldog mixed with maybe a corgi, bounced on her lap and licked her face and even gave a surprised L.B. a few hello licks, too.

"Where'd you go, Dozer?" Loud footsteps echoed down the hall, and Serena looked up to find Gabrielle standing in the doorway.

"Is this your puppy?"

Gabrielle crossed her arms and leaned against the frame. "You say it like it's a bad thing." She smiled hesitantly at Serena.

Serena stood with Dozer in her arms and leaned back from his incessant licking so she could talk. "No, no. It's great and I'm amazed and I already love him." She leaned down and let him kiss her until he was done. His tongue fell out and he panted, looking back at Gabrielle.

"You're getting a lot of attention, mister." She took a few steps closer to them. "Hey, L.B. How are you?" She patted the side of her leg, and L.B. obediently went to her for ear scratches.

Gabrielle's relaxed body didn't go unnoticed by Serena. "What are you doing here?" she asked and shook her head. "I don't mean that in bad way. You have every right to be here." It was an unexpected surprise that made her heart skip several beats and her breath hitch in her throat. Gabrielle looked beautiful. Her hair was down, her makeup light, and it was nice to see her relaxed in jeans and a form-fitting black sweater. The scarf was something they'd found at a shop a few months ago before the weather turned bitter. Serena missed her face, her touch, her lips, and the wonderful way she made her feel. Treasured. She took a deep breath and waited for Gabrielle to answer.

"I wanted to make sure the project was progressing. Jake said he put in the windows, and usually that's one of the last things they do before they start walling things in. I'm very pleased with the work his crew has done." Gabrielle took a few steps closer. "I'm sorry I'm here. I didn't expect to run into you."

Serena nervously waved her off. "It's not a problem. This is your project. You deserve to see it, too." She stood up and took a step closer to Gabrielle. "This whole thing has been amazing from start to finish." Serena gently put Dozer on the floor, where he instantly jumped on L.B. and starting nipping at his lips and paws. Within seconds they were chasing one another around the room, barking and playing. "Great name. Dozer is very fitting." They laughed as Dozer ducked his head and ran into L.B. when he couldn't reach L.B.'s paws.

"Obviously my dog doesn't play fair."

"He's adorable." They watched the dogs until it became obvious that they either needed to talk or go their separate ways.

"How are you?" Gabrielle turned to Serena and quickly looked her over from head to toe. "You look great."

Serena automatically reached up and smoothed down her hair. Even though it was fashionable and cute, her hat had a terrible way of collecting static. Oh, and why did she wear this sweater? Pink made her looked washed out, and she was sure there was a snag on the side where L.B.'s nail got caught as she'd dried off his paws that morning. "I'm a mess at the moment, but thank you. You look great, too." So much so that Serena felt her heart clench and beat faster than normal. Gabrielle looked fantastic. There was something different about her, something Serena couldn't identify. Maybe it was because she hadn't seen her in over a month and she was starting to forget the softness of her skin and how graceful she was. She watched Gabrielle reach down and rub Dozer's belly. The look on her face was pure. Gabrielle was at peace. And she had a dog now. The cutest puppy ever, if she was being truthful.

"When did you get him?"

"He's been with me for almost a month now. Rosie and I went to the animal shelter, and when I saw him, I knew it was meant to be."

"How old is he?" Serena lightly clapped her fingers until Dozer scrambled up and raced over to her. "He has only one speed." She laughed as he bowled her over to lick her face.

"He's about four months old. I love him, but he has flaws."

"He's perfect. What could this perfect cuddly puppy do that's so bad?"

Gabrielle snorted and squatted on the other side of him. "Well, let's see. He's chewed up three pairs of my favorite shoes. He ate the rug in the kitchen, chewed up the legs of my bed, and we've been to the vet almost once a week because of small items that suddenly disappeared."

Serena smiled. "You're not very good at doggie-proofing a house. You need help." She looked at Gabrielle and was overcome with emotions she thought she had tamped down, locked up, and walked away from. Without her consent, without any regard to her heart, they flooded every part of her. She felt heavy, as if the weight of every emotional decision she'd ever made came crashing down at that moment. She looked away from Gabrielle and tried hard not to make a sound. Why now? Please not now. The first sob was lost in the sounds of Dozer snorting and playing. By the second sob, Gabrielle had her arms around her and was holding her tightly. By the third sob, her arms were around Gabrielle's neck. She stopped holding back and gave in. She was tired of fighting it.

"Hey, hey. It's okay. It's going to be okay. We're going to be okay."

Gabrielle stroked her head softly. Serena missed Gabrielle's strength and the way she made her feel safe.

"I'm so tired of fighting my feelings." She wasn't sure if she yelled it or whispered it, if Gabrielle even heard it.

"Then don't. Come back to me. I miss you so much," Gabrielle said.

Serena felt Gabrielle's warmth and couldn't let go. Wouldn't let go. She clutched her tightly and finally, agonizingly opened up. "I've missed you, too."

"I'm so sorry I hurt you. I never meant to hurt you. I promise never to do it again."

Serena loosened her grip, took a half a step back, and wiped her tears with the pink sleeve of her sweater. Crying was a weakness she didn't allow herself. "I was being stupid and then I didn't know how to get back to you. I don't know how to do this. I've never been in love before and I don't know what the rules are or anything."

Gabrielle reached out and pulled her back into her arms. "You're in love with me?"

Serena looked at her boots. A whirlwind of emotions blew through her mind. Why did she tell her that? Why did it slip from her mouth? She had never told another woman she loved her. Except for Faith. She might have told her mother at one time, but she didn't remember because it would have happened when she was very young. The word didn't flow out of her mouth freely. Not in the true sense of the word. The way the word was intended to be used. With heart. For a split second, she thought about backpedaling and denying the whole thing, but when she looked at Gabrielle, she saw nothing but hope and happiness. She nodded.

Gabrielle's fingers lifted Serena's chin up so their eyes met. "This is a very good thing. Look, I know you haven't had it easy. At all. I know that love has been very hard to come by, but I want you to know that it's here. Right in front of you. I love you, and I'm not going to let you slip away again." She wiped away more tears that spilled down Serena's cheeks.

Serena's chin trembled when a wave of new tears threatened to spill. "You love me." She pointed to Dozer. "And you got a dog for me."

Gabrielle laughed and pulled her into her arms. "Technically, he's still a puppy, and I got him for me, but I got him because I see how much you love L.B. and how much he means to you. Rosie and I have been working with Muppet and decided a smaller dog would feel less threatening to me." She put her arm around Serena and they watched their boys play.

"I wonder if I should add a little play section here in the front?" Serena pointed to the open space where Dozer and L.B. were playing. That was a designated space where there was going to be a display of toys, personal bedding, and cute sweaters that clients who were feeling guilty for dropping their pets off could purchase for them.

"You know, your architect will probably need to know that sooner rather than later so that she can make changes."

Serena smiled through her tears and nodded. "Or I can just leave it because it's beautiful and perfect and all I ever wanted."

"We should go. It's too cold in here and we have a lot of catching up to do," Gabrielle said.

Serena hadn't even noticed the cold until Gabrielle pointed it out. Her body and heart hummed with warmth. "Let's round up the boys. Do you want to come over? I can fix us lunch." Serena hoped her voice didn't sound too desperate.

"Yes, but Dozer is still not one hundred percent potty trained."

"Most of the floors are wooden and can be easily cleaned. Plus L.B. has become very good at using the doggie door, and Dozer will follow him everywhere."

Gabrielle captured Dozer before his chunky stout body banged into them another time. "Okay, big guy, settle down. Let's get out of here before you destroy the place before it's open."

Gabrielle waited as Serena locked the door. "So, new dog and a new car."

"The convertible was completely ill-fitted for Colorado and a new puppy." Gabrielle opened it to secure Dozer in his carrier and allow Serena to look around.

"I should have looked at this instead of my Jeep. It's beautiful." Serena touched the black leather seats and ran her hand over the touchscreen. When she finally had her fill of admiring Gabrielle's new SUV, she ushered L.B. into her Jeep.

"Follow you home?" Gabrielle asked.

"Yes. Please." Serena held her gaze and smiled. She waited until she saw Gabrielle pull in behind her before she turned onto the highway to go home. A place that now had a future. She wasn't going to get too excited, but she just got her girlfriend back. Her beautiful, smart, funny, caring girlfriend who said things to her she never thought she was good enough to hear. Things that filled her so completely she had to smile and let some of that energy out with a few happy squeals. L.B.'s ear cocked and stood at attention. "Sorry, buddy. I got a little excited. Let's go home and play with Dozer and Gabrielle. You'd like that, wouldn't you?" L.B.'s small bark startled her. "I guess you would."

❖

Serena didn't know what to do with so many people. This time, though, her life was completely different and she welcomed them. The Barneses' annual Christmas party took place the Saturday before Christmas. This was the first time Serena and Gabrielle had been together in front of Gabrielle's family since their unnecessary breakup. Not to mention all of their friends. When Piper, Shaylie, and Maribelle showed up, Piper couldn't stop hugging Serena.

"I told you this was all going to work out. You two are made for each other," Piper whispered in Serena's ear.

"I should listen to you more."

"Piper's right about everything," Shaylie said. She kissed Piper's temple and handed Maribelle off to her. "I'm going to bring in the rest of the presents."

"Do you need any help?" Serena hated standing around when other people were working. It wasn't in her nature to be idle.

"No, thanks. It's only one trip. You stay here and entertain my wife and daughter."

"That's a job I can do," Serena said.

"Tell me everything and leave nothing out." Piper put Maribelle down and watched as she ran to Gabrielle on the other side of the room.

"We ran into one another at the Pet Posh Inn and just talked through things."

Piper put her hands on her waist. "Really? That's all I get? I want the romance, I want the little details. Who made the first move?"

"I saw her and just fell apart. Is crying a move?"

Piper laughed and pulled Serena into a quick hug. "And that's what makes love so wonderful. It's strips you down to nothing except you and everything that's real in your life."

"I tried to be strong, but I saw her and her new puppy and started crying. I told her I loved her but didn't know how to get back to her. Piper, I've never said the words before."

Piper leaned closer. "I don't think Gabrielle has really been in love before. Maybe when she was in high school or college, but not since I've known her. You're perfect for her."

That gave Serena a burst of energy. Gabrielle didn't talk about her ex-girlfriends, and now she knew why. She didn't have any. Not that having a string of one-night stands was really something to be proud of, but that meant she wasn't emotionally invested in anyone. At least not in the last ten years. "She's perfect for me."

"There you are. Hello, Serena." Meredith pulled her into a tight hug and held her a little bit longer than normal. Serena felt the love and almost burst into tears again.

"Hi, Mrs. Barnes. It's so nice to be here again."

"It's Meredith. And I couldn't be happier right now. It's about time Gabrielle came to her senses and won you back."

Serena smiled at her. Gabrielle only had to show up. "Don't tell anyone, but Dozer is really the one who stole my heart."

"Wait a minute. Wait a minute. Are you all talking about me? Because my ears are burning." Gabrielle stood beside them holding Maribelle on her hip.

"I want to hold her now before she gets too big." Serena reached out to Maribelle, who crawled into her arms.

"Don't worry about that. We've got you covered," Piper said.

"What do you mean?" Serena took a small bite of cookie that Maribelle put up against her lips.

"Want to tell them?" Piper looked at Shaylie, who nodded.

"We're expecting."

"Shut the—oh, my God. Congratulations!" Serena lowered her voice. "Is it public knowledge yet?"

"It can be. We're ready to tell people, but we didn't want to take away from your special day either."

"You're not. We're treating every day as a special day," Gabrielle said.

Serena blushed. Gabrielle was telling the truth. Since getting back together, they were inseparable. Gabrielle had driven to Vail two weekends in a row and even made a few trips during the week. Dozer was getting used to Serena's place and got excited whenever they turned into Serena's driveway.

"Oh, it's the office. I should take this." Gabrielle waved her phone at the small group and excused herself. Serena watched as Gabrielle slipped into her father's den.

"Is that the call?" Meredith whispered.

Serena's anxiety amped up the moment the door closed. She knew in her heart it was the call they were waiting for. The board was getting together before the holidays to make the decision. The new partner would be introduced January first. All of Gabrielle's hard work was about to pay off, and either her dream was going to come true or the other dream of starting her own business was going to come true. Either way, something life changing was going to happen in the next few minutes.

"What's going on over here? Everyone looks so nervous." Rosie bit another chip and stared at the small group that had gathered outside of the den.

"Gabrielle got the call," Meredith said.

"The call? The big one? The one we've been stressing about for months?" Rosie asked. Serena nodded and reached for Rosie's hand. Rosie pulled her into a hug. "I can't tell you how wonderful it is to see you again. I told Gabrielle she needed to get you back, and I'm so happy she did."

"I've missed you."

Everybody stilled when the door opened. Serena's heart sank at the small smile on Gabrielle's lips. It wasn't the kind of smile she was hoping for, but she put on a brave front and smiled back.

"Are you going to tell us what happened or are we going to have a staring contest? You forget, I have children. I'll win this battle." Rosie didn't beat around the bush.

"Well, I got it." Everyone cheered and congratulated her at once. Gabrielle held up her hand. "Wait. I'm not done. I kind of turned it down."

"You did what?" Meredith's voice boomed above all other gasps and murmurs.

"I gave them another option." Gabrielle walked into the group and reached for Serena's hand. "Can I talk to you?"

Serena nodded and followed her into the den. "What's going on?" She couldn't keep the concern from her voice or the small line that formed on her forehead when she was stressed.

Gabrielle pulled her close. "I told them I wanted Arnest & Max to open an office in Vail and I would run it. I could do that as a partner or a very well paid employee. They're going to talk about it and get back to me on Monday."

"So, what does that mean?" It sounded wonderful, but was this sacrifice too much? "I don't want you to turn down partner because of me. You've worked too hard to just say no."

Gabrielle cupped her face. "Don't worry about it. It took me forever to find you, a bad decision to lose you, love to win you back, and I'm never letting you go again. Work isn't my life. You, Dozer, L.B., my parents, Rosie and her family, Shaylie and hers. You all are my life."

"But Denver is your home. Everyone is here."

"My life is with you. The Pet Posh Inn isn't even up and running. Your life's in Vail."

Serena told herself not to cry. Nobody had ever sacrificed anything for her. Not their time and definitely not their heart. For the first time, somebody was putting her first. She nodded and hugged Gabrielle.

"If it does really well, then maybe we can open a second place in Denver and split our time between the two," Serena said. "I don't want you to sacrifice everything for me." Serena was only just learning that she was worth it.

Gabrielle cupped her chin and kissed her softly. "I'm not sacrificing anything. I want to be with you. I can do my job anywhere. I love you so much. You know that, right? I ask myself all the time, how did I get so lucky?"

Serena put her arms around Gabrielle's neck. "No, love. You have it all wrong." She kissed the confused look off her face. "I'm the lucky one."

Epilogue

The Weather Channel was the only thing Gabrielle and Serena watched all weekend. Spring weather in the Rockies was unpredictable, and opening day was tomorrow. Gabrielle tried to get Serena to relax, eat, and rest, but she knew what the rush was like. Serena's dream was about to become a reality. She had a full staff including a full-time veterinarian, two techs, a dog trainer, an office manager, and four concierges who greeted clients and were there to offer the facility's top-notch treatment for their pets. Three college students were scheduled to start later in the week after finals and would work with the trainer behind the scenes.

"I love how many people have reserved rooms already." Gabrielle looked over the guest list and smiled at Serena. "You already have sixty-five percent capacity in the Canine Cabins, thirty percent in the Feline Fort, and how is it possible that you already have reservations in the Bird Bungalow?"

Serena wrapped her arms around Gabrielle's waist and looked over her shoulder. "Look at the Critter Chateau. We have bunnies, a guinea pig, and twin ferrets. Remember when you thought I was crazy when I insisted on this room?"

Gabrielle pulled Serena's arms tighter around her and leaned her head on Serena's shoulder. "I still think you're crazy, but smart. Very smart. You'll be opening up another branch in no time."

"I'll have to leave the country for six months the next time I do this," Serena said.

Gabrielle told Serena delays always happened, especially when they were gambling with the weather. Even though the structure had been done for at least a month, they had to wait for the temperature to be above freezing before they could paint the outside, install the wrought iron fence, and pave the parking lot. "Six months, huh? Well, Arnest & Max's Vail location will be fine for a few months, but six might be stretching it, although as partner, I can work from anywhere. Let's go to Italy or Rome," Gabrielle said.

"We can't leave our boys." Serena kissed her cheek. "Come on. We should go to bed because you know I want to get up early."

"Can I interest you in a distraction?" Gabrielle smiled devilishly at Serena.

"As long as it comes with a full body massage, I'm all in."

"You go upstairs and get ready, and I'll round up the boys," Gabrielle said. She brushed her lips across Serena's and gave her waist a quick squeeze on her way into the kitchen. Dozer and L.B. raced to her after she whistled, and even though she knew them and knew they would never hurt her, dogs rushing at her still put her on edge. "Slow down." They both stopped short and waited for her to open the door. "Are you calm? Are you ready to go night-night?" She made sure they had a drink of water before she ushered them into Faith's room. "You have to stay in here tonight. I'll come and get you later." Gabrielle blew them both kisses and quietly closed the door.

"Where are the boys?" Serena tied the sash of her robe and looked around the room.

"Oh, they wanted a slumber party, so I put them in Faith's room and told them to keep it down." She pulled Serena into her embrace and kissed her. "I don't even know why you're wearing this." Her fingers slid down the lapels of the robe, paying special attention to Serena's nipples along the way.

"I don't know why either." Serena slowly untied the sash and dropped her hands.

"My favorite part of every day. You." Gabrielle leaned forward and placed a soft kiss on the soft spot above Serena's collarbone. "Get into bed. I'll be there in five minutes." She put the massage oil on the warmer and hopped into the shower for a quick rinse. True to her word, she was back in bed in five minutes.

"I missed you." Serena had the covers and sheets pulled back. Her robe was on the floor in front of the bed.

"This is my favorite time of day," Gabrielle said. She climbed into bed and reached for the oil.

"Wait a minute. Why do you get to wear clothes?"

Gabrielle looked down at the long threadbare T-shirt that barely covered her. "This isn't about me right now. It's about you." She poured warm oil in her hand and motioned for Serena to turn over. She did with enthusiasm and moaned when Gabrielle straddled her and started massaging her back.

"I don't know what I'm more excited about, the massage and how good it feels, or how wet you are."

"You can find out later," Gabrielle said. She rubbed Serena's arms and back until she was limp and relaxed. She smiled when Serena's body twitched when her hands moved lower. She slid lower to massage the back of her thighs. She smiled at Serena's moans and how she spread her thighs and lifted her ass every time Gabrielle's fingers got close to her wet core.

Serena mumbled into the pillow, "You're driving me crazy."

"How's this? Is this better?" Gabrielle easily slid two fingers inside Serena.

"Oh, God, yes." Serena lifted her hips up to greet each thrust from behind.

When Serena was this relaxed, her inhibitions disappeared. Gabrielle leaned forward and whispered in her ear, "Do you want me to get out one of our toys?"

Serena didn't hesitate. She nodded immediately.

Gabrielle's heart swelled. She opened the drawer and found her favorite dildo. It wasn't too big, but long enough to hit Serena's sweet spot. She added some of the massage oil that also served as a safe lubricant and rubbed the tip up and down Serena's slit. Serena spread her legs more and moved her hips up and down until Gabrielle slid the full length inside her. Serena hissed and moaned with complete pleasure. It was the sexiest noise Gabrielle had ever heard and empowered her to be a better lover. It was always her intent to give Serena more pleasure every time they made love, but that noise, that raw, uninhibited noise did something else to Gabrielle. Her body exploded with a need to please Serena.

Chills sped across her skin as her heart filled with love for this woman. She crept between Serena's legs and pulled her up so she was on her knees. "I love you." She said it over and over, building Serena up every time she said it, and thrust deeper and faster inside her. When Serena finally came, Gabrielle teared up at the raw beauty of the moment.

"I love you, too." Serena slid down on the bed, breathing heavily.

Gabrielle pulled up the sheet and a thin blanket and covered her. "I'm going to wash up, but I'll be right back." Serena nodded. Gabrielle was gone for two minutes but when she returned, naked and ready, she found Serena fast asleep. She smiled and slipped into bed. The feeling would keep. She nestled behind her, put her arm around her waist, and drifted off to sleep.

❖

"This is amazing, big sis." Faith showed up for the grand opening even though she'd only got off work six hours earlier. "You even have the press here." KCNC-TV and KMGH-TV both had vans covering the big day.

Gabrielle turned to Serena and put her hands on her shoulders. "I need you to breathe, babe. It's going to be fine. They're probably going to bring up the lottery, so remember what we talked about. You look beautiful. Now go make this dream come true and open those doors."

Serena bounced on the balls of her feet a few times and took a deep breath. "I've got this." She nodded to all of her new employees lined up to start the first day of the Pet Posh Inn.

Gabrielle loved her girlfriend. So much change had happened to her over the last year. She'd gone from pauper to instant wealth, but managed to stay humble. After thirty years of being a prisoner to a shell of a family that wasn't there no matter how hard she wanted it, she'd ended the toxic relationship with her mother but was closer to Faith than ever before. Gabrielle watched the reporter interview Serena, and a bubble of pride burst in her chest. Her girlfriend was a survivor. She was beautiful, kind, and full of love that she was desperate to share with the world. Gabrielle smiled because not only did Serena change her for the better, she gave her the one thing money couldn't buy. She gave her true love.

About the Author

Award-winning author Kris Bryant was born in Tacoma, WA, but has lived all over the world and now considers Kansas City her home. She received her BA in English from the University of Missouri and spends a lot of her time buried in books. She enjoys hiking, photography, spending time with her family, and her world-famous fur baby, Molly (who gets more attention than Kris does on Facebook).

Her first novel, *Jolt*, was a Lambda Literary Finalist and Rainbow Awards Honorable Mention. Her second book, *Whirlwind Romance*, was a Rainbow Runner-up for Contemporary Romance. *Taste* was also a Rainbow Awards Honorable Mention for Contemporary Romance. *Forget Me Not* was selected by the American Library Association's 2018 Over the Rainbow book list and was a Golden Crown Finalist for Contemporary Romance. *Breakthrough* won a 2019 Goldie for Contemporary Romance.

Kris can be reached at krisbryantbooks@gmail or www.krisbryant.net, @krisbryant14.

Books Available From Bold Strokes Books

All the Paths to You by Morgan Lee Miller. High school sweethearts Quinn Hughes and Kennedy Reed reconnect five years after they break up and realize that their chemistry is all but over. (978-1-63555-662-9)

Arrested Pleasures by Nanisi Barrett D'Arnuck. When charged with a crime she didn't commit, Katherine Lowe faces the question: Which is harder, going to prison or falling in love? (978-1-63555-684-1)

Bonded Love by Renee Roman. Carpenter Blaze Carter suffers an injury that shatters her dreams, and ER nurse Trinity Greene hopes to show her that sometimes hope is worth fighting for. (978-1-63555-530-1)

Convergence by Jane C. Esther. With life as they know it on the line, can Aerin McLeary and Olivia Ando's love survive an otherworldly threat to humankind? (978-1-63555-488-5)

Coyote Blues by Karen F. Williams. Riley Dawson, psychotherapist and shape-shifter, has her world turned upside down when Fiona Bell, her one true love, returns. (978-1-63555-558-5)

Drawn by Carsen Taite. Will the clues lead Detective Claire Hanlon to the killer terrorizing Dallas, or will she merely lose her heart to person of interest urban artist Riley Flynn? (978-1-63555-644-5)

Lucky by Kris Bryant. Was Serena Evans's luck really about winning the lottery, or is she about to get even luckier in love? (978-1-63555-510-3)

The Last Days of Autumn by Donna K. Ford. Autumn and Caroline question the fairness of life, the cruelty of loss, and what it means to love as they navigate the complicated minefield of relationships, grief, and life-altering illness. (978-1-63555-672-8)

Three Alarm Response by Erin Dutton. In the midst of tragedy, can these first responders find love and healing? Three stories of courage, bravery, and passion. (978-1-63555-592-9)

Veterinary Partner by Nancy Wheelton. Callie and Lauren are determined to keep their hearts safe but find that taking a chance on love is the safest option of all. (978-1-63555-666-7)

Forging a Desire Line by Mary P. Burns. When Charley's ex-wife, Tricia, is diagnosed with inoperable cancer, the private duty nurse Tricia hires turns out to be the handsome and aloof Joanna, who ignites something inside Charley she isn't ready to face. (978-1-63555-665-0)

Journey to Cash by Ashley Bartlett. Cash Braddock thought everything was great, but it looks like her history is about to become her right now. Which is a real bummer. (978-1-63555-464-9)

Love on the Night Shift by Radclyffe. Between ruling the night shift in the ER at the Rivers and raising her teenage daughter, Blaise Richilieu has all the drama she needs in her life, until a dashing young attending appears on the scene and relentlessly pursues her. (978-1-63555-668-1)

Olivia's Awakening by Ronica Black. When the daring and dangerously gorgeous Eve Monroe is hired to get Olivia Savage into shape, a fierce passion ignites, causing both to question everything they've ever known about love. (978-1-63555-613-1)

The Duchess and the Dreamer by Jenny Frame. Clementine Fitzroy has lost her faith and love of life. Can dreamer Evan Fox make her believe in life and dream again? (978-1-63555-601-8)

The Road Home by Erin Zak. Hollywood actress Gwendolyn Carter is about to discover that losing someone you love sometimes means gaining someone to fall for. (978-1-63555-633-9)

Waiting for You by Elle Spencer. When passionate past-life lovers meet again in the present day, one remembers it vividly and the other isn't so sure. (978-1-63555-635-3)

While My Heart Beats by Erin McKenzie. Can a love born amidst the horrors of the Great War survive? (978-1-63555-589-9)

Face the Music by Ali Vali. Sweet music is the last thing that happens when Nashville music producer Mason Liner and daughter of country royalty Victoria Roddy are thrown together in an effort to save country star Sophie Roddy's career. (978-1-63555-532-5)

BOLDSTROKESBOOKS.COM

Looking for your next great read?

Visit BOLDSTROKESBOOKS.COM
to browse our entire catalog of paperbacks, ebooks,
and audiobooks.

Want the first word on what's new?
Visit our website for event info,
author interviews, and blogs.

Subscribe to our free newsletter for sneak peeks,
new releases, plus first notice of promos
and daily bargains.

SIGN UP AT
BOLDSTROKESBOOKS.COM/signup

Bold Strokes Books
Quality and Diversity in LGBTQ Literature

Bold Strokes Books is an award-winning publisher
committed to quality and diversity in LGBTQ fiction.

Flavor of the Month by Georgia Beers. What happens when baker Charlie and chef Emma realize their differing paths have led them right back to each other? (978-1-63555-616-2)

Mending Fences by Angie Williams. Rancher Bobbie Del Rey and veterinarian Grace Hammond are about to discover if heartbreaks of the past can ever truly be mended. (978-1-63555-708-4)

Silk and Leather: Lesbian Erotica with an Edge, edited by Victoria Villaseñor. This collection of stories by award-winning authors offers fantasies as soft as silk and tough as leather. The only question is: How far will you go to make your deepest desires come true? (978-1-63555-587-5)

The Last Place You Look by Aurora Rey. Dumped by her wife and looking for anything but love, Julia Pierce retreats to her hometown only to rediscover high school friend Taylor Winslow, who's secretly crushed on her for years. (978-1-63555-574-5)

The Mortician's Daughter by Nan Higgins. A singer on the verge of stardom discovers she must give up her dreams to live a life in service to ghosts. (978-1-63555-594-3)

The Real Thing by Laney Webber. When passion flares between actress Virginia Green and masseuse Allison McDonald, can they be sure it's the real thing? (978-1-63555-478-6)

What the Heart Remembers Most by M. Ullrich. For college sweethearts Jax Levine and Gretchen Mills, could an accident be the second chance neither knew they wanted? (978-1-63555-401-4)

White Horse Point by Andrews & Austin. Mystery writer Taylor James finds herself falling for the mysterious woman on White Horse Point who lives alone, protecting a secret she can't share about a murderer who walks among them. (978-1-63555-695-7)